NEW YORK REVIEW BOOKS
CLASSICS

GOING TO THE DOGS

ERICH KÄSTNER (1899–1974) was born in Dresden and
after serving in World War I studied history and philosophy
in Leipzig, completing a PhD. In 1927 he moved to Berlin and
through his prolific journalism quickly became a major
intellectual figure in the capital. His first book of poems was
published in 1928, as was the children's book *Emil and the
Detectives*, which quickly achieved worldwide fame. *Going to
the Dogs* appeared in 1931 and was followed by many other
works for adults and children, including *Lottie and Lisa*, the
basis for the popular Disney film *The Parent Trap*. In 1933 the
pacifist Kästner was banned from German publication and
subsequently found employment as a film scriptwriter. After
World War II, he worked as a literary editor and continued to
write, mainly for children.

CYRUS BROOKS translated works by Alfred Neumann,
Friedrich Dürrenmatt, and Leonhard Frank as well as
Kästner's *Emil and the Detectives*, *Emil and the Three Twins*,
and *Lottie and Lisa*.

RODNEY LIVINGSTONE is a professor emeritus in
German studies at the University of Southampton and a
translator of books by Theodor W. Adorno, Max Weber, and
Walter Benjamin, among others. In 2009 he was awarded the
Ungar German Translation Prize of the American Translators
Association.

GOING TO THE DOGS

The Story of a Moralist

ERICH KÄSTNER

Translated from the German by
CYRUS BROOKS

Introduction by
RODNEY LIVINGSTONE

NEW YORK REVIEW BOOKS

New York

THIS IS A NEW YORK REVIEW BOOK
PUBLISHED BY THE NEW YORK REVIEW OF BOOKS
435 Hudson Street, New York, NY 10014
www.nyrb.com

First published under the title *Fabian* by Deutsche Verlagsanstalt, Stuttgart, 1931
Original English translation first published by Jonathan Cape, 1932
This complete translation and introduction first published under the title
Fabian by Libris, 1990
Reprinted by arrangement with Libris, London

Library of Congress Cataloging-in-Publication Data
Kästner, Erich, 1899–1974.
[Fabian. English]
 Going to the dogs : the story of a moralist / by Erich Kästner ; introduction and edited
by Rodney Livingstone ; translation by Cyrus Brooks.
    p. cm. — (New York Review Books Classics)
 ISBN 978-1-59017-584-2 (alk. paper)
 I. Livingstone, Rodney. II. Brooks, C. Harry (Cyrus Harry), b. 1890. III. Title.
PT2621.A23F313 2012
833'.912—dc23

                    2012018730

ISBN 978-1-59017-584-2
Available as an electronic book

Printed in the United States of America on acid-free paper.
10 9 8 7 6 5 4 3 2 1

CONTENTS

INTRODUCTION

I

Erich Kästner's *Fabian* first appeared in 1931. Presenting, as it did, a vivid picture of life in contemporary Berlin, it was savagely criticized on the right because its candid account of contemporary morals was felt to be offensive and immoral, while its satirical attack on Germany's traditions was thought unpatriotic. However, the novel was praised by the Communist paper, *Die Rote Fahne*, despite Kästner's rejection of Communism in the text. When *Fabian* was reprinted after the war it remained controversial, this time because it seemed to epitomize the attitudes and fate of the petty bourgeois liberal intellectual in the Weimar Republic. The passivity which characterizes Jacob Fabian was held responsible for the failure of bourgeois liberalism and thus for the bankruptcy of the entire republic.

The controversies which the book has continued to attract are a sign of its vitality. It is increasingly perceived as one of the key novels of the Weimar Republic, the book which catches most faithfully and precisely the atmosphere of the republic in its dying years. Other works are acknowledged to have greater literary stature – Thomas Mann's *Magic Mountain* or Rilke's *Duino Elegies*, for example. But as the products of literary high modernism, their connections with the society that produced them are more indirect and subterranean. And even Brecht's *Threepenny Opera* or Alfred Döblin's *Berlin Alexanderplatz* fail to render as brilliantly as Kästner the tangible immediacy of Berlin in those last frenetic years before 1933. There are some parallels with Christopher Isherwood's Berlin books, but Kästner's novel appeared earlier and he tells his story as an insider. Moreover, as the poised and ironic voice of a liberal democracy tragically doomed to destruction, Kästner speaks to us with an immediacy which other, perhaps greater writers lack. It is significant that Peter Rühmkorf, one of Germany's leading contemporary poets and satirists, should have seen in

Kästner's writings the foundation of the regeneration of democracy after 1945 and credited him with making possible 'a sort of unofficial process of re-education', implying perhaps that his influence was in its way as important as the official programmes of re-education launched by the Allied Occupation.*

2

Erich Kästner was born in 1899 in Dresden, a city which bears a marked resemblance to Jacob Fabian's home town.† His father was a saddler who, like many small craftsmen in the eighteen nineties, was forced into factory work, a luggage factory in his case. His mother came from a rather wealthier family of bakers, butchers and horse-dealers, some of whom became millionaires. However, the Kästner family was always poor, and after her marriage his mother worked at home, sewing trusses and corsets. At the age of thirty-four she trained to become a hairdresser. Despite these efforts it was still necessary to eke out the family income by taking in lodgers, mainly teachers. One of these had a strong influence on Kästner, who decided that he too wished to become a teacher and who was always to be quite frank about the didactic element in his writings; his quite remarkable rapport with children would have stood him in good stead in such a career.

In 1913, after primary school, Kästner went to a teachers' training college, but his studies there were interrupted by the First World War. He was called up in 1917 and once in the army his heart was damaged by the strain of basic training under a brutal sergeant by the name of Waurich whom he commemorated in a satirical poem. Fabian too has a weak heart and the meeting at the end of the book with his former officer, Knorr, evidently reflects that experience.

After the war Kästner completed his teacher's training

* See the *Süddeutsche Zeitung*, 3 March 1979.
† There is a brief account of Kästner's life in English in R. W. Last's *Erich Kästner* (London, 1974). The best in German are to be found in Luiselotte Enderle, *Erich Kästner in Selbstzeugnissen und Bilddokumenten* (Hamburg, 1966) and, more recently, Helga Bemmann, *Humor auf Taille. Erich Kästners Leben und Werk* (East Berlin, 1983). Luiselotte Enderle was Kästner's companion for many years.

(unlike Fabian, who did not take his state examination) but was then awarded a scholarship which enabled him to study at university. Following the German pattern he studied in Leipzig, Rostock and Berlin. Kästner's educational background gives a clue to that of his hero, Jacob Fabian, since it was unusual at the time for a man of such lowly origins to acquire an education, to say nothing of a doctorate.

In 1925 Kästner completed a doctoral thesis on the responses to Frederick the Great's polemical tract, *De la Littérature Allemande* of 1778, in which Frederick attacked the writings of emerging writers like Goethe, Schiller and the 'Sturm und Drang' generation, and defended the disappearing ideals of French classicism. However, Kästner had earlier begun a thesis on Lessing, and he evidently identified strongly with that hero of the German Enlightenment.

While studying in Leipzig Kästner was friendly with a student called Ralph Zucker whose fate anticipates that of Labude in *Fabian*. A brilliant medical student, Zucker shot himself after being told by a fellow student that he had failed in ophthalmology, a subject in which he had in reality passed with top marks. While studying, Kästner had begun to freelance for newspapers in Leipzig, and in 1927 he moved to Berlin where he supported himself in the same way, writing theatrical reviews and also songs for cabarets. Between 1928 and 1932 he published four volumes of poetry which made his reputation as a perceptive and witty satirist. In 1928 he achieved fame with the publication of *Emil and the Detectives*, the first in a long line of books for children. *Emil* was made into a film by UFA* in 1930, Kästner collaborating on the script with Emil Pressburger and Billy Wilder. The same year saw *Emil*'s publication in English, in New York. The fame of *Emil* was such that it was exempted from the ban imposed on Kästner's works by the Nazis in 1933.

When the Nazis came to power Kästner found himself in Switzerland. Unlike most of the radical intelligentsia he set out to return to Germany after the burning of the Reichstag and, grotesquely, was met at the station by friends and acquaintances fleeing from the new regime. According to the memoirs of the

---

* UFA (short for Universum-Film Aktiengesellschaft) which was founded in 1917, was the dominant German film production company in both the Weimar Republic and the Third Reich. It ceased to exist in 1945.

novelist Hermann Kesten, he gave as his reasons the need to stay with his mother and the wish to act as witness to the horrors to come. Kästner's intention was to write a novel describing the Nazi dictatorship and he wished to have been present throughout so as to be able to step forward as their accuser later on. His decision prompted much discussion, of course, most of it hostile. In the event the novel about Nazism failed to materialize and he confined himself largely to writing children's books, which replaced the social criticism of *Fabian*, and to his poetry expressing the wish-fulfilments of a world without conflict.

It has been suggested that Fabian's policy of inaction and the retreat to his home town and mother represent a regression which foreshadows ideologically the 'inner emigration' of the years following 1933. However, it was not just right-wing or 'unpolitical' writers who chose to stay in Germany. The courageous pacifist journalist Carl von Ossietzky made the same choice and paid for it with his life. For Kästner the price was less exacting, but he was forced to accept two invitations to visit the Gestapo, in 1934 and 1937, from which he was lucky enough to emerge unscathed.

On 10 May 1933 Kästner was among the authors whose books were publicly burned. In Berlin the ceremony was conducted on the Opernplatz by Goebbels himself. Kästner's books were consigned to the flames alongside those of Heinrich Mann because of their affront to 'discipline and morality in the family and the state'. Of all the writers whose books were burned that day, Kästner was the only one to be present. Henceforth his books were banned from Germany but could be printed abroad, and he lived on the income from these foreign sales. However, in 1943 he worked anonymously on the script of the UFA film *Baron Münchhausen*, and when this became known to Hitler and Goebbels the ban on his writings was made absolute.

After 1945 Kästner emerged from the shadows and lived the life of a celebrated writer. However, little of his writing since then is of note, apart from *Notabene 1945*, a diary of the final year of the war. He campaigned actively in the cause of peace and against nuclear weapons. He was President of the West German PEN and received numerous awards, including the prestigious Georg-Büchner Prize in 1957. He died in 1974.

In a speech given to the Zurich PEN in 1957 Kästner provides an interesting characterization of his own writings:

> Our guest, Ladies and Gentlemen, is no belletrist, but a schoolmaster! If you look at the whole range of his works from this point of view – from picture books to the most risqué poem – the situation becomes crystal clear. The man is a moralist. He is a rationalist. He is a descendant of the German Enlightenment, the sworn enemy of all the false 'profundity' which never goes out of fashion in the land of poets and thinkers. He is wholly devoted to three inalienable imperatives: integrity of feeling, clarity of thought and simplicity in word and sentence.

In his writings Kästner is associated with the trend known as the *Neue Sachlichkeit* ('New Sobriety' or 'New Objectivity').* This movement is usually regarded as a reaction to the emotional excesses of expressionism and as the ideological reflex of Weimar Germany's period of stabilization between 1925 and 1930. It influenced Brecht on the left and Ernst Jünger on the right of the political spectrum, but its characteristic products, apart from Kästner, were Erich Maria Remarque's *All Quiet on the Western Front* (published in 1929), the plays of Ödön von Horváth and Carl Zuckmayer, the paintings of Georg Grosz and Otto Dix and the music of Paul Hindemith (whose notion of functional music is similar to Kästner's idea of functional poetry).

What these artists share is a response to the emergence of technological mass society. They are the authentic voice of the Weimar Republic itself and Kästner is typical of them. His point of view is that of the 'kleiner Mann', the ordinary man in the street speaking to other ordinary men and women. He is sceptical, intelligent and clear-sighted. He has no faith in systematic panaceas. In his poetry, which he called 'functional poetry', the main features of the movement can be seen: the cult of the factual statement, the use of non-figurative language, a habit of cool wit and understatement. His poems have titles like

* For the background of Kästner's poems and the New Objectivity see J.J. White, 'Functional Poetry in the Weimar Period', in Alan Bance, *Weimar Germany. Writers and Politics*, Scottish Academic Press, 1982.

'Berlin in Figures', 'Sober (*Sachliche*) Romance' or 'The Führer-Problem, Looked at Genetically'. With its satire on German militarism a poem like 'Kennst du das Land, wo die Kanonen blühn?' ('Knowest thou the land where the cannon bloom?') could arouse the fury of right-wing nationalists. In 'Kurzgefaßter Lebenslauf' ('Short CV') the flavour of his poetry is caught to perfection.

> Now I am 31 or so they say,
> With a small poetry business of my own.
> Alas, my hair is starting to go grey,
> And all my friends are getting overblown.
>
> I like to be caught sitting on the fence,
> Cut down the branch on which I choose to sit.
> I walk through gardens filled with sentiments
> Long dead, and scatter there a little wit.*

This is also the flavour of *Fabian*, which as the Austrian writer and parodist Robert Neumann observed, consists of Kästner poems steamrollered flat.

4

Fabian is set in contemporary Berlin; the Berlin, that is, of the years between the Wall Street Crash and the Nazi takeover. These were the years of rapidly rising unemployment.† In Berlin alone there were 350,000 unemployed in September 1930, increasing to 650,000 two years later. One Berliner in four depended on welfare payments. Major companies like Karstadt, the department store, were on the verge of collapse. The Dresdner Bank and the Darmstadt National Bank followed the

---

* Translated by Patrick Bridgwater in Erich Kästner, *Let's Face It . . .* , edited by Patrick Bridgwater (Jonathan Cape, 1963), quoted by kind permission of Atrium Verlag, Zurich, and Jonathan Cape Ltd.

† Of the many books on the last years of the Weimar Republic Alex de Jonge's *The Weimar Chronicle* (Paddington Press, 1978) makes particularly fascinating reading. John Willett's *The New Sobriety 1917–1933: Art and Politics in the Weimar Period* (Thames and Hudson, 1978) is an indispensable sourcebook. For the Berlin background Annemarie Lange, *Berlin in der Weimarer Republik* (Berlin, 1987), contains much information unavailable elsewhere.

Vienna Creditanstalt into liquidation. The fall of the Social Democrat Müller government in 1930 signalled the end of democracy. Heinrich Brüning, Müller's successor, ruled by emergency decree.

In the elections of September 1930 five and a half million people voted for the NSDAP – the National Socialist German Workers' Party – i.e. for the Nazis, making it the second largest party after the Social Democrats. By April 1932 the NSDAP was the biggest party in Prussia, outnumbering the Socialists and Communists combined. In the arts the predominant atmosphere was right-wing. Although these were the so-called 'golden years' of the Republic it was the heyday of nationalist and extremist writing. Alfred Rosenberg's *Myth of the Twentieth Century* and Hans Grimm's *Volk ohne Raum* appeared in 1930 and 1926. We now remember mainly the glittering intellectual and literary achievements of those years, but what most people read were Nazi and quasi-Nazi writers. Progressive writers were under attack. The premiere of Brecht's *Mahagonny* in Frankfurt in 1930 was disrupted by the Nazis as was Lewis Milestone's film of *All Quiet on the Western Front* the same year. The Communist playwright and doctor Friedrich Wolf was sent to gaol because his play *Potassium Cyanide* had offended against the abortion laws; Erwin Piscator was imprisoned on tax charges. The Communist cabaret artist and poet, Erich Weinert, was arrested for subversion, and Agitprop art was banned at political meetings. In July 1931 the Kroll Opera, where Klemperer was the chief conductor, was closed down, as was Walter Gropius's Bauhaus in January 1932.

The contrast is striking between Kästner's Berlin and Berlin as it had been before the First World War, in Theodor Fontane's novels, for example. That world had been refined, elegant, a little staid but highly civilized despite its underlying problems. Alex de Jonge has remarked that post-war Berlin had a hole in the heart: with the loss of the court its social centre had disappeared. Instead there were the garish lights and frenetic pace of a Berlin dominated by nightclubs and dance-halls, and the 6-day cycling races. These nightclubs had sprung up in secret during the war in response to a ban on dancing in public places. After the war establishments which had operated before 1914 were allowed to reopen until ten in the evening, but dancing in bars and other cafés was still banned. The number of illicit dance places – the defining feature of Berlin in the twenties – grew almost nightly.

5

Fabian tells the story of Jacob Fabian, 'aged thirty-two, profession variable, at present advertising copywriter, 17 Schaperstrasse, weak heart, brown hair'. He is ideally suited to enable Kästner to explore the reality of contemporary Germany. On the one hand, he is typical of the growing class of white-collar workers which came into existence during the twenties. On the other, he is highly educated and his outlook is broad enough to comment on developments in society as a whole. However, despite his education, he is condemned to a menial and certainly low-paid job, and even that lacks security. In other words, Fabian is upwardly mobile, but he is caught up in a social conjuncture in which the new class of white-collar workers is being forced by the recession back towards the proletariat from which it had so recently sprung. From this complicated vantage-point Kästner is able to give a sharply perceived picture of the problems of Weimar Germany.

This picture is not an unfamiliar one. Thousands are thrown on the scrapheap. According to Malmy, the city editor, there is a huge mismatch between supply and demand. Technical progress has brought about a massive increase in the supply of goods; yet that same progress throws people out of work, thus denying them the means with which to purchase the goods produced. The ill-effects of technological progress are reinforced by the story of Professor Kollrepp (in Chapter XI), an inventor who is so shocked by the unemployment caused by his innovations in textile machinery that he has abandoned his work and lives the life of a down-and-out.

Kästner gives a quasi-factual account of the effects of unemployment that rings very true. Fabian earns 200 Marks a month. This was roughly the wage of a skilled worker, such as a toolmaker. From this he has to pay 80 Marks in rent. The plight of people who live in rented rooms and the power exercised by their landladies is a theme both here and in his poetry ('Coughing three times costs 1 Mark'). A lodger is seen as a prisoner whose love life must be carried out on the sly. The only solution, he suggests in 'Möblierte Melancholie' ('Furnished Melancholy'), is to tie a knot in your penis.

Love is less inhibited in *Fabian*, but the economic constraints are very apparent. Once forced into the ranks of the unemployed you are driven from pillar to post, hedged about with notices stating that 'everything is forbidden', and reduced to an income of 24.50 Marks. At the other end of the scale there are disreputable nouveaux-riches like the film director Makart and the slippery Zacharias, a newspaperman, who aged twenty-eight earns 2,500 Marks. At Fabian's level competitiveness is extreme. Labude's death is caused by the sheer malice of Weckherlin, the jealous assistant of the professor examining Labude's dissertation. When Fabian's colleague Fischer hears of Fabian's dismissal in Chapter XI, he goes green and comments, 'Good Lord, my luck's in again!' Even a commercial rationality appears to be missing: Fabian is more talented than Fischer and earns more money for the company, but it is he who gets the sack just because Fischer is paid even less. The triumph of short-term commercial thinking leads to an inhumanity that permeates the whole of society. It ranges from the casual callousness of the letter announcing Fabian's dismissal, via the indignant censoriousness of the crowd eager to condemn and punish a little girl who has stolen an ashtray, right down to the 'Anonymous Cabaret', where people come to laugh at performers who are evidently insane.

In the last analysis Kästner feels that the evils of society are spiritual, rather than economic. The suggestion (in Chapter III) that economic cures might be available or should be sought is derided. In Chapter XXI Fabian too rejects a materialist approach: 'Did he want conditions to improve? He wanted men and women to improve.' Malmy, the editor who cynically refrains from writing the truth in his newspaper, gives it as his diagnosis that Germany is suffering from 'spiritual slothfulness' and what is needed is a 'change of heart'. Such beliefs place the novel in a long tradition going back to Balzac's *Lost Illusions* and Flaubert's *Sentimental Education*, each of which is concerned with a young man from the provinces who becomes disillusioned by the corruption of the capital. In both cases the heroes suffer, as does Fabian, from 'spiritual slothfulness'.

However, Kästner is ambivalent about this slothfulness. Is

Fabian the typical representative of Germany or is he its critic? In the novel he stands somewhere between Malmy, a cynic, and his friend Labude, a scholar from a wealthy family. Labude is an idealist who shares Fabian's moralistic attitude towards society, but believes in taking action, mobilizing the uncommitted but progressive centre. Fabian is sceptical about the scope for action. He regards himself as a free-floating intellectual. Basing himself on the idea that the entire continent is just living provisionally and that people are 'swine', he feels that he can do nothing but observe. 'Let us assume for the moment that I really have some function. Where is the system in which I can exercise it?', he asks Labude in Chapter V. Since no such system appears to exist he is left with nothing to do but sit around in brothels and nightclubs cultivating 'the mixed emotions' and waiting for 'the triumph of decency'.

In a key passage in Chapter IV Fabian expresses his admiration for Descartes who like him had been a lodger in furnished rooms, but who, far from the world of action, had accomplished an 'overthrow of opinions'. At the same time Fabian is convinced of the futility of this ambition and this gives him a tragi-comic sense of his own impotence. He regards events with an ironic detachment which provides the novel with its satirical perspective, but at the same time this irony is directed towards himself. At the end of the book, he can wonder if there is any point in becoming 'a useful member of Society Ltd', as if he were somehow independent of it. Equally he can wryly record his own defeats. In his initial encounter with Frau Moll, for example, he is nearly raped and is generally humiliated. Defeats like this paradoxically strengthen his case against the immorality of the world while lending dignity to his own moral stance. They justify his refusal to adopt any course of action.

Fabian's ironic pessimism is also validated by comparison with Labude's idealism. Labude's ideas are characteristic of the day. He places his faith in the younger middle-class generation. Their fathers, like his own parents, had brought Europe to the brink of bankruptcy. Reform would be achieved by international agreements, the voluntary restriction of private profit, and other constraints on capitalism and the onward march of technology. Labude hopes to bring this about by means of a left-of-centre alliance. He is defeated by the setbacks to his career and in his personal life – the rejection of his thesis and the infidelity of Leda, his girlfriend. The novel appears to endorse Fabian's deeper pessimism ('. . . when you've got your Utopia the people there will still be punching each other on the nose!' he says in Chapter V). But equally, Kästner clearly believes that something should be done and Fabian himself, for all his scepticism about political parties, is prompt to act at a personal level. He intervenes to rescue the little girl who is accused of theft in the department store. He helps to rescue the Communist and Fascist who have wounded each other in the street fight in Chapter VI. And at the end he does not hesitate to leap into the Elbe to rescue the drowning boy. Despite the ironies surrounding this last intervention Kästner probably identifies as much with the desire to act as with Fabian's sense of futility.

6

The novel devotes much space to unconventional sexual behaviour. This is of course something of a cliché about the age in which it was written. As Henry Pachter has observed, 'Going through the memoirs of some famous people who had access to high society, such as Oskar Maria Graf, Carl Zuckmayer, Ludwig Marcuse, I get the impression that they were all writing about the same party, the same one-legged prostitute, the same supplier of cocaine.'*

In fact Kästner by no means confines his attentions to high society. Indeed he barely touches on it, in the lives of Labude's parents. However, this apart, his novel is raised above the stereotype by its satirical wit and the overall moral point of view. In the 1950 preface, he insists that he writes as a moralist:

> The present book . . . does not describe what things were like; it exaggerates them. The moralist holds up not a mirror, but a distorting mirror to his age (p. 4 below).

As Fabian drifts through the Exotic Bar where he meets Frau Moll, the Anonymous Cabaret, where the performers are insane, La Cousine, the lesbian bar, or the studio of Ruth Reiter, the lesbian sculptress, the sexual practices he witnesses

* Henry Pachter in his autobiographical *Weimar Etudes* (New York, 1982), p. 89.

are not just deviant: in Kästner's view they are deeply pathological.

In her polemical study of Kästner, Marianne Bäumler argues that by adopting such a narrative strategy Kästner can only depict private life. He can criticize Labude's father for his frivolity and his amorality, but since the latter is a highly placed lawyer it would have been more to the point to criticize him in his public role as a lawyer in a corrupt legal system.* However, in Kästner's eyes there is no caesura between private and public life. We are meant to make inferences about the legal profession from the fact that Herr Moll, for example, has drawn up a contract regularizing his wife's nymphomania, and that he would be willing to consider making Fabian an allowance in return for Fabian's satisfying his wife's insatiable needs. At every point the private and public overlap. In Haupt's dance-hall, for example (in Chapter V), where the tables have telephones to facilitate introductions, one of the prostitutes has rough hands from having worked in a factory. She has been sacked for blackmailing her former employer. She and her friend eat ravenously because they are now so poor. The prize offered for the most beautiful girl is a swindle: it has to be returned to the management. Or again, there is the story in Chapter II of the woman sitting with one man in a café while flirting outrageously with another, a deception only made possible by the fact that the first man is blind. This story, together with the landlord's evident relish at it is clearly intended as a general comment on social morality.

What Kästner portrays is a rampant sexuality which reflects a widespread social dislocation of which women were frequently the victims. This theme is crucial to Kästner. In an earlier poem he had noted that women playing pianos in the nineteenth century were replaced by women clattering away on typewriters in the twentieth. Another poem, 'Jahrgang 1899' ('The Generation of 1899') relates that disorientation to the war:

> While the men were in Flanders fighting,
> We tumbled their wives into bed;
> We had thought it would be more exciting;
> We understood less than we said.

* Marianne Bäumler, *Die aufgeräumte Wirklichkeit des Erich Kästner* ('Erich Kästner's Cheery Reality') (Cologne, 1984).

After the war the economic situation made marriage highly problematic. As Fabian tells his girlfriend Cornelia in Chapter IX, 'Either a man accepts the responsibility for a woman's future, and then, if he loses his job the week after, he realizes how irresponsibly he has acted. Or his sense of responsibility forbids him to make a mess of a woman's future, and if, for this very reason, he plunges her into misfortune, he finds out that his decision was as irresponsible as the other fellow's.' Cornelia rejects this analysis as itself irresponsible. In her view Fabian is making a plea for women to accept a status somewhere between marriage and prostitution: 'Of course, we are to come and go as you wish. But we are to cry when you send us away. And we are to be blissful when you allow us to come back. You want us to be an article of commerce, but the article is to be in love with you.'

Fabian's relationship with Cornelia stands out as an idyll amidst the decadence and corruption. It is nonetheless doomed. When Fabian loses his job she leaps at the chance to make her fortune in films. But this road runs through the bed of the brutish film-maker Makart. She mourns her betrayal of Fabian, but accepts it philosophically as the inevitable consequence of the economic situation: 'The only way to get out of the mud is to get yourself thoroughly muddy.' She clings to the hope that her self-sacrifice will save their love, but the book hints that she will be transformed into the kind of woman she portrays in Makart's film, 'vulgar and domineering'.

Since so much space is given to the description of sexual mores, the question naturally arises about the nature of Kästner's moralizing. His concern is not with the moral law, but with the health of society. Fabian is no shocked innocent but a man of the world who 'had spent his nights busily knocking about'. One senses that in this respect, too, he is not unlike his creator. The depth of Kästner's love for his mother seems to have made for difficulties in his relationships with women. His letters to her abound in negative comments on his various girlfriends, perhaps because this is what she wanted to hear, but partly at least because his perpetual disappointments were genuine. However in 1944, having been bombed out of his own home, he moved in with Luiselotte Enderle, a journalist whom he had known in Leipzig and with whom he stayed for the rest of his life.

Recent criticism, such as that of the critic Helmut Lethen,

has attacked Kästner from a feminist point of view.* According to Lethen Kästner is not interested in sexual liberation. Instead he creates a gallery of voracious and predatory women. One is Frau Moll, a nymphomaniac who brings her lovers home for her husband to inspect and who later sets up a male brothel where she personally subjects new employees to an entrance examination. Another is Mucki whom Fabian picks up on the rebound from Cornelia. Although Fabian may seem to take the initiative, in reality it is she who is the predator. Kästner draws an oppressive picture of a woman eager to spoil Fabian by stuffing him full of food, while devouring him sexually. In Chapter XVII she even combines these activities when she brings in the coffee, unbuttons her blouse and announces, 'Now for the dessert.'

Although there are exceptions, such as the sympathetic portrayal of the prostitute in Dresden, most of the women are shown to be in the grip of uncontrollable sexual desire. Instead of accepting that women should have the right to express their sexuality as they see fit, Kästner responds repressively. It is strongly suggested that men like Labude's father or Dr Moll are at fault in failing to keep their wives under control. Lesbianism, too, is not treated as either a biological or psychological constant, but as a perhaps wilful turning away from men. It is true that men are guilty of the opposite failing. The brutal Wilhelmy, the candidate for death, beats Kulp senseless, and Makart uses his power unscrupulously to subdue Cornelia. Nevertheless, despite the general case that relations between the sexes have been disrupted by underlying social processes, there is some truth in the argument that Kästner's criticism of a society that debases women is shot through with a sub-text that blames women for the havoc they wreak.

This point is reinforced by Kästner's depiction of children and of his mother. Kästner is at his most charming in his

* There is little critical literature on Kästner in English. For those who know German the most interesting contributions include two essays by Egon Schwarz, in Reinhold Grimm and Jost Hermand (eds), *Die sogenannten Zwanziger Jahre* (Bad Homburg, 1970), and in H. Wagener (ed.), *Zeitkritische Romane des 20. Jahrhunderts* (Stuttgart, 1975). There is a solid monograph from a pluralist standpoint by Dirk Walter, *Zeitkritik und Idyllensehnsucht* (Heidelberg, 1977). The best critique of Kästner from the left is Helmut Lethen, *Neue Sachlichkeit 1924–1932* (Stuttgart, 1970).

portrayal of both. But it is their essential innocence, including sexual innocence, that enables him to place them at the opposite pole to his principal adult characters. The portrayal of Fabian's mother echoes his relationship with his own as reflected in his letters and autobiographical writings. They remained close throughout her life. The symbol of their love was the washing. On becoming an independent adult he insisted on perpetuating the illusion of dependence by always obeying her request to send home his washing, even when he was famous and wealthy and there was an express laundry round the corner. The deep affection, and an almost collusive intimacy which extends to a 'sharing' of Kästner's girlfriends, are evident in *Fabian* too. The mutual solicitude which governs their relationship is most beautifully summed up in the episode at the end of Chapter XIII where each surreptitiously slips the other a twenty-mark note.

Children, too, represent a realm of innocence. In fact the whole of Kästner's work is made radiant by the presence of children. He would undoubtedly have approved of Novalis's aphorism, 'Where there are children, there is the Golden Age.' The child who steals an ashtray in the department store as a birthday present for her father does not thereby lose her innocence in Kästner's eyes. Later on, in Fabian's dream (in Chapter XIV), when Labude appeals to the crowd, the adults raise one hand in support while continuing to pick each other's pockets with the other. Only the little girl raises both hands in support of 'decency'.

However, children's innocence is undermined by school, by 'that lie which stealthily filled the place, that evil, secret power that transformed whole generations of children into obedient officials and narrow-minded bourgeois' (Chapter XXII).

7

Having lost his job, his best friend and his girl, Fabian decides to abandon Berlin and return to his home town. Although it is given no name there is little doubt that it is a description of Dresden, Kästner's birthplace. Unlike other literary flights from the corrupt capital to the provinces, this one is not portrayed in an idyllic light. If the atmosphere in Berlin is too febrile, in his home town the temperature is below normal. Like

Kästner Fabian has no relationship with his father, who is unaware that he even had a best friend to lose.

The places he visits and the people he meets fail to trigger nostalgic memories. His school friend, Wenzkat, belongs to the reactionary 'Stahlhelm' and in the brothel takes a sadistic pleasure in beating the prostitutes. Fabian is unable to re-establish a relationship with his former girlfriend, Eva, a harassed mother of two, now completely provincialized. A visit to his old school merely reminds him of the rigidly traditional and patriotic education with its eternal round of senseless discipline. The fact that half the members of his class had died in the war has not been enough to introduce any changes or to dent the complacency of his headmaster. Kästner's bitter line, 'Whatever Germans build turns into barracks', applies to everything in Fabian's entire home town. He could obtain work, but it would be with a right-wing newspaper, so that he would be unable to escape the cynical compromises of the Berlin journalists he had so disapproved of earlier on. Even his mother is shown to be worn down by the recession and her magic powers are not enough to salvage the situation.

There is some disagreement among critics about how to interpret Fabian's death. Is it the ultimate regression, a quixotic action which ironically confirms the wisdom of his earlier passivity? Or does Kästner turn against his hero at the end with the suggestion that it is high time that he learnt to swim? However it is regarded, it underlines the fact that the Germany of the future would have no place in it for people like Fabian.

8

The most important contemporary criticism of Kästner came from Walter Benjamin, who scathingly reviewed some of Kästner's poetry in an essay called 'Left-wing Melancholy', in which he fastened on his pessimistic outlook.

In short, this left-wing radicalism is precisely the attitude which fails to correspond to political action of any kind. It stands to the left not just of this or that position, but of every conceivable course of action. For right from the start its only aim is to relax into a negativistic inertia. . . . It is the fatalism of those who stand at the furthest remove from the processes of production, and whose dull efforts to identify economic trends are comparable with the attitude of a man who submits completely to the inscrutable forces of his own digestion.*

For Benjamin the solution to Kästner's problem was presumably a committed literature in the style of Brecht. Beyond that it was often implied on the left, though not perhaps by Benjamin himself, that the only way out was to join the left-wing parties. However, quite apart from the fact that the Social Democrats and the Communists were at each others' throats, it is by no means obvious that this was an effective course of action at the time. Certainly, Kästner is not simply to be condemned because he rejected it. He believed that it was important to defend the republic which, as he saw it, was being torn apart by extremists of right and left. This is represented in Chapter VI in the shoot-out between the Fascist and the Communist. The novel seems to endorse the doctor's judgement that such episodes are a curious way of trying to reduce the unemployment problem. In doing so it adopts the ironic distancing tactics of the non-political ideology which claims the right to stand above the contending parties; but since at this stage there was perhaps no remaining viable course of action, one can at least say in Kästner's favour that his novel is not a tract in favour of abolishing the republic, as was the case in the work of progressive radicals like Kurt Tucholsky.

It is for this reason that modern West German critics can look back to Kästner as an ideological founding father of the Federal Republic after 1945. Kästner's pessimism reflects his sad perception that the middle ground had disappeared from Weimar. Yet the values for which Kästner pleads, decency, rationality and genuine human warmth, were worth defending. It was not so much Kästner's inadequacy as Germany's tragedy that the liberal bourgeois democracy which would have underpinned them was no longer available.

Rodney Livingstone

* 'Linke Melancholie', first published in *Die Gesellschaft* in 1931, in Benjamin's *Gesammelte Werke*, vol. III (Frankfurt, 1972), p. 283. The liberal *Frankfurter Zeitung* had refused to publish Benjamin's political attack.

NOTE ON THE TRANSLATION

This translation of Kästner's *Fabian* appeared originally in 1932, one year after the German publication. The translator, Cyrus Brooks, was a writer of detective stories and a translator of other books by Kästner as well as by Alfred Neumann, Leonhard Frank and others. During the Second World War he was Chief Executive Officer in the PWE – the Political Warfare Executive – and in this capacity he was active in the re-education of German prisoners of war.

The present edition adopts his elegant translation of *Fabian* with only minor changes. It also includes the Epilogue which had been rejected by the original publisher, and the new Preface which Kästner added for the 1950 German reprint.

Despite its excellence Brooks's translation turned out to be by no means complete. The omissions appear to reflect a conscious decision to tone down Kästner's sexual explicitness. This resulted in a version which seriously understates Kästner's candour and wit in erotic matters. It also blurs the picture he gives of Weimar Germany. Moreover, it may have escaped earlier English readers that the language Kästner uses in *Fabian* is not the same as in *Emil*. There the little boys and girls speak in a tough, streetwise language, but are too polite to say that the thief, Herr Grundeis, has left his hotel room to go to the lavatory. In *Fabian* there are no such inhibitions. Since we have long been accustomed to greater explicitness there is no reason to abide by Brooks's – or his publisher's – practice, so all the omitted passages have been restored.

R.S.L.

GOING TO THE DOGS

This book, which is approaching its twenty-fifth anniversary, has been subjected to a variety of judgements, and even those who have praised it have often misunderstood it. Will people understand it any better today? Of course not! How should they? The fact that judgements of taste were nationalized during the Third Reich, packaged in slogans and consumed by the million, has ruined the taste and judgement of broad sections of the public down to our own times. And even today, before they have had time to regenerate themselves, new, or rather, very ancient powers are fanatically engaged in inoculating the masses with new standardized opinions which are not so very different from the old ones. Even now many people do not know, and many others have forgotten, that we all both can and should form judgements for ourselves. Even those who make the attempt do not know how to set about it. And we already find laws in preparation against modern art and literature, ostensibly for the protection of the young. The word 'subversive' is once again to be found at the top of the list of reactionary vocabularies. Such verbal abuse is just one of the means which not only justify the end, but all too often bring it about as well.

Hence people nowadays understand even less well than twenty-five years ago that *Fabian* is a highly moral book, and by no means an 'immoral' one. Its original title was *Going to the Dogs*. Together with a number of crass chapters, that title was rejected by the original publisher. It was meant to make it clear, already on the front cover, that the author had a particular aim in view. He wished to utter a warning. He wanted to warn people about the abyss into which Germany was in danger of falling and threatening to take all Europe with it. He wanted to force people to listen and reflect before it was too late. To do this he used the appropriate means, which in this case meant every available means.

The great wave of unemployment, the spiritual depression which followed in the wake of the economic one, the craving to anaesthetize the mind, the activities of unscrupulous parties –

3

these were the storm signals which heralded the approaching crisis. Nor was the uncanny silence before the storm lacking – that spiritual lethargy which spread paralysis like an epidemic.

It drove many to oppose both the storm and the silence preceding it. They found themselves pushed to one side. People preferred to listen to the fairground criers and drummers who sang the praises of their mustard plasters and poisonous patent medicines.

People ran to follow the Pied Pipers, following them right into the abyss in which we now find ourselves, more dead than alive, and in which we try to make ourselves comfortable, as if nothing had happened.

The present book which depicts life as it was in the big city, is no poetic photograph album, but a satire. It does not describe what things were like; it exaggerates them. The moralist holds up not a mirror, but a distorting mirror to his age. Caricature, a legitimate artistic mode, is the furthest he can go. If that doesn't help nothing will. It is not unusual that nothing should help, nor was it then. But it would be unusual if the moralist were to be discouraged by this fact. His traditional task is the defence of lost causes. He fulfils it as best he may. His motto today is as it has always been: to fight on notwithstanding!

Erich Kästner
Munich, May 1950

I

A WAITER AS ORACLE
THE OTHER DECIDES TO GO NOTWITHSTANDING
A CLUB FOR INTELLECTUAL CONTACTS

Fabian was sitting in a café, by name Spalteholz, reading the headlines of the evening papers: English Airship Disaster near Beauvais, Strychnine Stored with Lentils, Girl of Nine Jumps from Window, Election of Premier – Another Fiasco, Murder in Lainz Zoo, Scandal of Municipal Purchasing Board, Artificial Voice in Waistcoat Pocket, Ruhr Coal-Sales Falling, National Railways – Presentation to Director Neumann, Elephants on Pavement, Coffee Markets Uncertain, Clara Bow Scandal, Expected Strike of 140,000 Metal Workers, Chicago Underworld Drama, Timber Dumping – Negotiations in Moscow, Revolt of Starhemberg Troops. The usual thing. Nothing special.

He took a sip of coffee and shuddered. The stuff tasted sweet. Ten years before, in a students' hostel at the Oranienburg Gate, he had forced himself, three times a week, to swallow macaroni with saccharine; since then he had loathed everything sweet. He hurriedly lit a cigarette and called the waiter.

'Yes, sir?'

'Please answer me a question.'

'Yes, sir.'

'Shall I go or not?'

'Where to, sir?'

'I want you to answer questions, not ask them. Shall I go or not?'

The waiter mentally scratched his head. Then he shifted from one flat foot to the other and said with some embarrassment: 'You'd better not go. Keep on the safe side, sir.'

Fabian nodded. 'Right. I'll go. The bill.'

'But I said, don't go.'

'That's why I'm going. The bill, please.'

'So if I'd said, go, you wouldn't have gone?'

5

'Oh yes I should. The bill, please.'

'It's beyond me,' declared the waiter, in an irritable tone. 'Why did you ask me at all?'

'I wish I knew,' replied Fabian.

'One cup of coffee, one roll and butter, fifty, thirty, eighty, ninety pfennigs,' recited the waiter.

Fabian placed a mark on the table and left the café. He had no notion where he was. If you board a No. 1 bus at Wittenbergplatz, get out at Potsdam Bridge and take a tram, without knowing its destination, only to leave it twenty minutes later because a woman suddenly gets in who bears a resemblance to Frederick the Great, you cannot be expected to know where you are.

He followed three workmen who were striding along at a good pace, stumbled over planks of wood, passed hoardings and grey, dubious hotels and arrived at Jannowitz Bridge Station. In the train, he found the address which Bertuch, the manager at his office, had written down for him: 23 Schlüterstrasse, Frau Sommer. He got out at the Zoo. In the Joachimsthaler Strasse, a thin-legged young lady, rising and falling on her toes, asked him what about it. He rejected her advances, wagged his finger at her and escaped.

The town was like a fair-ground. The house-fronts were bathed in garish light to shame the stars in the sky. An aeroplane droned above the roofs. Suddenly there was a shower of aluminium thalers. The passers-by looked up, laughed and bent to pick them up. Fabian fleetingly recalled the story of the little girl who lifted her frock to catch the small change that fell from heaven. Then he took one of the thalers from the stiff brim of a stranger's hat. It bore the words: 'Come to the Exotic Bar, 3 Nollendorfplatz, Beautiful girls, Nude tableaux, Pension Condor in same house.' Suddenly Fabian had the impression that he was up there in the aeroplane, looking down at himself, at that young man in the Joachimsthaler Strasse, who stood in the bustle of the crowd, in the glare of street lamps and shop windows, in the turmoil of the inflamed and feverish night. How small the fellow was, and yet it was himself!

He crossed the Kurfürstendamm. On one of the gables a figure in neon lights, that of a youthful Turk, was rolling its electric eyeballs. Then something struck Fabian violently on

6

the heel. He turned round disapprovingly. It was a tram. The conductor swore.

'Look where you're going,' shouted a policeman.

Fabian raised his hat. 'I'll do my best.'

In Schlüterstrasse the door was opened by a Lilliputian in green livery, who climbed an ornamental ladder, helped the visitor out of his coat, and vanished. Scarcely had he gone when a well-developed woman, undoubtedly Frau Sommer, came rustling through the curtains. 'Will you kindly come to my office?' she said. Fabian followed her.

'Your club was recommended to me by a Herr Bertuch.'

She flicked over the pages of a ledger, and nodded. 'Bertuch, Friedrich Georg, manager, aged forty, medium height, dark, 9 Karlstrasse, fond of music, prefers slim blondes of twenty-five and under.'

'That's him.'

'Herr Bertuch became a member last October and has been here five times since.'

'That speaks well for the place.'

'The entrance fee is twenty marks, and there is a further fee of ten marks for each visit.'

'Here are thirty marks.' Fabian put the money on the desk. The well-developed woman slipped the notes into a drawer, took up a fountain-pen and said: 'Your name and address?'

'Fabian, Jacob, aged thirty-two, profession variable, at present advertising copywriter, 17 Schaperstrasse, weak heart, brown hair. What else do you want to know?'

'Have you any special wishes in the matter of ladies?'

'I would rather not tie myself down. My taste is for blondes, but my experience is against them. I have a preference for tall women. But the attraction is not mutual. Better leave that column blank.'

A gramophone was playing somewhere. The well-developed woman rose and said gravely: 'Before we go in I must make you acquainted with the more important rules. There is no objection to members approaching each other, indeed they are expected to do so. The ladies enjoy the same rights as the men. The existence, address and practices of the club must not be revealed except to trustworthy persons. Despite the idealistic aims of our establishment, refreshments must be paid for on consumption.

No couple may claim exemption from interference while on the club premises. Couples are requested to leave the club if they wish to be undisturbed. The establishment serves to initiate acquaintanceships, but does not cater for them once made. Members who give each other temporary opportunities for identification are requested to forget them, as otherwise complications are inevitable. Do you understand, Herr Fabian?'

'Perfectly.'

'Then please follow me.'

There must have been thirty or forty persons present. In the first room they were playing bridge. Next door they were dancing. Frau Sommer led the new member to an unoccupied table, said that he could apply to her at any time in case of need, and took her leave. Fabian sat down, ordered a brandy and soda from the waiter, and looked round him. Was he at a birthday-party?

'They look more innocent than they are,' remarked a small, dark-haired girl, and sat down at his side. Fabian offered her a cigarette.

'I rather like you,' she said. 'You were born in December.'

'In February.'

'Oh, Pisces with a spot or two of Aquarius. Rather cold. You've come here out of curiosity?'

'The supporters of the atomic theory maintain that even the smallest particle of matter consists of charges of electrical energy revolving round each other. Do you regard this merely as a hypothesis or as an actual statement of fact?'

'So you are sensitive too?' cried the young woman. 'But that doesn't matter. Have you come to look for a wife?'

He shrugged his shoulders. 'Is that a formal proposal?'

'Nonsense! I've been married twice, and that's enough to go on with. Marriage does not provide me with the right form of self-expression. I'm much too interested in men. I picture every man I meet, provided I like him, as a husband.'

'In his most salient aspects, I hope.'

She laughed as though she had a hiccup, and placed her hand on his knee. 'Quite so. They say I suffer from an inventive imagination. If, in the course of the evening, you should feel a desire to take me home, my flat and I are small but substantial.'

He removed that restless, alien hand from his knee, and said: 'All things are possible. Now I'm going to take a look round.'

That was as far as he got. When he rose and turned away from her, he found a tall woman with a figure that answered the programme standing in front of him. 'They are just going to dance,' she said. She was taller than he and blonde into the bargain. The little black-haired buccaneer observed the regulations and vanished. A waiter started the gramophone. People rose from their tables. They were dancing.

Fabian examined the blonde. She had a pale, infantile face and an air of greater restraint than, to judge by her dancing, she possessed. He said nothing, and felt that in a few minutes they would reach that stage of taciturnity when conversation, especially trivial conversation, becomes impossible. Luckily he trod on her toe. She grew talkative. She pointed out the two ladies who had recently boxed each other's ears and torn the clothes off each other's backs for the sake of a man. She informed him that Frau Sommer was engaged in an intrigue with the green Lilliputian, the details of which she dared not imagine. Finally she asked whether he wanted to stay; she was going. He went with her.

In Kurfürstendamm she signalled to a taxi-cab, gave an address, climbed in and constrained him to take a seat at her side. 'But I've only two marks left,' he objected.

'That doesn't make much difference,' she replied, and ordered the driver to put out the lights. They were in darkness. The car started and drove off. At the first turn in the road she fell upon him and bit his lower lip. He struck his temple against the frame of the window, caught his head in his hands and said: 'Ah-oo! That's a good beginning.'

'Don't be so touchy,' she said, and smothered him with her attentions.

The assault was too sudden for him. He had a pain in his head, and his heart was not in the business.

'I really wanted to write a letter,' he groaned, 'before you throttle me.'

She punched him on the collar-bone, laughed up and down the scale with complete self-possession, and went on strangling him. Evidently his attempts to defend himself against the woman were misinterpreted. Every turn of the road led to new entanglements. He asked the gods to spare them further swerves. But the gods were having a day off.

At last the car stopped. Outside the door of a block of flats the blonde powdered her face, paid the fare and said: 'Your cheeks are covered in red smudges, and you're coming up for a cup of tea.'

He rubbed the traces of lipstick from his face, and replied: 'I'm honoured by the invitation, but I've got to be early at the office tomorrow.'

'Don't make me angry. You're going to stay with me. The maid will wake you.'

'But I shan't get up. No, I must sleep at home. I'm expecting an urgent telegram at seven in the morning. My landlady will come into my room and shake me till I wake.'

'But how do you know about this telegram?'

'I even know what's in it.'

'What?'

'It will say, "Get out of bed. Yours ever, Fabian." My name is Fabian.' He blinked up at the leaves of the trees and noted with delight the yellow gleam of the street lamps. The street was completely empty. A cat ran silently away into the darkness. If only he could go now and saunter along in front of those grey house-fronts!

'But your story about the telegram is not true.'

'No, but that's purely a matter of chance,' he said.

'What makes you come to the club if you don't want to take the consequences?' she said irritably, and unlocked the door.

'Someone gave me the address and I'm very curious.'

'Well, come along,' she said. 'We'll set no limits to your curiosity.' The door slammed to behind them.

II

A VERY IMPORTUNATE LADY
A SOLICITOR WHO MADE NO OBJECTION
BEGGING RUINS THE CHARACTER

There was a mirror on one side of the lift. Fabian took out his handkerchief and rubbed the red blotches from his face. His tie was askew. His temple was burning; and the pale blonde was looking down at him. 'Do you know what a megaera is?' he asked. She put her arm round him. 'Yes, but I'm prettier.'

The name was on the door-plate: 'Moll.' The maidservant opened the door. 'Bring some tea.'

'The tea is in your room, madam.'

'Good. Go to bed.' The girl vanished down the passage.

Fabian followed the blonde. She led him straight into her bedroom, poured out tea, produced cognac and cigarettes, and said with a comprehensive gesture: 'Help yourself.'

'Lord, you're a quick worker. Your name is Moll, isn't it?'

'Yes. Irene Moll. So that people with a good education have something to laugh at. Sit down, I'll be back in a moment.'

He held her back and kissed her.

'Well, you're coming on slowly,' she said, and left him. He took a sip of tea and a glass of cognac. Then he examined the room. The bed was low and broad. The lamp gave a reflected light. The walls were covered with mirrors. He drank another cognac and went to the window. It was not barred.

What was she going to do with him? Fabian was thirty-two, and had spent his nights busily knocking about; the situation began to attract him. He drank his third cognac and rubbed his hands.

For some time he had cultivated mixed emotions as a hobby. If a man wants to study such things he must have them. He can only observe them while he is experiencing them. Fabian was a surgeon, dissecting his own soul.

'There. Now the little fellow's going to be slaughtered,' said the blonde. She was wearing pyjamas of black lace. He retreated a step. But she shouted 'Hurrah!' and sprang at his neck with such verve that he lost his balance, reeled and found himself sitting on the floor with her.

'Isn't she appalling?' asked a strange voice.

Fabian looked up in astonishment. A thin man with a big nose, dressed in pyjamas, was standing yawning in the doorway.

'What do you want here?' asked Fabian.

'I beg your pardon, my dear sir, but how was I to know that you were crawling round the room with my wife.'

'With your wife?'

The intruder nodded, yawned desperately, and said in a reproachful voice: 'Irene, how could you place this gentleman in such an awkward predicament? If you want me to inspect your new acquisitions, you might at least present them to me with some regard for etiquette. On the carpet! I'm sure this gentleman objects. And I was sleeping so peacefully when you woke me . . . My name is Moll, sir. I am a solicitor and also,' he yawned heartbreakingly, 'and also the husband of the woman who is now reclining on you.'

Fabian pushed the blonde from off him, stood up and smoothed the parting of his hair. 'Does your wife keep a male harem? My name is Fabian.'

Moll came up and shook him by the hand. 'I'm pleased to meet so charming a young man. The circumstances are both usual and unusual. It depends on your point of view. But if the information reassures you: I am used to it. Do sit down.'

Fabian sat down. Irene Moll slid on to the arm of his chair, stroked him and announced to her husband: 'If you don't like him, I'll break our contract.'

'But I do like him,' protested the solicitor.

'You talk about me as though I were a slice of seed-cake or a bobsleigh,' said Fabian.

'You are a bobsleigh, little man!' cried the woman, and pressed his head against her full, black-latticed bosom.

'Almighty God!' he cried. 'Will you let me alone?'

'You must not annoy your visitors, dear Irene,' said Moll. 'I'll take him into my study and tell him all he need know. You're forgetting that he must find the situation unusual. Afterwards I'll send him over to you. Good night.' He shook hands with his wife.

She climbed on to the low bed and stood, disconsolate and forlorn, among the pillows. 'Good night, Moll,' she said. 'Sleep well, but don't talk his head off. I shall want him.'

'Yes, yes,' answered Moll, and went out, taking his guest with him.

They sat down in his study. The solicitor lit a cigar, shivered, wrapped a camel-hair blanket round his knees, and searched among a bundle of documents.

'Of course it's no business of mine,' began Fabian, 'but the things you put up with from your wife are beyond all reason. Does she often fetch you out of bed to size up her lovers?'

'Very often, my dear sir. At first, I made her sign a document giving me the right to give or withhold my approval. At the end of our first year of married life we made a contract, of which the fourth paragraph runs as follows: "The said Irene Moll undertakes first to present to her husband, the said Felix Moll, any person with whom she wishes to enter into intimate relations. Should the said Felix Moll express disapproval of such person, the said Irene Moll undertakes immediately to forgo her intentions. Any infringement of this undertaking shall entail the forfeiture of one half of the said Irene Moll's monthly allowance." The contract is a very interesting one. Shall I read the whole of it?' Moll produced from his pocket the key of his desk.

'Please don't trouble,' protested Fabian. 'What I should like to know is why you hit on the idea of ever making such a contract.'

'My wife had such bad dreams.'

'What?'

'Dreams. She dreamt the most terrible things. It was obvious that her sexual needs increased proportionately to the length of our married life and produced wish-dreams of whose content, my dear sir, you can, happily, form no conception. I retired, and she peopled her bedroom with Chinamen, pugilists and dancers. What else could I do? We made a contract.'

'Don't you think that a different sort of treatment might have been more suitable and more successful?' asked Fabian, impatiently.

'For instance?' The solicitor leaned forward in his chair.

'For instance, twenty-five across the pants every night.'

13

'I tried it. It hurt me too much.'

'I can well appreciate that.'

'No,' cried the solicitor, 'you cannot appreciate it. Irene is very strong, sir.'

Moll bowed his head. Fabian took a white carnation from a vase on the writing-desk, stuck the flower in his buttonhole, rose and walked about the room, putting the pictures straight. Probably the tall old fellow had quite enjoyed being put across his wife's knee.

'I'm going,' he said. 'Give me the front-door key.'

'Are you serious?' inquired Moll, anxiously. 'But Irene's expecting you. For heaven's sake, don't go! She'll fly into a passion when she finds you've gone. She'll think I sent you away. Please stay. She's been so looking forward to it. Don't grudge her her little pleasures.'

The man had sprung to his feet. He seized his visitor by the coat. 'Do stay. You won't regret it. You'll come again. You will be one of our friends. And I shall know Irene is in good hands. Do it as a favour to me.'

'Perhaps you'd like to guarantee me a regular income?'

'We might talk that over. I am not without means.'

'Give me that key, and kindly be quick about it. I am not qualified for the job.'

Dr Moll sighed, rummaged on his writing-desk and handed Fabian a bunch of keys. 'What a pity!' he said. 'I took a fancy to you from the very first. Keep those keys for a day or two. Perhaps you'll think better of it. I assure you I should be very glad to see you again.'

Fabian growled 'Good night,' went softly down the passage, took his hat and coat, opened the door, closed it gently behind him and ran down the stairs. In the street, he took a deep breath and shook his head. Out here, people were sauntering past along the pavements without any idea of the crazy things that happened behind the house-fronts. The fairy-tale gift of looking through walls and curtained windows was nothing compared with the fortitude required to endure the sights one would see there.

He had told the blonde creature he was curious; now he was running away instead of feeding his curiosity on Dr and Frau Moll. He was the poorer by thirty marks. He still had two marks in his pocket. Supper was out of the question. He whistled for it, walked at random through strange, gloomy avenues and came by accident to Heerstrasse Station. He took a train to the Zoo; there he boarded an underground train, changed at Wittenbergplatz and came up out of the underworld at Spichernstrasse to stand beneath the open sky.

He went to his usual café. No, Dr Labude had gone. He had waited till eleven. Fabian sat down, ordered coffee and smoked.

The landlord, a certain Herr Kowalski, inquired after his health. That evening, by the way, something very funny had happened. Kowalski laughed till his false teeth flashed. Nietenführ, the waiter, had noticed it first. 'There was a young couple sitting over there at the round table. They were getting on like a house on fire. The girl kept stroking the man's hand; she laughed, lit his cigarette and was altogether more charming than girls generally are.'

'But that's not funny.'

'Wait a bit, Herr Fabian, wait a bit. The girl – she was pretty, I grant you – was carrying on at the same time with a man at the next table. You should have seen it. Nietenführ quietly fetched me over. You'd never have believed it. At last the fellow handed her a note. She read it, nodded, wrote a word or two and threw it back to his table. And all the while she went on talking to her friend, telling him things to make him laugh – I've seen some smart women, but this little juggler beat the lot of them.'

'But why did the man put up with it?'

'Just a minute, Herr Fabian. I'm just coming to the point. Well, of course we wondered why he let her carry on so. He sat there at her side, quite satisfied, smiled in a simple sort of way, put his arm round her, while all the time she was nodding to the man at the next table. He nodded back, made signs to her. We couldn't make head or tail of it. Then they called for their bill and Nietenführ went over to them.' Herr Kowalski threw back his massive head and threw his laughter towards the ceiling.

'Well, what was it?'

'The man she was with was blind!' The landlord bowed and walked off, laughing heartily. Fabian looked after him in astonishment. The progress of humanity was unmistakable.

There was some trouble near the door. Nietenführ and the second waiter were busy hustling a shabbily dressed man out of the café. 'Get out of here, and quick! Always this everlasting

begging. It's a disgrace,' said Nietenführ, through his teeth.
And the second waiter jerked the man to and fro. He was pale
and never said a word.

Fabian jumped up and ran across to them. 'Hands off that
gentleman!' he cried to the waiters. They obeyed reluctantly.

'So you've got here safely,' cried Fabian, and shook the
beggar by the hand. 'I'm awfully sorry these men insulted you. I
beg your pardon. Come over to my table.' He led the man, who
did not know what was happening to him, to his corner, invited
him to sit down, and said: 'What will you have to eat? You'll
take a glass of beer, won't you?'

'It's very good of you,' said the beggar, 'but I shall only make
things uncomfortable for you.'

'Here's the menu. Won't you find something?'

'It won't do. They'll only come and fetch me and chuck me
out.'

'They won't. Pull yourself together! You're afraid to sit
properly on your chair, and all because your coat's patched and
your belly's grumbling. It's partly your own fault if you always
find the door slammed in your face.'

'If you'd been out of work for two years you would see things
in a different light,' said the man. 'I sleep in a doss-house on the
Engel Embankment, and get ten marks a week from the poor
relief. My digestion's ruined with too much caviare.'

'What's your trade?'

'Bank-clerk, if I remember rightly. I've been in prison too.
Lord, you have to look round a bit. The only experience I've
never had is suicide. But there's still time for it.' He sat on the
edge of his chair, holding one shaking hand before the opening
in his waistcoat to hide his dirty shirt.

Fabian did not know what to say. He tried over several
sentences in his head, but none would do. He stood up and said:
'Just a minute, the waiter wants a deputation to go and fetch
him.' He went to the buffet, called the head-waiter to account,
took him by the arm and hauled him across the café.

The beggar was gone.

'I'll pay you tomorrow!' cried Fabian, and ran into the street.
He looked round. The man had vanished.

'Who are you looking for?' asked a voice. It was Münzer, the
journalist. He buttoned up his overcoat and lit a cigar. 'Hell,' he

said, 'I should have won easily, if Schmalnauer hadn't played such a rotten game. But I must get down to the office. The German people will want to know, in the morning, how many houses have caught fire while it slept.'

'But you're the political editor,' objected Fabian.

'Houses catch fire in all departments,' said Münzer. 'Especially at night. It must be the way they're constructed. I'll tell you what – you come along. Come and take a look at our circus.'

Münzer climbed into a small car. Fabian took his seat beside him. 'How long have you had a car?' he asked.

'I bought it from our city editor. It was costing him too much to run,' explained Münzer. 'It is splendid to see how much it annoys him to see me climb into his former pride and joy. That in itself is worth it. Do you know you're riding at your own risk? If you break your neck you'll have to pay for it.'

Then they drove off.

III

FOURTEEN DEAD IN CALCUTTA
IT IS RIGHT TO DO WRONG
SNAILS THAT CRAWL IN A CIRCLE

The corridor was empty. There was a light in the city editor's office, but no one was there, and the door was open. 'Pity Malmy's in the building,' said Münzer, ill-humouredly. 'Now he's missed seeing his car again. One moment. Let's hear what's going on in the universe.' He threw open a door. Typewriters were clattering. From a row of telephone-cabins along one wall came the voices of stenographers, seeming to sound from a great distance.

Münzer shouted into the noise: 'Anything important?'

'The Chancellor's speech,' a woman answered.

'That's right,' said Münzer. 'The fellow's upsetting my whole front page with his clap-trap. Have you got it all?'

'Cabin two is just taking the second third.'

'Straight into the typewriter with it and then up to me!' commanded Münzer. He slammed the door and led Fabian to the offices of the political section. As they took off their coats, he pointed to his table. 'Look what they've sent me. A paper earthquake.' He rummaged in a heap of recent messages, cut off a few snippets with his scissors, like a tailor's cutter, and put them on one side. The rest he threw into the wastepaper basket. 'Come on. In you go,' he said. He rang the bell, gave the uniformed messenger some money and asked for a bottle of Moselle and two glasses. The messenger collided at the door with an excited young man who was trying to get in.

'The Chief has just phoned,' explained the young man, breathlessly. 'I was to cut five lines from the leading article. Some more news has come in and superseded it. I've just come from the composing room. I've taken out the five lines.'

'You're a magician,' declared Münzer. 'Let me introduce you. Dr Irrgang – he has a great future before him. Irrgang is his pen-name – Herr Fabian.'

They shook hands.

'But,' said Herr Irrgang, nervously, 'now there are five lines missing.'

'What is one to do in such an extraordinary situation?' asked Münzer.

'Fill up the column,' volunteered the trainee.

Münzer nodded. 'Nothing in type?' He searched among the galleys. 'Sold out,' he said. 'The silly season.' Then he examined the messages he had just put on one side, and shook his head.

'Perhaps something usable will turn up,' suggested the young man.

'You ought to have been St Simeon Stylites,' said Münzer, 'or a prisoner awaiting trial, or some other chap with plenty of leisure. If you need a paragraph and haven't got one, invent one. Watch me!' He sat down without reflecting, quickly wrote a few lines and handed the sheet to the young man. 'There! Clear off, young column-filler. If it's too short use extra leads.'

Herr Irrgang read what Münzer had written, and said softly: 'God Almighty!' He sat down on the couch, amid a crunching mass of foreign newspapers, as though he had suddenly been taken ill.

Fabian bent over and read the paragraph that trembled in Irrgang's hand. 'Street fighting between Mohammedans and Hindus has broken out in Calcutta. Although the police soon had the situation in hand the casualties were fourteen dead and twenty-two injured. Order has now been fully restored.'

An old man in slippers shuffled into the room and put down several typewritten sheets in front of Münzer. 'Chancellor's speech, continuation,' he murmured. 'The rest will be through in ten minutes.' Then he shuffled out again. Münzer took the six pages of which the speech provisionally consisted, and pasted them end to end, till they looked like a medieval scroll. Then he began to edit them. 'Buck up, Jenny,' he said, with a sideways glance at Irrgang.

'But there's been no fighting in Calcutta,' returned Irrgang, with some hesitation. Then he looked down and murmured helplessly: 'Fourteen dead!'

'No fighting in Calcutta?' asked Münzer, indignantly. 'Will you kindly prove that? There's always fighting in Calcutta. Are we to report that a sea-serpent has been sighted in the Pacific?

Just remember this: reports that are never proved untrue – or at least not for a week or so – are true. And now run away like lightning, or I'll have you made into a stereo and sent out as a supplement to the final edition.'

The young man went.

'And that wants to be a journalist,' groaned Münzer. He sighed and worked at the Chancellor's speech with his blue pencil. Gossip-column consultant – there's a job for the lad. No such thing, more's the pity.'

'So you calmly slaughter fourteen Hindus in Calcutta and send twenty-two more to the municipal hospital?' said Fabian.

Münzer went on working at the Chancellor. 'What's one to do?' he asked. 'Besides, why all this sympathy for the fellows? They're still alive, all thirty-six of them, and sound as a bell. Believe me, old man, what we make up is not half as bad as what we leave out.' And as he spoke he cut another half page from the Chancellor's speech. 'You can influence public opinion more effectively by printing news than by printing articles, but the most effective way of all is to print neither. The most convenient kind of public opinion is the public lack of all opinion whatsoever.'

'Then give up publishing your paper,' suggested Fabian.

'And what should we live on?' asked Münzer. 'Moreover, what should we do instead?'

The uniformed messenger returned, bringing the wine and glasses. Münzer filled the glasses and raised one to his lips. 'Long live the fourteen dead Hindus!' he cried, and drank. Then he fell upon the Chancellor again. 'The august head of the state is once more producing drivel,' he declared. 'It's nothing but a schoolboy's essay on Germany's future, floating where it won't sink. He would get half marks for it in the lower fifth.' He turned to Fabian and asked: 'What shall we put at the top of this comic speech?'

'I'd rather know what you are going to put underneath it,' said Fabian, angrily.

His companion took another drink, rolled the wine slowly round his mouth, swallowed, and said: 'Not a syllable. Not a word. We've had instructions not to stab the government in the back. If we attack it we do ourselves harm, and if we keep quiet we help the government.'

'Let me make a suggestion,' said Fabian. 'Why not support the government?'

'Oh, no,' cried Münzer. 'We're respectable people. Evening, Malmy.'

A slim, smartly-dressed man was standing at the door. He nodded generally into the room.

'You mustn't mind anything he says,' said the city editor to Fabian. 'He's been a journalist for twenty years and has reached the stage of believing his own lies. Herr Münzer has piled ten feather beds over his conscience, and he sleeps the sleep of the unjust on top of them.'

The old messenger came in with more pages of typescript. Münzer reached out for the paste-pot, completed the Chancellor's scroll and went on editing.

'You disapprove of your colleague's inertia,' said Fabian to Herr Malmy. 'What else do you do?'

The city editor smiled, though only with his lips. 'I lie too,' he answered. 'But I know I'm lying. I know the system is wrong. A blind man could see that if he were in my job. But I serve the wrong system with devotion. For, within the frame of this wrong system, at whose disposal I have placed my modest talents, the wrong measures are right by the very nature of things, and the right are obviously wrong. I am an admirer of rigid consistency, and I am also –'

'A cynic,' threw in Münzer, without looking up.

Malmy shrugged his shoulders. 'I was going to say "a coward". That's even more to the point. My character is inferior in every way to my reason. I'm sincerely sorry for it, but I've given up doing anything about it.'

The young Dr Irrgang came in with a copy of the early edition. He discussed with Münzer which stories should come out and which should take their place in the final edition. There had been two fires. A few nebulous words had been dropped in Geneva concerning the German minority in Poland. The Minister of Agriculture had promised the big north-eastern landowners an increased tariff. The case against the directors of the Municipal Purchasing Board had taken a critical turn.

'And what shall we make the headline for the Chancellor's speech?' asked Münzer. 'Come on gentlemen. Ten pfennigs for a good headline. They're waiting to set it. If the matrices are late we shall have another row with the printer.'

The young man thought with such effort that the sweat came out on his brow. 'Chancellor Demands Confidence,' he suggested.

'So-so,' judged Münzer. 'Fetch a tumbler and have a drop of wine.' The young man took this advice as though it were a command.

'Germany, or Spiritual Sloth,' said Malmy.

'Don't talk such rot,' cried the political editor. Then he took his blue pencil and wrote six words in block letters at the head of the manuscript. 'The ten pfennigs are mine,' he declared.

'What have you put?' asked Fabian.

Münzer pressed the bell and declaimed with pathos: 'Optimism a Duty, Says the Chancellor!' The messenger fetched the copy. The city editor felt in his pocket and without a word placed a ten-pfennig piece on the table.

His colleague looked up in surprise.

'With this contribution,' said Malmy, 'I open a fund for a most deserving object.'

'What is it?'

'A fund to pay you back your school-fees,' said Malmy. Irrgang, the apprentice in political journalism, laughed gently. Then he rushed to the telephone. The buzzer had sounded. 'A subscriber wants to know something,' he announced after some time, and covered the transmitter with his hand. 'They're sitting in a pub and they've made a bet on whether it ought to be "It's me" or "It's I".'

Münzer took the receiver from him. 'One moment,' he said. 'We'll tell you in one moment, sir.' Then he signed to Irrgang and whispered: Literary editor.'

The young man ran out, but came back shrugging his shoulders. 'I've just discovered that it should be "It's I". Not at all. Good night.' Münzer hung up the receiver, shook his head, and pocketed Malmy's ten pfennigs.

Later on they were sitting in a little wine-bar not far from the newspaper office. A compositor on his way home had brought Münzer a copy of the paper so that he could see that all was in order. He grumbled over a few printers' errors but was pleased with the headline on the front page. Then Strom, the dramatic critic, joined them.

Now they were busy drinking. The young Dr Irrgang was

already half tight. Strom, the critic, likened several well-known producers to window-display artists. According to Strom, the contemporary theatre was a symptom of the decline of capitalism, and when someone interjected that there were no playwrights, Strom maintained that there were.

'You're no longer quite sober,' said Münzer thickly, and Strom laughed pointlessly.

Rather against his will, Fabian was allowing Malmy to enlighten him on the subject of short-term loans. 'The whole country, politically and economically, is falling more and more into the hands of foreigners,' he maintained. 'A pin prick and the whole thing will blow up. If once the money is recalled in large quantities, we shall all go broke – the banks, the municipalities, the joint-stock companies, and the Reich.'

'But you never put that in the paper,' said Irrgang.

'I help to do the wrong thing consistently. Anything that assumes gigantic proportions may be imposing, even stupidity.' Malmy scrutinized the young man. 'You'd better go out quickly. There's a small gale blowing up in you.' Irrgang laid his head on the table. 'Get on the sporting staff,' advised Malmy. 'Sport won't make such demands on your sensitive constitution.' The young man stood up, staggered across the room to the back door, and went out.

Münzer sat down on the sofa and began suddenly to weep. 'I'm a swine,' he murmured.

'A strongly Russian atmosphere,' said Strom. 'Alcohol, self-torment, and tears from grown-up men.' He was touched, and stroked the political editor's bald head.

'I'm a swine,' murmured the other. He insisted on it.

Malmy smiled at Fabian. 'The state bolsters up the bankrupt landowners. The state supports the heavy industries. The industrialists sell their goods to foreign countries at a loss and to the home market at a figure above the world price-level. Raw materials are too dear; the manufacturers reduce wages; the state accelerates the decline in the purchasing power of the masses by imposing taxes which it dare not impose on the rich; capital still flees by the milliard across the frontiers. Isn't that consistency? Can you say that madness has no method? It makes my mouth water.'

'I'm a swine,' murmured Münzer, and thrust out his lower lip to catch the tears.

'You think too much of yourself, old man,' said the city editor. Münzer continued to weep, but his face assumed an injured expression. He was deeply hurt by this attempt to prevent him being what he thought himself – even if only in a state of drunkenness.

Malmy went on cheerfully with his task of explaining the situation. 'Technical improvements increase production. Technical improvements decimate the ranks of labour. The purchasing power of the masses is attacked by galloping consumption. Grain and coffee are being burnt in America to keep up the prices. In France the wine-growers are grumbling because the harvest is too good. Just think of it! Mankind is desperate because the earth is too fruitful! Too much grain – and elsewhere people are starving! If a thunderbolt doesn't fall and destroy such a world, then all the lessons of history should be put in a sack and buried.' Malmy got up, a little unsteadily, and tapped on his glass. Those sitting near looked up at him.

'Gentlemen,' he said, 'I'm going to make a speech. If any one objects, let him stand up.'

Münzer arose with difficulty.

'Let him stand up,' cried Malmy, 'and leave the room.'

Münzer sat down again. Strom laughed.

Malmy began his speech: 'When the disease from which our esteemed world is now suffering attacks an individual, we simply say that he's paralysed. And I'm convinced you all know that the cure for this extremely unpleasant complaint, with all its attendant results, is a matter of life and death. What treatment is being applied to the world? It is being dosed with camomile tea. Everybody knows that this drink is harmless and ineffectual. But it is also painless. Wait and go on drinking tea, they think, and thus the softening of the public brain progresses till it's a pleasure to think of.'

'Enough of these beastly medical metaphors!' cried Strom. 'I've got a weak stomach!'

'Enough of these beastly medical metaphors,' cried Malmy. 'The fact that a few of our contemporaries are particularly villainous is not enough to ruin us, nor that a few others are particularly weak-minded, nor even that both classes are represented among those who manage the affairs of this globe. What will ruin us is the spiritual sloth of all concerned. We want things to change, but we do not want to change ourselves. Why not the other fellows? we think, and go to sleep in our rocking-chairs. Meanwhile money is shifted from places where there is plenty to places where there is none. The shifts and the usury never come to an end and the improvement never begins.'

'I'm a swine,' murmured Münzer. He raised his glass and held it to his lips without drinking. He sat like this for some time.

'The circulation of the blood is poisoned,' cried Malmy. 'And we content ourselves with putting sticking-plaster on the earth's surface at those spots where the inflammation breaks out. Can this blood-poisoning be cured? It can not. One day the patient, smothered from head to foot with sticking-plaster, will die on our hands.'

The dramatic critic wiped the sweat from his brow and looked appealingly at the speaker.

'Enough of these medical metaphors,' said Malmy. 'We are failing because of our spiritual slothfulness. I am an economist, and I tell you that all attempts to overcome the present crisis economically, without a previous change of heart, are just quackery!'

'The mind moulds the body,' said Münzer, and banged down his glass. Then he began to sob. The screaming misery of things assaulted him with considerable force. And Malmy had to raise his voice still higher to outshout his colleague. 'You will object that two great mass-movements are already in the field. But these people, whether they mobilize on the right or on the left, intend to remove the poison from the patient's blood by chopping off his head with an axe. Of course that will be the end of the blood-poisoning, but it will also be the end of the patient – and that's carrying therapy too far.'

Herr Strom had had enough and to spare of these metaphors of disease, and sought the open air. A fat man at the corner table rose with difficulty and endeavoured to turn his head towards the speaker. But his neck was too fat, so he said, speaking in another direction: 'You ought to have gone in for medicine.'

Then he fell back with a thud into his chair. Sitting there, he was seized by a sudden violent fury, and roared: 'We want money. Money! And then more money!'

Münzer nodded and whispered, 'Montecuccoli was a swine, too.' Then he resumed his weeping.

The fat man at the corner table refused to be pacified.

25

'Absolute rot!' he growled. 'Change of heart! Spiritual slothfulness! Absolute rot! Give us money, and we shall be all right.'

A woman, every bit as fat as himself, was sitting opposite him. 'But where's the money to come from, Arthur?' she asked.

'Did I ask you?' he shouted, his excitement rising again. Then he calmed down for good, seized the passing waiter firmly by the tail of his coat, and said: 'Another pickled pork cutlet, with vinegar and oil.'

Malmy pointed across at the fat man. 'Am I not right?' he asked. 'Are we to stand and be shot at for idiots like that? No thanks. Carry on with the lying. It's right to do what's wrong.'

Münzer had made himself at home; he was lying on the sofa, already snoring, although he was not yet asleep. 'All the same, I've got your car,' he grunted, and looked out of the corner of his eye at Malmy.

Shortly afterwards Strom and Irrgang came back. They returned arm-in-arm, looking as though they both had jaundice. 'I can't stand alcohol,' explained Irrgang, apologetically. They sat down.

'A product of the war,' said Strom. 'A pitiable generation.' He might say the most obvious and undeniable things, but when they came from his lips they sounded quite incredible, and compelled his hearers to contradict. If he had declared, with his air of reach-me-down conviction, that two and two made four, Fabian would suddenly have doubted the accuracy of this calculation. He turned away from him and looked at Malmy. Malmy was sitting stiffly on his seat, and his eyes were elsewhere. When he felt himself observed, he seemed to pull himself together; he looked at Fabian and said: 'One ought to take oneself in hand more. Schnaps loosens the gag.'

Münzer was now snoring permissibly; he was asleep. Fabian rose and shook hands with the journalists. Last of all he took leave of the city editor.

'But perhaps you're right,' said Malmy, and smiled sadly.

'I am no longer quite sober,' remarked Fabian to the night, when he found himself outside the door. He was fond of that early stage of intoxication which leads a man to believe that he can feel the earth revolving. The trees and houses still stand quietly in their places, the street-lamps have not yet acquired a twin, but the earth revolves; you feel it at last! But today even

26

that displeased him. He walked on beside his intoxication and pretended they did not know each other. What a queer globe it was, whether it revolved or not! He could not help thinking of a drawing by Daumier, entitled 'Progress'. Daumier had drawn a number of snails crawling after each other; that was the pace of human development. But the snails were crawling in a circle.

And that was the worst of it.

IV

When he reached the office next morning, Fabian was tired. Moreover he was the worse for wear. Fischer, his companion in the office, began his work as usual by taking breakfast.

'Where on earth do you get that permanent hunger?' asked Fabian. 'Your wages are less than mine. You are married. You have money in the savings bank. And yet you eat so much that I have enough by merely looking at you.'

Fischer went on chewing. 'It's in our family,' he explained. 'We Fischers are famous for it.'

'They ought to put up a monument to your family,' said Fabian, with feeling.

Fischer shuffled uneasily on his chair. 'Before I forget it, Kunze has made a series of drawings for newspaper advertisements, and we've got to fix them up with rhymed couplets. That will just be in your line.'

'I am honoured by your trust,' said Fabian, 'but I'm still busy with the captions for those photographic posters. You carry on quietly with the poetry. What good is that breakfast to you and your esteemed family if you can't compose a few rhymes?' From the window, he looked across at the cigarette factory, and yawned. The sky was as grey as the surface of a cycle track. Fischer walked up and down, frowned to show extreme annoyance, and searched for rhymes.

Fabian unrolled a poster, fastened it to the wall with drawing pins, went over to the farthest corner of the room and stared at it. It revealed a close-up of Cologne Cathedral, with a cigarette of equal size which the poster-artist had erected on one side of it. He jotted down: Nothing can equal . . . Two great products . . . Towers above all . . . Absolutely unbeatable . . . He did his duty, though he could not see why.

Fischer found neither peace nor rhymes. He began a conversation. 'Bertuch says there'll be some more fellows sacked.'

'Very likely,' said Fabian.

'What shall you do,' asked the other, 'if you lose this job?'

'Do you think I've spent my life since the day I was confirmed making good publicity for bad cigarettes? When these people kick me out, I shall look for a new profession. One more won't make much difference to me.'

'You've never told me anything about yourself,' said Fischer.

'During the inflation period I looked after the shares for a limited company. Twice a day I had to reckon out the gold value of their shares so as to let them known how much capital they had.'

'And then?'

'Then I bought a greengrocer's shop for a pile of shares.'

'Why a greengrocer's?'

'Because we were hungry. There was a signboard over the window: Dr Fabian – Delicatessen. Early in the morning, while it was still dark, we used to push a ramshackle hand-cart round to the market.'

Fischer rose from his seat. 'What, are you a doctor too?'

'I passed my examination the year I was given a job as auxiliary envelope-addresser at the municipal offices.'

'What was the subject of your thesis?'

'It was entitled: "Heinrich von Kleist – Did He Stammer?" First I wanted to prove from internal stylistic evidence that Hans Sachs had flat feet. But that meant spending too much time in research. Well, never mind. Get on with the poetry.' He fell silent and walked up and down before the poster. Fischer looked across at him inquisitively. But he did not trust himself to renew the conversation. He turned in his chair with a sigh, and read through the rhymes he had jotted down. He decided to rhyme 'smoke' with 'folk', smoothed out the sheet of paper that lay before him and half closed his eyes, relying on inspiration.

Just then the telephone rang. He lifted the receiver. 'Yes,' he said. 'He's here. One moment, Dr Fabian is just coming.' And, turning to Fabian: 'Your friend Labude.'

Fabian took the receiver. 'Morning Labude, how goes it?'

'How long have these cigarette johnnies been calling you doctor?' asked his friend.

'I've been telling tales out of school.'

'Serves you right. Can you come and see me tonight?'

'Yes.'

'Flat number two. So long.'

'So long, Labude.' He hung up the receiver. Fischer took hold of him firmly by the sleeve.

'This Herr Labude is a friend of yours, isn't he? Why don't you call him by his Christian name?'

'He hasn't one,' said Fabian. 'His parents forgot to give him one when he was born.'

'Hasn't he a Christian name at all?'

'No, just imagine! He's been trying for years to get one retrospectively. But the police won't allow it.'

'You're having me on,' said Fischer, offended.

Fabian patted him approvingly on the shoulder. 'There's not much you don't notice,' he said. Then he devoted himself once more to Cologne Cathedral, wrote down a few captions and took them to Director Breitkopf.

'You might just try to think out a nice little prize-competition,' said the director. 'We thought quite a lot of your prospectus for the retailers.'

Fabian made a slight bow.

'We want something new,' went on the director. 'A prize-competition or something of that sort. But it mustn't cost any money, you understand? The board decided recently they might have to reduce the advertising budget by fifty per cent. You can guess what that would mean for you. Well, young man, get a move on. Bring me something new as soon as you can. But I repeat: as cheap as possible. Good morning.'

Fabian went out.

Late that afternoon, when he entered his room – eighty marks a month, morning coffee included, lighting extra – he found on the table a letter from his mother. He could not have a bath. The hot water was cold. He contented himself with a wash, changed his underclothes, put on his grey suit, took up his mother's letter and sat down by the window. The noise of the street drummed like a storm of rain upon the panes. Someone on the third floor was practising the piano. Next door the conceited old accountant was shouting at his wife. Fabian opened the envelope and read:

'My dear, good boy,

'So that you don't worry, I must tell you at once the doctor says it is nothing serious. It is probably something wrong with

30

the glands, and elderly people often get it. So don't worry about me. At first I was very anxious, but now the old crock will soon be all right again. Yesterday I went to the Palace Gardens for a bit. The swans have had young ones. At the Park Café they charged me seventy pfennigs for a cup of coffee. Such impudence!

'Thank heaven the washing's done. Frau Hase couldn't come at the last minute. I think she's got a haemorrhage. But I managed it all right. I shall post yours back to you tomorrow morning. Take care of the cardboard box and mind you tie it up firmly next time. Things can so easily get lost in the post. Kitty is sitting on my lap. She's just had a bit of lights, and now she's rubbing her head against me and wants me to stop writing. If you put money in my letter, like you did last week, I'll pull your ears for you. We can manage, and you need your money for yourself.

'Do you really enjoy writing advertisements for cigarettes? I liked the things you sent very much. Frau Thomas said it is an awful pity that you write such stuff. But I said, it's not your fault. If you don't want to starve nowadays – and who does? – you can't wait for the right job to fall into your lap. And besides that, I told her it was only temporary.

'Father still finds something to do. But there seems to be something wrong with his back. He walks all bent double. Yesterday Aunt Martha brought a dozen eggs from the garden. The hens are laying well. She's a good sister, if only she hadn't so much trouble with her husband.

'My dear boy, if only you could soon come home for a bit. You were here at Easter. How time flies. I've got a boy and yet I don't seem to have him at all. Just for a few days in the year. If I had my way I should go straight to the station and come to Berlin to see you. It was lovely before you went. Almost every night, before I go to bed, I look at the photographs and picture postcards. Do you remember when we used to pack the ruck-sack and go off together? Once we came back with a whole pfennig. I can't help laughing when I think of it.

'Well, good-bye, my dear boy. I suppose we shan't see you before Christmas. Do you still go to bed as late as ever? Remember me to Labude. Tell him to look after you. How about the girls? Do take care. Father sends love. Much love and many kisses, from, Your Mother.'

31

Fabian put the letter in his pocket and looked down into the street. Why was he sitting here, in this strange, godforsaken room, which belonged to the widow Hohlfeld who hadn't always had to let? Why wasn't he sitting at home with his mother? What did he want here in this city, in this crazy mass of brickwork boxes? Writing flowery nonsense to make humanity smoke more cigarettes than ever? He could wait for the breakdown of Europe just as well in the place where he was born. All this came of his conceited notion that the world would only turn so long as he stood and watched it. This ridiculous anxiety to be on the spot! Other men had genuine professions, got on, married, fathered children, and believed that that was somehow relevant. And he had to sit on the fence, voluntarily, looking on and despairing by instalments. Europe had been let out of school. The teachers were gone, the time-table had vanished. The old continent would never get through the syllabus. Never get through any syllabus!

Then his landlady, Frau Hohlfeld, knocked on the door. She came in, and said: 'Beg pardon, I didn't know you were back.' She came closer. 'Did you hear the noise Herr Tröger was making last night? He had women up there again. You should see the state the sofa's in. If that happens once more, I shall give him notice. What will the young lady think that's just taken the next room?'

'If she still believes in the stork, she's in real trouble.'

'But Herr Fabian, my house is not a low-class hotel.'

'It is a well-known fact, madam, that at a certain age desires stir in the human heart that are at variance with the morals of landladies.'

Frau Hohlfeld grew impatient. 'But he had at least two women with him!'

'Herr Tröger, madam, is a Don Juan. You had better inform him that he is not to bring home more than one lady per night. And if he doesn't act accordingly, we will have him castrated by the watch committee.'

'I move with the times,' declared Frau Hohlfeld, not without pride, and came still nearer. 'Manners have changed. You have to adapt yourself. I make allowances. After all I'm not so old as all that.'

She was standing just behind him. He could not see her, but her misunderstood bosom was probably heaving. Things were getting worse by the day. Was there no one to be found for her? At night she probably stood barefoot outside the door of Tröger, the commercial traveller, and reviewed his orgies through the key-hole. She was slowly going mad. Sometimes she looked at him as if she were just itching to pull his trousers down. This type of woman had formerly turned pious. He got up and said: 'A pity you haven't any children.'

'I'm going.' Frau Hohlfeld left the room dejectedly.

He looked at the clock. Labude was still at the library. Fabian went over to his table, which was piled with books and pamphlets. On the wall, above the table, there hung a piece of embroidery. It bore the legend, 'Just Fifteen Minutes'. On taking the rooms, he had removed this maxim from the sofa and fastened it above his books. Sometimes he read a page or two in one of them. It had rarely done any harm.

He took up one of the volumes. It was by Descartes, and was entitled *Meditations on the First Philosophy*. He had studied it six years ago. It was the sort of thing Professor Driesch used to ask about in the viva. Six years can be a long time. There had been a signboard on the other side of the street: 'Chaim Pines. Skins Bought and Sold.'

Was that all he remembered of those days? Before he was called in to the examiner, he had walked down the corridor, wearing another student's top-hat, and given the porter a fright. Vogt, the owner of the top-hat, had failed, and gone to America.

He sat down and opened the book. What had Descartes to say to him? 'Several years have now elapsed since I first became aware that I had accepted, even from my youth, many false opinions for true, and that consequently what I afterwards based on such principles was highly doubtful; and from that time I was convinced of the necessity of undertaking once in my life to rid myself of all the opinions I had adopted, and of commencing anew the work of building from the foundation, if I desired to establish a firm and abiding superstructure in the sciences. But as this enterprise appeared to me to be one of great magnitude, I waited until I had attained an age so mature as to leave me no hope that at any stage of life more advanced I should be better able to execute my design. On this account, I have delayed so long that I should henceforth consider I was doing wrong were I still to consume in deliberation any of the time that now remains for action. Today, then, since I have opportunely

33

freed my mind from all cares (and am happily disturbed by no passions), since I am in the secure possession of leisure in a peaceable retirement, I will at length apply myself earnestly and freely to the general overthrow of all my former opinions.'

Fabian looked down into the street; his eyes followed the omnibuses that rolled along the Kaiserallee like elephants on roller-skates; then he closed his eyes for a moment. He turned the pages, skimming through the introduction. Descartes had been forty-five when he announced his revolution. He had taken some small part in the Thirty Years War. A little fellow with a huge head. 'Freed from all cares.' A revolution in solitude. In Holland. Beds of tulips before the house. Fabian laughed, laid the philosopher aside, and put on his overcoat. In the corridor he ran into Herr Tröger, the commercial traveller with the inordinate appetite for women. They raised their hats to each other.

Labude's number two flat was in Central Berlin. It was known to very few. Hither he retired when the West End, his smart relations, society women and the telephone began to get on his nerves. And here he followed his own scientific and social inclinations.

'Where did you get to last week?' asked Fabian.

'Very well thanks,' said Labude, absently, and drank off the glass of cognac that stood in front of him. 'I was in Hamburg. Leda sends her love.'

'And how's the affianced bride?'

'We'll talk about that later.'

'Heard anything from the Professor? Has he read your work?'

'No, he's never got the time, always full up with doctorates, examinations, lectures, seminars and meetings of the senate. By the time he's read my research thesis I shall have a beard down to my knees.' Labude filled his glass and drank.

'Don't worry. Those fellows will have the surprise of their lives when they see how you've reconstructed the brain and thought-processes of Lessing from his collected works. Until you came along they always represented him as the freewheeling Logos. They never understood him.'

'I'm afraid the surprise will be too much for them. It will only annoy them to find the canonized logic of a dead writer evaluated psychologically; they won't like to see errors of

34

thought exposed and their individual and general significance demonstrated; they'll hate to see a classic, already labelled and done with, now treated as the typical instance of a man of genius wavering between two epochs. Well, we must wait and see. Let's leave the old chap in peace. For five years I've been dissecting him, taking him to pieces and putting him together again. A fine job for a grown-up man, poking about in the eighteenth century as though it were a dustbin. Get yourself a glass.'

Fabian took a liqueur glass from the cupboard and filled it. Labude sat staring ahead. 'When I was in the National Library this morning, they arrested one of the professors – a sinologist. For twelve months he's been taking rare prints and pictures from the library, and selling them. When they arrested him, he went as white as a sheet and had to sit down on the steps for a bit. They gave him a drink of cold water and carted him off.'

'A square peg in a round hole,' said Fabian. 'Why did he trouble to learn Chinese if he was to finish up by living on theft? Things look bad. The philologists have started thieving now.'

'Drink up and come along!' cried Labude.

They walked along beside the market, passing through a thousand foul odours until they came to the bus-stop.

'We'll go to Haupt's,' said Labude.

V

That evening there was, as usual, a 'seaside carnival' at Haupt's dance-hall. At ten o'clock sharp, two dozen street-girls did the goose-step as they marched down from the gallery. They were dressed in bright-coloured bathing-suits, stockings rolled below their knees and high-heeled shoes. All who came thus undressed were given free admission and a glass of schnaps into the bargain. Such privileges were not to be despised in view of the scarcity of clients. The girls danced together at first, so that the men should have something to look at.

This panorama of feminine profusion, presented to the accompaniment of music, stimulated the clerks, book-keepers and shopkeepers who jostled each other along the barrier. The MC called upon them to 'go for' the ladies, which they thereupon did. The plumpest and boldest women received the preference. The alcoves, where wine was served, were quickly occupied. The barmaids manipulated their lipsticks. The orgy was ready to begin.

Labude and Fabian were sitting beside the barrier which separated the tables from the dance-floor. They were fond of the place because they did not belong there. The number-plate of their table-telephone glowed uninterruptedly. The buzzer buzzed. People wanted to speak to them. Labude took the receiver from its holder and put it under the table. Now they were at peace again. For the noise that remained, the music, the singing and the laughter, were not meant personally and therefore could not disturb.

Fabian told his friend of the newspaper-office, the cigarette-factory, the voracious Fischer family and Cologne Cathedral. Labude looked at him, and said, 'It's time you began to make some progress.'

'But I can't do anything.'

36

'You can do a great deal.'

'The same thing,' said Fabian. 'I can do a great deal and don't wish to do anything. Why should I get on? What for and what against? Let us assume for the moment that I really have some function. Where is the system in which I can exercise it? There isn't one; nothing has any meaning.'

'Oh, yes. You could earn money, for instance.'

'I'm not a capitalist.'

'All the more reason.' Labude laughed a little.

'When I say I'm not a capitalist, I mean I have no pecuniary instinct. Why should I earn money? What should I do with it? You can get enough to eat without getting on. It's a matter of indifference, to me and to the rest of the world, whether I address envelopes, write couplets for advertisements or deal in pickled red cabbage. Are these jobs for a grown man? Pickled red cabbage, wholesale or retail, where's the difference? I'm not a capitalist, I tell you. I don't want dividends, I don't want surplus value.'

Labude shook his head. 'That is inertia. If you earn money and don't want it, you can exchange it for power.'

'And what should I do with power?' asked Fabian. 'I know you want power. But what should I do with power, when I don't want to be powerful? The love of power and the love of money are members of one family, but it's not my family.'

'You can use power for the good of others.'

'But who does? One man uses it for his own advantage, another for that of his family, one for his fellow supertax-payers, another for people with fair hair, a fifth for those over six feet tall, a sixth in order to test some mathematical formula on humanity. To hell with money and power!' Fabian brought down his fist on the balustrade, but it was upholstered and covered in plush. His blow made no sound.

'If only there were such a place as the nursery I sometimes dream of! I should take you there, bound hand and foot, and have a life's purpose grafted into you!' Labude was seriously troubled and laid his hand on his friend's arm.

'I just look on. Is there nothing in that?'

'Whom does it help?'

'Who can be helped?' asked Fabian. 'You want to gain power. You dream of marshalling and leading the lower middle class. You want to control capital and implant a civic sense in

37

the proletariat. And then you want to help build up a civilized state, which looks to me devilishly like Utopia. And I tell you, when you've got your Utopia the people there will still be punching each other on the nose! Quite apart from the fact that you'll never get it . . . I know of a life's purpose, but unfortunately it's not a purpose at all. I should like to help to make people decent and sensible. At present I'm busy watching them to find out whether they are suited to such treatment.'

Labude raised his glass and cried: 'I wish you luck.' He drank and put it down. 'First you must get a rational system,' he said, 'then people will adapt themselves to it.'

Fabian drank in silence.

Labude went on excitedly: 'You see that, don't you? Of course you do. But you would rather imagine some goal of unattainable perfection than work towards an imperfect goal which might be realized. It's easier for you. You have no ambition, that's the worst of it.'

'Lucky for me I've not! Suppose our five million unemployed were not content with their claim to unemployment-pay. Suppose they were ambitious!'

Just then two angels in bathing-suits came up and leaned against the balustrade. The one was blonde and fat, and her bosom bulged over the plush as if it were being offered on a salver. The other was thin, and looked as if she might be knock-kneed. 'Give us a cigarette,' said the blonde. Fabian offered the packet, Labude struck a match. The women smoked and looked expectantly at the young men. After a pause the thin one announced in a rusty voice: 'Well, there you are.'

'Who'll stand a schnaps?' asked the fat one.

All four of them made their way towards the bar. Vine-leaves and vast bunches of grapes, all of cardboard, hemmed in their path. They sat down in a corner. The Palatinate near Caub was painted on the wall. Fabian thought of Blücher's victory at Caub, Labude ordered the liqueurs. The women whispered together. Probably they were deciding the allotment of the two cavaliers, for immediately afterwards the fat blonde threw one arm round Fabian, placed her hand on his leg and made herself thoroughly at home. The thin one emptied her glass at a gulp, tweaked Labude's nose and giggled inanely. 'There are some alcoves upstairs,' she said, rolled back the blue stockinet from her thighs, and twinkled.

'Why are your hands so rough?' asked Labude.

She shook her finger at him. 'Not what you think,' she cried, and choked with roguishness.

'Paula used to work in a jam factory,' said the blonde. She took Fabian's hand and moved it to and fro across her breasts until the nipples stood out large and hard. 'Shall we go on to a hotel?' she asked.

'I'm shaved all over,' confided the thin one, and was not unwilling to provide proof. Labude with difficulty restrained her.

'You can sleep better afterwards in a hotel,' said the blonde to Fabian, and stretched out her fat legs.

Lottchen, the barmaid, filled the glasses. The women drank as though they had eaten nothing for a week. They could hear the muffled strains of the band. A giant of a man was sitting at the bar, gargling with kirsch. His hair-parting went down to the back of his neck. An electric bulb was shining behind the Palatinate near Caub. It sparkled on the Rhine, though only from behind the canvas.

'There are some alcoves upstairs,' said the thin one again, and they went up. Labude ordered supper. As soon as the dish of cold meat and sausage was placed before the girls, they forgot all else and fell upon it. Downstairs, on the dance floor, a competition was being held for the handsomest figure. The women in their scanty bathing-suits revolved in circles, spread out their arms and fingers and smiled seductively. The men stood round as though at a cattle-market.

'The first prize is a big box of sweets,' explained Paula, chewing busily. 'And the girl who gets it has to take it back to the manager.'

'I'd rather eat,' said the blonde. 'Besides they always say my legs are too fat. And yet fat legs are the finest thing you can have. Once I went with a Russian prince. He still sends me picture-postcards.'

'Rubbish!' growled Paula. 'They all want something different. I knew a gentleman, an engineer, he liked consumptives. And Victoria's friend has a hump on his back, and she says she couldn't live without it. What do you say to that? I reckon the main thing is to know your job.'

'What you've learnt, you've learnt,' pronounced the fat one, and fished the last slice of ham from the dish. Down on the dance-floor they were just announcing the name of the girl with the handsomest figure. There was a flourish from the orchestra and the manager handed a large box of sweets to the winner. She thanked him delightedly, bowed to the howling, stamping crowd and went off with her prize, probably to hand it back to the manager.

'Why have you given up working in your jam factory?' asked Labude, and his question sounded reproachful.

Paula pushed back her empty plate, passed her hand across her stomach, and replied: 'First of all it wasn't my factory at all, and secondly I got the sack. Luckily I happened to know something against the managing director. He'd seduced a girl of fourteen. Seduced is an exaggeration. But anyhow he swallowed the dope. And so I rang him up every fortnight and said I must have fifty marks or people would begin to hear of it. Then next day I went to the cashier and collected the money.'

'But that's blackmail!' cried Labude.

'That's what the lawyer said when the director put him on my track. I had to sign a paper; he gave me a hundred marks, and that was the end of what I thought was a pension for life. Well, well, now I'm here and earn my living on my back.'

'It's terrible,' said Labude to Fabian. 'It's terrible, the number of directors who abuse their hold over their employees.'

'Oh Lord, what are you talking about?' cried the fat one. 'If I were a man and director of a factory I should always be carrying on with the work-girls.' Then she ruffled Fabian's hair, gave him a kiss, seized his hand and laid it flat on her full stomach. Labude and Paula danced together. Yes, she had knock-knees.

In the next alcove, a woman was singing in a loud, drunken voice:

> 'Love is a hobby
> For which you use your body.'

The fat one said: 'She's a one next door. She doesn't belong here at all. Comes in fine fur coats, and what she wears underneath is so thin you can see through it. They say she's got plenty of money and comes from the West End. Married too. She gets young chaps in an alcove, pays for them and gives them a hell of a time.' Fabian rose and looked over the low partition.

A tall, well-built woman in a green silk bathing-suit was sitting there singing songs. She was also engaged in undressing a

40

soldier who was defending himself desperately. 'Now then,' she cried. 'Don't be such a wet blanket. Come on! Show your passport!' But the brave infantryman drove her back. Fabian remembered that well-known Egyptian minister whose wife so shamefully molested poor Joseph, the gifted great-grandson of Abraham. Suddenly the women in green stood up, seized a champagne glass and staggered towards the edge of the balcony.

It was not Frau Potiphar but Frau Moll. That Irene Moll whose keys he had in his overcoat pocket.

She stood swaying beside the balustrade, raised the glass then threw it down into the hall below. It broke to splinters on the floor. The orchestra put down their instruments. The dancers raised their heads in alarm. Everyone looked up towards the alcove.

Frau Moll stretched out her hand and cried: 'Do you call these men? They fall to pieces if you touch them. Ladies, I propose we lock up the whole bunch. Ladies, we want male brothels! Those in favour hold up the right hand!' She struck herself an emphatic blow on the chest, and began to hiccup. The crowd laughed. The manager was already bearing down on her. Irene Moll began to weep. The cosmetic on her eyelashes became liquid and the tears ruled black lines down her face. 'Let us sing,' she cried, sobbing and hiccupping. 'Let us sing that lovely Piano Song!' She spread out both arms and shouted at the top of her voice:

'Man's a beast, you will agree,
Bad alone, but worse in pairs.
Come and play a tune on me,
Come and play a tune on me,
Practise all your naughty airs.
That is what I'm for—'

The manager put his hand over her mouth. She misunderstood his intentions and fell on his neck. In doing so she caught sight of Fabian looking over the partition, and tore herself free. 'I know you,' she cried, and tried to get at him. But the manager and the soldier, who had meanwhile recovered, seized her and forced her down on to a chair. The orchestra struck up and the dancing began afresh.

During this scene Labude had paid the bill. He gave money to Paula and the fat girl, took Fabian's arm and drew him away.

In the cloakroom, he asked: 'Does she really know you?'

'Yes,' said Fabian. 'Her name is Moll. Her husband is a solicitor, and pays you anything you care to mention if you'll sleep with her. I've still got the keys of this comic family in my pocket. Here they are.'

Labude took the keys from him. 'I won't be a minute,' he cried. And ran back in coat and hat.

VI

THE DUEL BY THE MÄRKISCHES MUSEUM
WHEN WILL THE NEXT WAR BREAK OUT?
A DOCTOR UNDERSTANDS DIAGNOSIS

When they reached the street Labude asked angrily: 'Did you have anything to do with that lunatic?'

'No. I just went to her bedroom and she got undressed. Then another fellow turned up and said he was her husband but I wasn't to let that disturb me. Then he quoted some extraordinary contract that these two had made. After that I went.'

'Why did you take the keys?'

'Because the street-door was locked.'

'What a ghastly female!' said Labude. 'She was lying across the table, dead-drunk, and I stuck the keys quickly into her hand-bag.'

'You didn't care for her?' asked Fabian. 'And yet she's got a most impressive figure, and that cheeky school-girl face above it is so wonderfully incongruous.'

'If she'd been ugly you would have handed the keys to the porter long ago.' Labude drew his friend down the street. They turned slowly into a by-road, came to a pedestal on which Herr Schulze-Delitzsch was standing, and passed the Märkisches Museum. The statue of Roland leaned darkly in an ivied corner, and a steamboat was complaining noisily on the Spree. They stopped on the bridge, and looked at the dark river and the windowless warehouses. The sky was afire above the Friedrichstadt.

'My dear Stephan,' said Fabian, gently, 'the way you look after me is really touching. But I am not more unhappy than our times. Do you want to make me happier than they? You won't succeed, even if you get me a directorship, a million dollars or a decent wife whom I could love, or, indeed, all three of them together.' A small black boat with a red lantern at the stern came floating downstream. Fabian put his hand on his friend's shoulder. 'When I said just now that I spend my time watching

43

curiously to see whether the world has any talent for decency, I was telling you only half the truth. There's another reason for all this loafing. I hang about waiting, as I did during the war, when we knew we were soon going to be called up. Do you remember? We wrote our essays and did our dictation, we appeared to be learning, and it was a matter of complete indifference whether we worked or not. We were going to be called up. We sat, as it were, under a glass case, out of which the air was being pumped, slowly but incessantly. We began to kick, but it was not high spirits; it was simply that we were gasping for breath. Do you remember? We didn't want to miss anything; we had a dangerous hunger for life, because we believed it was our last meal before execution.'

Labude leaned against the parapet and looked down at the Spree. Fabian walked excitedly up and down, as though he were pacing his room. 'Do you remember?' he asked again. 'And six months later our training was over. I got a week's leave and went off to Graal. I went there because I'd been there once as a child. It was autumn. I tramped miserably over the quaking earth of the alder woods. The Baltic seemed to have gone mad. You could have counted the visitors to the place. Ten passable women were available, and I slept with six of them. The near future had made up its mind to mince me into sausage-meat. What was I to do in the meanwhile? Read books? File the rough corners off my character? Earn money? I was sitting in a great waiting-room and its name was Europe. The train was due to leave in a week. I knew that. But no one could tell me where it was going or what would become of me. And now we are again seated in the waiting-room, and again its name is Europe! And again we do not know what will happen. We live provisionally, the crisis goes on without end!'

'Good God!' cried Labude. 'If everyone thinks as you do, we shall never get things stabilized. Don't I feel the provisional nature of this age? Is this dissatisfaction your personal privilege? But I'm not content to be a spectator, I try to act rationally.'

'The rational will never achieve power,' said Fabian, 'and still less the righteous.'

'Indeed?' Labude went up close to his friend and took hold of his coat-collar with both hands. 'But should they not dare to attempt it?' he asked.

At that moment they heard a shot, followed by a cry, and shortly afterward three further shots from a different direction. Labude ran across the bridge into the darkness, towards the museum. Another shot rang out. 'Good luck!' said Fabian to himself, as he ran, trying, despite the pain at his heart, to overtake Labude.

At the foot of the statue of Roland a man was squatting, waving a revolver. 'Just wait, you swine!' he shouted, and again fired across the street at some invisible enemy. A street lamp broke. Glass clattered on the pavement. Labude took the weapon from the man's hand, and Fabian asked: 'Why don't you stand up to shoot?'

'Because he got me in the leg,' growled the man. He was a young, burly fellow, and he wore a cap. 'You dirty dog!' he roared. 'But I know who you are.' And he threatened the darkness.

'Straight through the calf,' announced Labude. He knelt down, took a handkerchief from his coat-pocket and tried an emergency dressing.

'It all started over in the pub,' complained the wounded man. 'He scrawled a swastika on the table-cloth. I said something, then he said something and I landed him one behind the ear. The landlord turned us out. This chap ran after me, cursing the International. I turned round and he plugged me.'

'Are you, at least, convinced?' asked Fabian. He looked down at the man, who set his teeth, for Labude was probing the wound.

'The bullet's not there,' remarked Labude. 'Can't you see a taxi anywhere? This place is like a village street.'

'There's not even a policeman,' said Fabian, regretfully.

'That would just put the lid on it!' The wounded man tried to stand up. 'Nothing they'd like better than to lock up another workman, for having the cheek to let a Nazi put a bullet through him.'

Labude held him back, made him sit down again, and asked Fabian to find a taxi. Fabian ran off, crossed the street, turned the corner and followed the dark river-bank.

At the next turning a row of taxis were standing. He told one of the men to drive to the Märkisches Museum, where a fare was awaiting him by the statue of Roland. The taxi drove off. Fabian

45

followed on foot. He breathed deeply and slowly. His heart was pounding like mad. It hammered beneath his waistcoat. It throbbed in his throat. It pulsed inside his skull. He stopped and wiped the sweat from his forehead. Damn the war! Of course to have escaped with a weak heart was mere child's play, but the souvenir was enough for Fabian. They said there were isolated buildings, scattered about the provinces, still full of mutilated soldiers. Men without limbs, men with ghastly faces, without noses, without mouths. Nurses whom nothing could scare poured food into these disfigured creatures, poured it through thin glass tubes, speared into scarred and suppurating holes where once there had been a mouth. A mouth that could laugh and speak and cry aloud.

Fabian turned the corner. Across the road was the museum. The taxi was standing in front of it. He shut his eyes and remembered terrible photographs he had seen, which sometimes came back in his dreams to terrify him. Those pitiful creatures made in God's image! Still they lay there in those buildings, cut off from the world, still they must submit to be fed, to go on living. For of course it would be sin to kill them. But it had been no sin to eat away their faces with flame-throwers. Their families knew nothing of these husbands and fathers and brothers. Their families had been told they were missing. That was fifteen years ago now. Their widows had remarried, and the late lamented, who was still being fed through a glass tube somewhere in the Mark Brandenburg, existed at home merely as a handsome photograph above the sofa, a bunch of flowers in a rifle-barrel; and beneath the photograph sat his successor and tucked into his Sunday dinner. When would the next war break out? When would things reach that point again?

Suddenly someone called 'Hullo!' Fabian opened his eyes and looked round for the owner of the voice. He found him lying on the ground, propped up on his elbows and pressing one hand to his backside.

'What's wrong with you?'

'I'm the other fellow,' said the man. 'He plugged me too.'

Then Fabian planted his feet well apart and burst out laughing. From the other side of the street, from the walls of the museum, an echo laughed with him.

'Excuse me,' said Fabian. 'This is not very polite of me.'

46

The man drew in his knees, screwed up his face, looked at his hands, which were full of blood, and said grimly: 'As you like. The day will come when you'll laugh on the other side of your face.'

'What are you standing there for?' cried Labude, coming angrily across the street.

'Oh Stephan,' said Fabian. 'Here's the other half of the duel, with a bullet in his backside.'

They called the taxi-driver and hoisted the National Socialist into the taxi, placing him beside his Communist playmate. The two friends climbed in, and instructed the driver to take them to the nearest hospital. The car started.

'Does it hurt much?' asked Labude.

'Not so bad,' replied the two casualties, simultaneously, and looked grimly at each other.

'You traitor to the nation!' observed the National Socialist. He was taller than the workman, rather better dressed, and looked like a clerk.

'You traitor to the workers!' returned the Communist.

'You caveman!' cried the one.

'You ape!' cried the other.

The clerk put his hand in his pocket.

Labude caught his wrist. 'Give me that revolver,' he commanded. The man struggled. Fabian got hold of the weapon and pocketed it himself.

'Gentlemen,' he said. 'I am sure we all agree that Germany cannot go on like this. The attempt now being made to stabilize impossible conditions by a callous dictatorship is a crime, and will soon reap its reward. All the same, there is no sense in shooting additional holes in the remoter parts of the body. And even if your aim had been better, and you were now being driven to the mortuary instead of to the hospital, you would not have achieved very much. Your party,' he turned to the fascist, 'knows only whom it's fighting against, and that not very clearly. And your party,' he turned to the workman, 'your party –'

'We're fighting against the exploiters of the proletariat,' declared the Communist. 'And you're a bourgeois.'

'Certainly,' replied Fabian. 'I am a petty bourgeois, and today that is a great term of abuse.'

The clerk was in pain. He sat, leaning over to one side, on his

47

uninjured cheek, and found it difficult to keep his head from knocking against his opponent's.

'The proletariat represents a community of interests,' said Fabian, 'the greatest community of interests. It is your duty to demand your rights, and I am on your side. We have the same enemy, for I am a lover of justice. I am your friend, although you disdain my friendship. But, my dear sir, even when *you* attain power, the ideals of humanity will still sit apart and weep in secret. A man is not always good and wise simply because he's poor.'

'Our leaders –' began the man.

'The less said of them, the better,' interrupted Labude.

The taxi pulled up. Fabian rang the hospital bell. The porter opened the door. Attendants came and lifted the injured men out of the taxi. The doctor on duty shook hands with the two friends.

'You've brought me two politicians?' he said, with a smile. 'Altogether, we've had nine cases brought in tonight, one with a serious bullet-wound in the stomach. All workmen and clerks. Have you ever noticed that these fellows come from the suburbs, and generally know each other? These political brawls are indistinguishable from the dance-hall scraps. In both cases they represent a perversion of German social life. It looks as if they are trying to reduce the unemployment figures by potting each other off. A queer kind of self-help.'

'This excitement among the people is only natural,' said Fabian.

'Of course.' The doctor nodded. 'The whole continent is suffering from hunger-typhus. The patient is beginning to rave and strike out with his fists. Good-bye.' The door closed.

Labude gave the driver money and dismissed the taxi. They walked on in silence, side by side. Suddenly Labude stopped. 'I can't go home yet,' he said. 'Come along, we'll go to the Anonymous Cabaret.'

'But what's that?'

'I don't know myself yet. Some smart fellow has collected a crowd of semi-lunatics and gets them to dance and sing. He pays them a few marks and they let themselves be jeered at and abused by the audience. Probably they don't even notice it. I hear the place is very popular. That's just what you would expect. The people who go there are delighted to find there's someone else still madder than they are.'

Fabian agreed. He looked back once more at the hospital, above which the Great Bear was shining. 'We live in stirring times,' he said, 'and they get more stirring every day.'

VII

A number of private cars were parked outside the cabaret. A man with a red beard, wearing a plumed hat and carrying a huge halberd, was leaning against the door-post. 'Roll up!' he shouted. 'Into the padded cell!' Labude and Fabian went in, gave up their coats and hats, and after much searching through the crowded, smoke-filled room, found seats at a corner table.

A girl with a fatuous smile was hopping about on a ramshackle stage. Evidently, she was supposed to be a dancer. She wore a home-made dress of garish green material and carried a spray of artificial flowers. At regular intervals she threw herself and the spray of flowers into the air. On the left side of the stage was a piano, badly out of tune, on which a toothless old man was playing the Hungarian Rhapsody.

Whether the dance and the music bore any relation to each other was by no means manifest. The audience, all smartly dressed, drank wine, laughed and talked in loud voices.

'Fräulein, you're wanted urgently on the telephone,' cried a bald-headed man, who must have been at least a managing-director. The others laughed louder than ever. The dancer was not to be brought out of her tranced activity; she went on smiling and jigging as before. Suddenly the music stopped. The rhapsody was concluded. The girl on the stage threw an angry glance at the pianist and went on hopping, the dance was not concluded.

'Mother, your baby's crying,' called a woman with a monocle.

'So is yours,' cried someone at a distant table.

The woman turned round. 'I haven't a baby.'

'Lucky for the baby!' cried a man at the back.

'Order!' shouted someone else. The altercation ceased.

The girl was still dancing, though she must have been feeling the strain on her legs for some time. At last she decided she had done enough: she landed in an awkward curtsy, smiled more fatuously than ever, and spread out her arms. A fat man in a dinner-jacket stood up. 'Good, very good. You can come and beat the carpets in the morning!'

The audience shouted and clapped. The girl curtsied again and again. Then a man came out of the wings, dragged the dancer, still violently resisting, from the stage, and himself approached the footlights.

'Bravo, Caligula!' cried a woman in the front row.

Caligula, a plump young Jew with horn-rimmed glasses, turned to the man sitting beside her. 'Is that your wife?' he asked.

The man nodded.

'Then tell your wife to keep her mouth shut!' said Caligula. There was a burst of applause. The man in the front row flushed crimson. His wife felt flattered.

'Order, you fools!' cried Caligula, holding up his hands. There was silence. 'Wasn't that dance an absolutely new experience?'

'Yes,' they roared.

'But now I've something still better. I'm putting on a man named Paul Müller. He comes from Tolkewitz. That's in Saxony. Paul Müller speaks Saxon and claims to be a reciter. He is going to recite a ballad. Prepare for the worst. Unless appearances deceive, Paul Müller, of Tolkewitz, is a lunatic. I have spared no pains to secure this valuable turn for my cabaret. For I won't have it said that all the lunatics are in the audience.'

'That's going too far!' cried one of his auditors, whose face was decorated with duelling scars. He sprang to his feet and indignantly pulled down his dinner-jacket.

'Sit down,' said Caligula, screwing up his mouth. 'Do you know what you are? An idiot!'

The ex-student struggled for breath.

'I should add,' went on the proprietor of the cabaret. 'I should add that I use the word "idiot", not as an insult but as a simple statement of fact.'

The audience laughed and applauded. The man of scars and indignation was dragged back to his seat by his friends, and pacified. Caligula took up a hand-bell, swung it like a night-watchman, and called: 'Paul Müller!' Then he vanished.

An excessively lanky man, unusually pale and dressed in ragged clothes, approached from the back of the stage.

'How do, Müller?' they shouted.

'He's been growing too fast,' said someone.

Paul Müller bowed, a look of challenging gravity on his face. He ran his fingers through his hair and pressed them to his eyes. He was collecting himself. Suddenly he dropped his hands from his face, stretched out his arms, spread out his fingers, opened his eyes as wide as he could, and announced: 'The Death Drive, by Paul Müller.' Then he took another step forward.

'Don't fall off the stage!' cried the woman whom Caligula had ordered, through the medium of her husband, to keep her mouth shut.

Paul Müller took another short step, this time out of defiance, looked contemptuously down at the audience, and began again: 'The Death Drive, by Paul Müller.'

> 'It was the Count of Hohenstein,
> Who let his daughter weep and pine.
> A handsome officer loved she.
> Her father said, "You stay with me!" '

At that moment someone in the audience threw a lump of sugar on the stage. Paul Müller bent down, pocketed the sugar and went on, in an ominous voice:

> 'The countess took to flight, afar
> She sped in her ten horse-power car.
> The mists and darkness closed upon it,
> And death was seated on the bonnet.'

More sugar was thrown on to the stage. Probably there were regular visitors in the hall, who took into account the idiosyncrasies of the artistes. Others in the audience followed their example, and presently volleys of lump-sugar were being discharged, against which Müller could retaliate only by constant bendings and stoopings.

Thus there evolved a recitation combined with knee-bending. Müller also attempted to catch the flying lumps of sugar in his mouth. His face grew more and more threatening, his voice more and more grim. They gathered from the recitation that while the Countess Hohenstein was escaping in her car on that terrible night to reach her beloved, that handsome officer was driving towards the castle, where he believed her to be. Since the two lovers were following the same road, though in opposite directions, since it was a very wet and foggy night, and finally since the poem was entitled 'The Death Drive', it was to be feared with almost complete certainty that the two cars would collide. Paul Müller went on to remove the faintest doubt.

'Shut your mouth,' shouted a voice, 'or the sawdust will drop out of your skull!' But the accident was by this time inevitable.

> 'On one side came the officer's
> Car, on the other side came hers.
> The night was black, the fog was thick,
> And so Fate played its treacherous trick.
> A cry from here,
> A cry from there –'

'Which makes two cries, and that's a pair!' cried someone. The audience yelled and clapped. They had had enough of Paul Müller and had no further interest in the outcome of the tragedy.

He went on reciting. You could see his mouth moving, and that was all. Not a word could be distinguished. The death drive was swallowed up in the howls of the survivors. Then a white rage seized the lanky ballad-monger. He sprang from the stage, seized a woman by the shoulders, and shook her till the cigarette dropped from her lips into her blue silk lap. She jumped up with a cry. Her companion got on his feet and swore. It sounded as though a dog was barking. Paul Müller gave the fellow a push that sent him reeling back into his chair.

Then Caligula arrived. Gritting his teeth, he looked like an infuriated tamer of wild beasts. He seized the man from Tolkewitz by the ends of his tie and hauled him to the dressing-room.

'Good Lord!' said Labude. 'Sadists in the auditorium and loonies on the stage!'

'This particular sport is international,' said Fabian. 'They do the same thing in Paris, but there the crowd shouts "Tue le!", and a gigantic wooden hand comes out of the wings and shovels the poor devil out of sight. It just sweeps him away.'

'This chap calls himself Caligula. He knows what he's talking about. Even when it comes to Roman history.' Labude got up and went. He had had enough. Fabian was just rising when someone clapped him heavily on the shoulder. He turned round. The man with the duelling scars was standing in front of him, beaming all over his face. 'How are you, old thing?' he cried delightedly.

'All right, thanks.'

'Well, fancy meeting you again, old bean!' The ex-student gave Fabian a joyous punch in the chest, precisely on one of his shirt-studs.

'Come on,' said Fabian. 'Let us continue this scrap outside!' Then he pushed his way between the chairs and reached the vestibule. 'Be as quick as you can, old man,' he said to Labude, who was just getting into his coat. 'Some fellow has been addressing me as though I were his brother.' They got their hats. But it was too late.

The man with the scars arrived, pushing in front of him a freckled wife, as though she were incapable of walking alone. 'You see, Meta,' he explained to her. 'This gentlemen was top of the class in my old school.' And to Fabian he said: 'This is my wife, old boy. My better half, more or less. We're living at Remscheid. I've hung up my wig and gown and gone into my father-in-law's business. We make baths. If you ever want a bath you can have one wholesale. Ha-ha! Yes, I'm getting on fine, thanks. Happily married, nice flat with only one other family in the house, big garden at the back, and not short of a few marks. We've got a youngster too, but only lately.'

'It's no bigger than that,' apologized Meta, and showed with her hands how small the child was.

'It'll soon grow,' Labude comforted her. The woman looked at him gratefully and took her husband's arm.

'Well, old sport,' began the ex-student again. 'Now tell me what you've been up to all this time.'

'Nothing special,' said Fabian. 'At present I'm working on a space-rocket. I want to take a look at the moon.'

'Splendid!' cried the man who had married into baths. 'Germany still leads the way. And how's your brother?'

'My good sir,' said Fabian, 'you overwhelm me with joyous news. I've been wanting a little brother for a long time. Just one modest question: Where did you go to school?'

'In Marburg, of course.'

Fabian shrugged his shoulders regretfully. 'They say it's a most delightful town, but unfortunately I've never been there.'

'Then I beg your pardon,' returned the other, in a throaty voice. 'Slight mistake, extraordinary resemblance, no offence.' He clicked his heels together. 'Come, Meta!' he ordered, and marched off. Meta looked shyly at Fabian, nodded to Labude and followed her husband.

'What an utter ass!' Fabian was indignant. 'Accosts complete strangers, and pretends to be pally with them. I suspect that this Caligula encourages such behaviour as part of his show.'

'I don't think so,' said Labude. 'The baths were certainly genuine, also that terribly small child.'

They walked homeward. Labude's eyes were fixed disconsolately on the pavement. 'It's a shame,' he said, after a while. 'This ex-law-student has a flat, a garden, a job, a wife with freckles and everything else a man could want. And we vegetate about like a tramp with a wooden leg; we have no regular job, no regular income, no regular aim in life and not even a regular mistress.'

'But you have Leda.'

'And what troubles me most,' went on Labude, 'is that a man like that has a regular, home-made child of his own.'

'Don't be jealous,' said Fabian. 'This juristically educated bath-manufacturer is an exception. How many men of thirty can afford to marry nowadays? One is unemployed, another will lose his job tomorrow, a third has never had a job. The state today is not organized for the growth of future generations. If a man's having a rotten time, he'd better have it alone, instead of sharing it with a wife and child. And if he draws others into it, he is guilty at least of negligence. I don't know who made up the phrase about sorrow shared being sorrow halved, but if the idiot is still at large, I wish him two hundred marks a month and a family of eight. Then he can go on dividing his sorrow by eight till he goes black in the face.' Fabian gave a sideways glance at Labude. 'But why should you worry about that? Your father gives you an allowance. And when you get your job at the university you'll earn a few coppers extra. Then you will marry Leda and there will be no further obstacle to paternal joys.'

'There are other difficulties apart from finance,' said Labude. He stopped, and held up his hand for a taxi. 'Don't be angry with me, but I want to be alone now. Can you call for me tomorrow at my father's? I've got several things to tell you.' He pressed something into Fabian's hand, and climbed into the waiting taxi.

'Anything wrong with Leda?' asked Fabian, through the open window.

Labude nodded and bowed his head. The car drove off.

His friend gazed after the taxi-cab. 'I'll come,' he shouted. But the car was already far away, and the red rear-light shone like a glow-worm. Then he came to himself and realized what he was holding in his hand. It was a fifty-mark note.

VIII

STUDENTS ENGAGE IN POLITICS
LABUDE SENIOR IS IN LOVE WITH LIFE
A BOX ON THE EARS BY THE OUTER ALSTER

Labude's parents occupied a large Greek temple in Grunewald. In actual fact, it was not a temple but a villa. And they did not really occupy it. His mother spent much time abroad, generally in the south at a country-house near Lugano. For one thing, she preferred the Lago di Lugano to Grunewald Lake. For another, Labude's father felt that she required southern air for her delicate health. He loved his wife deeply, especially when she was away. His affection increased according to the square of the distance between them.

He was a well-known barrister. His clients had much money and many law suits, and consequently he had many briefs and much money. The excitements of his profession, to which he was greatly attached, were not enough for him. He could be found, almost every night, in some gambling club. The peace which brooded over his house was highly distasteful to him. And his wife's reproachful eyes drove him to despair. As each was afraid of meeting the other, they both avoided the villa as much as possible. And if their son Stephan wished to see his parents, he had to attend one of the parties they gave in the winter. These functions repelled him more and more as the years passed, until at last he gave up attending them altogether, so that he never met his parents except by accident.

Most of what he knew of his father he had once learned from a young actress. It was at a fancy-dress ball, and she had described to him in great detail the man who was at the time financing her. Light women occasionally try to acquire new lovers by revealing the intimate habits and customs of their former possessors. As they talked, it became evident that she was alluding to Labude Senior, and Stephan fled from the ball in panic.

Fabian did not like going to the villa in Grunewald. He regarded the expense that such houses involve as futile. He could not imagine how one could ever get rid, in the midst of

57

such luxury, of the feeling that one was there merely on a visit. And apart from all other considerations it seemed to him perfectly natural for Labude's parents to have fallen out in that inhabited museum.

'It's awful,' he said to his friend, who was seated at the writing-desk. 'Every time I come here I expect your butler to put felt slippers over my shoes and take me on a tour of the castle. If you were to tell me that the Great Elector rode on that chair at the battle of Fehrbellin, I should be quite willing to believe it. By the way, thank you for the money.'

Labude dismissed his thanks with a wave of the hand. 'You know I have more than I want. Don't speak of it. I asked you here because I want to tell you what happened in Hamburg.'

Fabian crossed over and sat down on the sofa. Now he was sitting behind Labude's back, so that his friend could talk without looking at him.

Both gazed out of the window at the green trees and the red roofs of the villas. The window was open and sometimes a bird alighted, hopped up and down the window ledge, looked into the room with its head on one side and flew back into the garden. Outside, they could hear someone raking the gravel path.

Labude looked fixedly into the branches of the nearest tree. 'Rassow wrote me he was speaking at the Auditorium Maximum in Hamburg to an audience of students of all parties. His subject was "Tradition and Socialism". He suggested I should follow him, or take part in the discussion, and explain something of my political plans. I went to Hamburg. The meeting began. Rassow described his visit to Russia, and told of his experiences and the talks he had had with Russian artists and scientists. He was constantly interrupted by representatives of the Students' Socialist Party. A Communist spoke next, and he, in his turn, was heckled by the members of the middle parties. Then it was my turn. I sketched the capitalist situation in Europe, claimed that the youth of the middle classes must become more radical, must oppose the ruin of the whole continent, towards which all parties are working, either passively or actively. Young people of the middle classes, I said, would soon be taking over the leadership in politics, industry, landed proprietorship and commerce; our fathers had brought us to bankruptcy, and it was our duty to reform the whole continental system. This was to be done by international agreements, by the voluntary restriction of private profit, by forcing capitalism and technical progress back within reasonable limits, by the increase in welfare legislation and by developing the cultural element in training and education. I said this new alignment was possible, this alliance across the frontiers of class, since our generation, or at least its best elements, was sick of unrestrained egoism, and had the sense to welcome a reversion to organic conditions in preference to the otherwise inevitable crash of the whole system. If we could not get on without class rule, I said, then let it be a class determined by age, that is, our own generation. My remarks were greeted with the usual merriment by the extremists. But when Rassow proposed that a radical bourgeois pressure group be formed, the motion was carried. We proceeded therefore to the formation of such a group. We drafted an appeal which we shall send to all the universities of Europe. Rassow, myself and a few others intend to visit the German universities and technical colleges, to speak to the students and form similar groups. We hope to achieve a sort of federation with the Socialist students. When we have formed branches at all the universities, these branches will proceed to approach other political and educational bodies. There's no doubt we shall get the thing going. I didn't mention this to you yesterday, because I know your scepticism only too well.'

'I'm glad,' said Fabian. 'I'm very glad that you can now set to work to bring your plan to fruition. Have you got in touch with the Independent Democratic Group? In Copenhagen they've started a "Europa Club", make a note of it. Don't worry too much because I doubt the essential goodness of youth. And don't be angry with me for not believing that you can ever make reason and power lie down together. Here you have, unfortunately, an antinomy. My conviction is that there are only two alternatives for humanity in its present state. Either mankind is dissatisfied with its lot, and then we bash each other over the head in order to improve things, or, and this is a purely hypothetical situation, we are content with ourselves and the universe, and then we commit suicide out of sheer boredom. The result is the same. What use is the most perfect system as long as people remain a lot of swine? But what had Leda to say to all this?'

'She expressed no opinion. She was not there.'

'But why not?'

'She did not know I was in Hamburg.'

Fabian got up in surprise, but sat down again without speaking.

Labude threw out his arms and grasped the corners of the writing-desk. 'I wanted to surprise her. I wanted to watch her without being seen. I've been getting suspicious. When two people are never together, except for two days and one night in every month, their friendship is bound to be undermined, and when that state of affairs goes on for years, as it has done with us, the whole relationship breaks down. That has little to do with the inherent quality of the two persons, the process is inevitable. Some months ago, I let you know that Leda had changed. She began to pretend. She was playing a part. Her greeting at the station, the tenderness she showed when we talked together, her passionate embraces, it was all play-acting.'

Labude threw back his head, and went on in a low voice: 'Of course we became alienated. Neither knew what troubles the other had; neither knew what friendships the other made. We didn't notice how we were changing nor why we were changing. Letters are no good. And then we met, kissed, went to the theatre, asked for the latest news, spent the night together, and separated again. Four weeks later the same thing was repeated. Mental proximity, and then love by the calendar, with your watch in your hand. It was hopeless. She in Hamburg, I in Berlin – geography spells the ruination of love.'

Fabian took a cigarette, and struck the match so gently that he might have been afraid of injuring the box.

'For the last few months I have always been afraid of these encounters. When she lay there with eyes closed, when she trembled beneath me, holding me clasped in her arms, I wanted to tear the mask from her face. She was lying. But whom was she trying to deceive? Only me, or both of us? I wrote to her repeatedly asking for explanations, but she always avoided them, and so there was nothing for it but to do what I did. That night, soon after our first group had been formed, I took leave of Rassow and the rest, and went to the house where she lives. The windows were dark. Perhaps Leda was already asleep. But I was in no mood for logic. I waited.'

Labude's voice faltered. He put out his hand, took several

pencils from the desk and rolled them nervously between his hands; their wooden clatter went on as he continued his story. 'The street is a wide one, with no houses except in one place. It is bordered, on the side opposite the house, by flower-beds, lawns, paths and bushes, and beyond them lies the Outer Alster. Across the road from the house there is a bench. I sat down on it, smoked innumerable cigarettes and waited. Whenever someone came down the street, I thought it must be Leda. I sat there from midnight till three in the morning while violent disputes and evil pictures passed through my mind. And time went by. Shortly after three, a taxi turned into the street and stopped outside the house. A tall, slenderly built man got out and paid the driver. Then a woman jumped out of the car, ran to the door, unlocked it, went in, held the door for the man to follow her, and locked it on the inside. The taxi turned round and drove off towards the town.'

Labude rose to his feet. He threw the pencils down on the writing-desk and paced rapidly up and down the room till he stopped in the farthest corner, close to the wall. He looked down at the pattern in the carpet and followed its lines with his finger. 'It was Leda. A light appeared in the window. I saw two shadows moving behind the curtains. The living-room grew dark. Then the bedroom was lighted up. The balcony-door was half open. At times I heard her laugh. She's got a strange, high laugh, you know. At times it was very still, up there in the house and down in my street, and I could hear nothing but the beating of my heart.'

At that moment the door was thrown open. Labude's father came in, without coat or hat. 'How do, Stephan?' he said. He came and shook hands with his son. 'Long time since I saw you. I've been away for a day or two. Had to ease off for once. Nerves, the nerves! Just come back. How are you keeping? You don't look very well. Worried? Heard anything about that thesis of yours? No? They're a hopeless crowd. Have you heard from mother? She'd better stay another week or two. Paradiso – good name for the place. Lucky woman! Evening, Herr Fabian. Serious conversation, what? Is there a life after death? In confidence, no. You have to get through it all beforehand. Keeps your hands full. Night and day.'

'Come along, Fritz!' cried a woman's voice from the stairs. 'What a time you are!' Labude senior shrugged his shoulders.

'Now you've got it. Little singer, lots of talent, but no engagements. Knows all the operas off by heart. Bit loud in the long run. Well, see you again one of these days. You ought to have a good time instead of redeeming the world. As I said, you've got to finish your life before you die. Further information if required. Not so serious, my boy!' He shook hands with them and went out, slamming the door behind him.

Labude put his hands retrospectively over his ears. He went across to the writing-desk, reflected for a moment, and then went on with his story: 'Towards five o'clock it began to rain. Just after six it cleared up. The sky brightened and another day began. The light in the bedroom was still on. That looked strange in the dawn. At seven o'clock, the man left the house. He whistled as he came out, and looked up. Leda appeared on the balcony in her kimono, and waved. He waved back. She spread out the kimono for a moment, so that he should see her body once more. He threw her a kiss. I was nearly sick. Then he went whistling off down the street. I looked away, and heard the balcony-door close above me.'

Fabian did not know what to say or do. He just sat there on the sofa. Suddenly Labude threw up his arm and brought his fist down on the writing-desk. 'The bitch!' he shouted. Fabian sprang up from the sofa, but his friend waved him back and said quite calmly: 'All right. Listen. At midday I telephoned. She was glad to hear I was back in Hamburg. Why hadn't I written? Could I come about five o'clock? The science students had been leaving work earlier for some weeks. I tramped about the docks till the hour named. Then I drove to her house. She had got tea ready, with cakes, and greeted me affectionately. I drank a cup of tea, talking trivialities. Then she began mechanically to undress, put on her kimono and lay down on the couch. At that I asked her what she thought of our breaking off the engagement. "What's the matter with you?" she asked. She thought it was a settled thing that we should marry as soon as I was installed as a lecturer at the university. Didn't I love her any more? I told her that was not the point. We were becoming increasingly alienated, and she was to blame for it. Therefore it seemed best for us to part.

'She stretched herself, allowed the kimono to slip to one side, and complained in a childish voice that I was so cold. The alienation, she said, as the present situation clearly demonstrated, was on my side rather than hers. She admitted it was hard to remain intimate across the distance from Hamburg to Berlin. Sexually, too, there were difficulties. When she wanted me, I was not there, and when I was there, we had to take our love like a luncheon-sandwich, whether we were hungry or no. But once we were married things would be different. And, by the way, I was not to be angry, but some weeks ago she had been to a doctor for a small operation. She wanted to bear our children when she was my wife, and not before. She had not told me earlier of that little affair, because she did not want to worry me. Now she was quite well again, and I was to hurry up and come and sit by her. She wanted me.

'I asked who was the father of the child she had got rid of. She sat up and assumed an injured expression.

' "And who was the man who slept with you last night?" I asked.

' "You must be seeing ghosts," she said. "You are jealous. It's absolutely idiotic."

'At this I slapped her face, and went. She ran after me down the stairs as far as the door. There she stood, naked beneath her fluttering kimono, at six in the evening, and called to me to stay. But I rushed off and drove to the station.'

Fabian went up behind Labude and put his hands on his friend's shoulders. 'Why didn't you tell me this last night?'

'Oh, I shall get over it,' said Labude. 'Deceiving me like that!'

'But what ought she to have done? Told you the truth?'

'I've reached a point where I can't think of it. I feel as though I've been very ill.'

'You are ill now,' said Fabian. 'You are still in love with her.'

'That is true,' said Labude. 'But I've managed to handle heftier fellows than myself.'

'What if she writes to you?'

'The matter is settled. I've spent the last five years living on a false assumption. That's enough. But I haven't told you the worst yet. She doesn't love me and never has loved me! Now that she's drawn a line under the bill, I can see what it amounts to. When she lay there beside me and told me those cold-blooded lies, I understood the years that have passed. In five minutes I understood everything. Now we'll put paid to it.'

Labude drew his friend towards the door. 'Let us go now.

Ruth Reiter has asked us to look in. Come on! I've got a good deal of catching up to do.'

'Who is Ruth Reiter?'

'I'd never met her before today. She has a studio and is a sculptress, according to her story.'

'I've always wanted to do a bit of posing,' said Fabian, and put on his coat.

STRANGE YOUNG WOMEN
A CANDIDATE FOR DEATH COMES ALIVE
A CLUB CALLED 'LA COUSINE'

'A couple of men at last!' cried Ruth Reiter. 'Make yourselves at home. Kulp's just been grumbling. She says she can't go on like this. She hasn't had a man for two days, and the last was only an accident. She's a fashion artist, and the bloke wouldn't give her an order without some little favour in return. An almost impotent old fellow, he was, she said.'

'They are the worst,' said Labude. 'They keep on trying so as to see whether the defect has disappeared.'

Labude looked round for the girl named Kulp. She was squatting with upraised knees on the sofa. She beckoned to him.

He sat down beside her. Fabian waited, irresolute. The studio was large. Under the lamp, in the middle of the room, in front of a row of sculptured figures, was a rough table, and on the table was sitting a naked woman with dark hair. Ruth Reiter crouched on a stool, took up a sketching-block, and began to draw. 'My nightly model,' she explained, without looking up. 'Her name's Selow. New position, darling. Stand up, legs apart, trunk turned at right angles. Clasp your hands behind your head. Hold it!' The naked woman whose name was Selow had risen, and was now standing with her legs apart on the table. She was beautifully built, and stared indifferently in front of her with melancholy eyes. 'Baron, something to drink. I'm cold,' she said, suddenly.

'Yes, Fräulein Selow has goose-flesh all over,' agreed Fabian. He had approached the model, and was standing in front of her like a connoisseur inspecting a female figure in bronze.

'Hands off!' The voice of the sculptress was most unfriendly.

Fräulein Kulp was expanding in Labude's arms as in a warm bath. 'Hands off the cake,' she called to Fabian. 'The Baron's jealous. She has an ongoing relationship with the model.'

'Don't go too far!' growled Ruth Reiter.

'Labude, if you and Kulp can't restrain yourselves, just go right ahead. I only have this one room, but it has seen everything.'

Labude confessed that he had moral reservations.

'It's amazing that such things still exist,' remarked Fräulein Kulp sadly.

Ruth Reiter looked up fleetingly from her pad and looked at Fabian.

'In case you would like a share in Fräulein Kulp, don't feel shy! All you need is a shilling. Labude chooses heads and you tails. Kulp will toss the coin, the exercise is good for her solar plexus. And whoever wins takes first turn.'

'What a profound statement!' exclaimed Fräulein Kulp. 'But only a shilling? You're depressing the prices!'

Fabian said politely that he did not like games of chance.

The nude woman stamped her foot. 'Something to drink!'

'Battenberg, there's some gin on a little table by your chair. Bring it here, will you?'

'Certainly,' said a voice. There was a tinkle of glass behind the statuary. Then a strange girl appeared in the circle of light cast by the lamp, and handed a full glass to the model.

Fabian was surprised. 'How many females are there here exactly?' he asked.

'I'm the only one,' declared Fräulein Battenberg, and laughed. Fabian looked into her face, and decided she did not fit into her surroundings. She went back to her place behind the statuary. He followed her. She sat down in an armchair. He stopped by a plaster Diana, put his arm round the waist of that athletic goddess, and looked through the studio-window at the arches and volutes of the modern gables outside. They heard the Baron's voice: 'Last pose, darling. Trunk forward bend, knees bend, bottom out, hands on knees. Good. Hold it.' And from the front part of the studio little high-pitched squeals could be heard. Fräulein Kulp was temporarily short of breath.

'How did you get into this pigsty?' Fabian asked Fräulein Battenberg.

'I come from the same town as Ruth Reiter. We went to school together. A few days ago, I happened to meet her in the street. And, as I have not been long in Berlin, she invited me to call and receive a little instruction. I shan't come here again. The instruction has been quite sufficient.'

'I'm very glad,' he said. 'I'm not altogether a defender of virtue, but it always depresses me to see a woman living below her level.'

She looked at him gravely. 'I'm not an angel. People have no time for angels in these days. What are we to do? When we love a man we give ourselves over to him. We cut ourselves off from all that happened before, and come to him. Here I am, we say, smiling pleasantly. Yes, here you are, he says, and scratches his head. Good God, he thinks, now I've got this woman tied round my neck. With a light heart we give him all we possess, and he curses. Our gifts are an embarrassment to him. At first he curses under his breath, but later aloud. And we are more completely alone than ever. I'm twenty-five and twice I've been left stranded by a man. They left me like an old umbrella that you forget somewhere on purpose. Do you mind my being so frank?'

'That happens to many women. We young men have cares of our own, and they leave us sufficient time for pleasure, but not enough for love. The family is disintegrating. After all, there are only two possible ways in which we can shoulder responsibility. Either a man accepts the responsibility for a woman's future, and then, if he loses his job the week after, he realizes how irresponsibly he has acted. Or his sense of responsibility forbids him to make a mess of a woman's future, and if, for this very reason, he plunges her into misfortune, he finds out that his decision was as irresponsible as the other fellow's. That particular dilemma used not to exist.'

Fabian sat down on the window-sill. Across the street was a lighted window. He looked into a modestly furnished room. A woman was sitting at the table with her head in her hands. And a man was standing in front of her. He waved his arms, moved his lips as though railing at her, snatched his hat from a peg and left the room. The woman took her hands from her face and stared at the door. Then she laid her head on the table, quite slowly, quite calmly, as though she were waiting for an axe to descend on her neck. Fabian turned away. He looked at the girl, sitting there in the armchair at his side. She also had watched the scene across the street. She looked at him sadly.

'Another frustrated angel,' he said.

'The second man I embarrassed with my love,' she said softly, 'left the flat one fine evening to post a letter. He went down the stairs and never returned.' She shook her head as though the experience were still beyond her comprehension. 'For three months I waited for him to come back from the pillar-box. Odd, wasn't it? Then he sent me a picture-postcard from Santiago, with heartiest good wishes. My mother called me a harlot, and, when I pointed out that she married her first husband at eighteen and had her first child soon after, she replied indignantly that that was something quite different. Of course! It was something quite different.'

'Why have you come to Berlin?'

'Formerly a woman gave herself and was valued as a gift. Now we are paid, and the day comes when we are thrown aside, like all goods that are bought and made use of. It's cheaper to pay cash, thinks the man.'

'Formerly a gift and a commodity were two quite different things. Now a gift is merely a commodity that can be bought for nothing. Its cheapness makes the purchaser suspicious. It must be a bad bargain, he thinks. And generally he is right. For later the woman presents him with the bill. Suddenly he is called on to refund the moral price of the gift. In moral currency. As a pension for life.'

'That is just how it is,' she said. 'That is just how men think. But in that case why do you call this studio a pigsty? The women here are more or less what you would like them to be. Are they not? I know what you need to complete your happiness. Of course, we are to come and go as you wish. But we are to cry when you send us away. And we are to be blissful when you allow us to come back. You want us to be an article of commerce, but the article is to be in love with you. You want all the rights and none of the obligations; we are to have all the obligations and no rights. That's what the man's ideal amounts to. But that's going too far. That's going much too far!' Fräulein Battenberg wiped her nose. Then she went on: 'If we're not to be allowed to keep you, we don't want to love you. If you want to buy us, you must pay dearly for us.' She was silent. Little tears were running down her face.

'Is that why you've come to Berlin?' asked Fabian.

She went on silently crying.

He went up to her and stroked her shoulder. 'You know, you

don't understand business,' he said, and looked between two plaster figures into the other end of the studio. The model was sitting on the table, drinking gin. The sculptress was leaning over the naked woman and kissing her on her almost flat belly and her breasts. Selow emptied her glass meanwhile and stroked her friend's back indifferently. One was kissing, the other drinking, and neither seemed quite to know what her companion was doing. In the background, the girl Kulp and Labude lay on the sofa, tangled in a confused, whispering heap.

The door-bell rang. Ruth Reiter got up and left the room with heavy steps. Selow put on her stockings. Then a huge man appeared in the doorway. He was gasping for breath. He had an artificial leg and walked with a stick.

'Is Kulp here?' he asked. Ruth nodded. He took some money from his pocket and gave it to the sculptress. 'The rest of you can clear out for an hour,' he said. 'You can leave Selow here if you like.' He dropped into a chair and laughed dully.

'No, no, Baron. I was only joking.'

Kulp crawled off the sofa, straightened her dress and shook hands with the newcomer. 'How do, Wilhelmy. Not dead yet?'

Wilhelmy wiped the sweat from his brow, and shook his head.

'But I can't go on much longer, or my money will be finished before me.' He gave her a few banknotes. 'Selow!' he cried. 'Don't drink all that gin. And hurry up and get dressed.'

'Go to "La Cousine". I'll come along later,' said Kulp. Then she shook Labude into wakefulness. 'You're going to be turned out now, my dear. The doctors have told Wilhelmy he'll die before the end of the month. He's waiting for death the way we wait for our periods, and I'm going to spend just fifteen minutes helping him to wait. I'll see you all again later.'

Labude got up. Ruth Reiter fetched her coat. Fabian came out from behind the statuary with Fräulein Battenberg. Selow had finished dressing. They went. Kulp and the candidate for death stayed behind.

'I hope he won't knock her about as badly as he did last time,' said the sculptress, on the stairs. 'It upsets him to think that other people have longer to live than he has.'

'She doesn't mind. She likes it,' said Selow. 'And besides, what she makes with her drawing is neither enough to live or die on.'

'What fine professions we have!' Ruth Reiter laughed savagely.

'La Cousine' was a sort of club, frequented mainly by women. They danced together. They sat arm-in-arm on little green sofas. They looked deep into each other's eyes. They drank schnaps, and some wore velveteen coats and high-cut blouses in order to look like men. The proprietress bore the same name as her establishment. She smoked black cigars and made people acquainted with each other. She went from table to table, chatting with her guests, telling spicy yarns and drinking like a fish.

Labude seemed ashamed of himself, and avoided Fabian. He danced with the model, went and sat at the bar with her, and turned his back on his friend. Ruth Reiter was jealous, but kept a firm hold on herself. She did not often glance towards the bar, but looked pale and began to drink. Later she moved to another table, and conversed with an elderly woman who was appallingly made up and cackled so loudly when she laughed that one expected her to lay an egg.

'I can't get our talk out of my mind,' said Fabian to Fräulein Battenberg. 'Do you actually think that all the women here are congenitally abnormal? The blonde over there was the mistress of an actor for years, till all of a sudden he turned her out of doors. Then she got a job in an office and slept with the manager. She had a child and lost her case. The manager denied paternity. The child was sent into the country, and the blonde got another job. But she's had enough of men, perhaps for good, but at all events provisionally, and many of the other women sitting here have been through the same sort of thing. Some could never find a man at all, others found too many, and others again are frightened to death of the consequences. Many of the women here are merely fed up with men. Selow, who's sitting over there with my friend, is one of them. She is lesbian only because she's angry with the other sex.'

'Will you take me home?' asked Fräulein Battenberg.

'You don't like it here?'

She shook her head.

Suddenly the door opened, and Kulp staggered into the room. She stopped before the table where the sculptress was sitting, and opened her mouth. She did not scream, she did not speak. She collapsed. The women jostled inquisitively round

70

her unconscious body. La Cousine brought whisky. 'Wilhelmy has been thrashing her again,' said Reiter.

'Three cheers for the men!' screamed a girl, and laughed hysterically.

'Fetch the doctor from the back room!' cried La Cousine. There was a confused running to and fro. The pianist, who was as witty as he was drunk, struck up Chopin's Funeral March.

'Surely that's not the doctor?' said Fräulein Battenberg. Through the side-door came a tall, thin woman in an evening gown. Her face was like a heavily powdered death's head.

'Yes, that's the doctor and a qualified man,' said Fabian. 'He once even belonged to a students' corps. Can't you see the duelling scars under the powder? Now he's a morphine addict and has a police licence to wear women's clothing. He gets his living by writing prescriptions for morphine. One day they'll catch him at it, then he'll take poison.'

They carried Kulp into the back room. The doctor in the evening gown followed her. The pianist began to play a tango. The sculptress fetched the model to dance, hugged her close and talked vehemently to her. Selow was completely drunk. She closed her eyes, scarcely listening. Suddenly she tore herself free, walked unsteadily across the floor, and slammed down the lid of the piano, making the instrument groan again. 'No!' she screamed.

There was a deathly silence. The sculptress stood alone in the middle of the dance-floor, her hands clenched tightly in front of her.

'No!' screamed Selow again. 'I've had enough. I'm fed up to the back teeth! I want a man! A man, do you hear me? Get away from me, you randy goat!' She hauled Labude from his stool, gave him a kiss, slammed her hat on her head, and dragged the young man to the door, scarcely giving him time to snatch up his coat. 'Vive la différence!' she cried. Then they both disappeared.

'I think we'd better go.' Fabian rose, put some money on the table, and helped Fräulein Battenberg into her coat. As they passed through the door, Ruth Reiter, known as the Baron, was standing in the middle of the floor. No one dared approach her.

X

TOPOGRAPHY OF IMMORALITY
LOVE NEVER ENDS!
VIVE LA DIFFÉRENCE!

'How comes it that this man is your friend?' she asked, when they reached the street.

'You don't know him yet.' He was angry at her question and angry at his answer. They walked on, side by side, without speaking. After a time he said: 'Labude's been unlucky. He went up to Hamburg and watched his future wife deceiving him. He's fond of organizing. His future, on the domestic side, was calculated to five places of decimals. And now, in the course of one night, he's found out that it was all wrong. He wants to forget it as soon as possible, and at the moment he's trying the horizontal method.'

They stopped in front of a shop. Despite the late hour, the windows were brightly illuminated, and the frocks and blouses and patent-leather belts lay there between the darkened houses as on a sunlit isle.

'Can you tell me the time?' asked a voice behind them.

Fräulein Battenberg started and caught her companion's arm. 'Ten past twelve,' said Fabian.

'Thank you. I shall have to hurry.' The young man who had accosted them bent down and made considerable show of tying up his shoe-lace. Then he stood up, and asked with an embarrassed smile: 'Have you by chance fifty pfennigs you could spare?'

'By chance I have,' returned Fabian, and gave him a two-mark piece.

'Oh, that's wonderful. Thank you very much, sir. Now I shan't need to spend the night at the Salvation Army shelter.' The stranger shrugged his shoulders apologetically, raised his hat and walked hurriedly away. 'An educated man,' observed Fräulein Battenberg. 'Yes, he asked the time before begging.'

They went on their way. Fabian did not know where the girl

lived. He let himself be guided, although he was better acquainted with the district than she. 'The worst of it all is this,' he said. 'Labude has discovered, five years too late, that Leda, the woman in Hamburg, has never loved him. She deceived him, not because she saw too little of him, but because she did not love him. She liked him as an individual, but he was not her type. Sometimes you meet the contrary. One person likes another because he incorporates the desired type, but can't stand him as an individual.'

'And does one never meet a person who is right in all respects?'

'You shouldn't let your hopes run to extremes,' returned Fabian. 'And what is it, apart from your bellicose project, that brings you to Sodom and Gomorrah?'

'I've passed my law examinations,' she said. 'I wrote my thesis on one aspect of international film rights, and a big Berlin film company is willing to take me as an apprentice in their copyright department. A hundred and fifty marks a month.'

'Why don't you become a film-actress?'

'Even that,' she said, resolutely, 'if it must be.'

Both laughed. They were walking through the Geisberg-strasse. It was seldom that a car traversed the nocturnal silence. Beds of flowers dispersed their scent in the front gardens. A pair of lovers were cuddling in a doorway.

'Even the moon shines in this city,' remarked the expert on international film rights.

Fabian gave her arm a slight squeeze. 'It's almost like it was at home, isn't it?' he said. 'But don't be deceived. The moonlight, the scent of flowers, the stillness, the rustic kiss in the doorway, are all illusions. There's a café over yonder on the square, where Chinamen sit with Berlin tarts, none but Chinamen. Straight ahead is an establishment where perfumed young homosexuals dance with over-dressed actors and smart Englishmen; they make known their accomplishments and their price, and to finish up a hennaed old woman pays the bill in return for the privilege of their company. On the right, at the corner, is a hotel entirely occupied by Japanese; next door is a restaurant where Russian and Hungarian Jews practise on each other the varied arts of cadging and swindling. In one of the side-streets is a pension where under-age high-school girls sell themselves in the afternoons to add to their pin-money. About six months ago there was a scandal that was never properly hushed up: a middle-aged man went to one of the rooms on pleasure bent and there, as he had expected, found a girl of sixteen waiting for him; but unfortunately it was his daughter, and that he had not expected . . . So far as this vast city consists of bricks and mortar, it is practically the same as of old. But so far as its inhabitants are concerned, it has long since resembled a madhouse. In the east resides crime, in the centre roguery, poverty in the north and vice in the west, and ruin dwells at every point of the compass.'

'And what comes after ruin?'

Fabian plucked a little twig that hung over the railings, and answered: 'I'm afraid, imbecility.'

'Where I come from, imbecility has arrived already,' said the girl. 'But what is one to do?'

'If you are an optimist, you should despair. I am a melancholic, so nothing much can happen to me. I don't tend towards suicide, for I feel nothing of that urge to action which makes others go on butting their heads against a wall till their heads give way. I look on and wait. I wait for the triumph of decency; when that comes, I can place myself at the world's disposal. But I wait for it as an unbeliever waits for miracles. My dear, I don't know you. None the less, or perhaps on that account, I should like to offer you, for your dealings with other people, a working hypothesis that has already justified itself. It does not need to be true in theory; it yields valuable results in practice.'

'And what is your hypothesis?'

'You should assume, until the contrary is indisputably proved, that every person you meet, except children and the very old, is a lunatic. Do as I say, and you will soon find how valuable this advice can be.'

'Shall I begin with you?' she asked.

'If you please,' he said.

They crossed the Nürnbergerplatz in silence. A car braked close in front of them. The girl trembled with fright. They entered the Schaperstrasse. Some cats were howling in a neglected garden. The rows of trees that lined the footpath spread their shadows across the road and hid the sky.

'This is where I live,' she said, and stopped outside No. 17. It was the very house where Fabian lived. He concealed his astonishment and asked if he might see her again.

74

'Do you really want to?'

'On one condition: that you want to also.'

She nodded and laid her head for one moment on his shoulder. 'Yes, I want to.' He pressed her hand. 'This city is so big,' she whispered, and stood silent and irresolute. 'Would you misunderstand me, if I asked you to come up for half an hour? I feel such a stranger in my room. There are no echoes of things said, no memories of things done, for I have never spoken to any-one in my room, and nothing has ever happened of which it could remind me. And at night black trees sway to and fro outside the window.'

Fabian's voice was louder than he had intended: 'I'll come up with pleasure. Won't you unlock the door?' She put the key in the lock and turned it. But before she opened the door, she turned to him again: 'I'm very anxious that you shouldn't misunderstand me.' He pushed back the door and switched on the stair-lighting. Then he was angry with himself, fearing that he had given himself away. But she took no account of it, locked the door behind him and walked on ahead. He followed, amused at the secrecy with which he was entering the house. Which floor did she live on? She stopped outside the widow Hohlfeld's door, outside the door of his landlady's flat, and opened it.

There was a light in the hall. Two girls in pink camiknickers were playing football with a green balloon. They started and began to giggle with fright. Fräulein Battenberg stood rigid. Then the lavatory door opened and Herr Tröger, the sensual commercial traveller, appeared in his pyjamas.

'You'd better keep your harem under lock and key,' growled Fabian.

Herr Tröger grinned, drove the girls into his seraglio and bolted the door. Without thinking, Fabian put his hand on his own door-handle.

'Good heavens!' whispered Fräulein Battenberg. 'That's not my room!'

'I beg your pardon.' He followed her down the corridor to the room at the end. He threw his hat and coat on the sofa, and she hung her coat in the wardrobe. 'A barn of a place,' she said, smiling. 'And eighty marks a month.'

'Just what I pay,' he comforted her.

There was a commotion in the next room. Springs creaked

unwillingly. 'They don't charge me extra for my neighbours,' she said.

'Bore a hole in the wall and demand admission.'

'Oh, I'm so glad!' She rubbed her hands as though she were standing before a fire. 'This room seems far worse when I'm alone. I'm grateful to you. Would you like to take a look at those ghastly trees?'

They went to the window. 'Even the trees seem friendlier now,' she informed him. Then she looked at him. 'It's because I'm always alone here,' she murmured. He drew her gently to him and kissed her. She returned the kiss. 'Now you'll think this is what I brought you up for.'

'Of course,' he said. 'But you didn't know it at the time.'

She looked out of the window and pressed her cheek against his. 'What is your name?' he asked.

'Cornelia.'

When they were lying side by side in bed, he closed his eyes and gently touched her face with his hands, trying to feel the outlines of her features. 'Do you know,' he said, genuinely troubled, 'that earlier this evening we were sitting in a studio behind a row of plaster goddesses, and you told me that you wanted to avenge yourself on men for their egotism?'

She covered his hands with little kisses. Then she took a deep breath. 'I've not changed my mind in the least,' she answered. 'Truly I've not. But with you I'll make an exception. I feel just as though I were in love with you.'

He sat up. But she drew him down to her again. 'Just now, when you took me in your arms, I cried,' she whispered. And as she recalled the fact, her eyes grew moist again, but she smiled through her tears, and he was almost happy for the first time for months. 'I cried because I love you. But my love for you is my own affair, do you hear? It is no concern of yours. You are to come and go when you wish. And when you come I will be glad, and when you go I will not be miserable. I promise you that.' She turned to him and pressed her body against his till both lay breathless. 'There,' she cried. 'And now I'm hungry.'

She laughed at the look of surprise on his face.

'It's like this,' she explained. 'When I love someone, I mean when someone has loved me – you know what I mean – afterwards I'm always frightfully hungry. There's only one

76

drawback in this case. I haven't anything here to eat. How was I to know that I should get hungry like this so soon in this awful city?' She lay on her back and smiled at the ceiling, including even the stucco cherubs.

Fabian got up. 'Then there's nothing for it but to go burgling,' he said. He lifted her out of bed, carried her across the room, put her down, opened the door, and drew the resisting Cornelia into the corridor. She struggled, but he took her arm, and, looking like Adam and Eve, they walked down the passage to Fabian's door.

'This is too bad,' she wailed, and tried to run back. But he pressed down the latch, and drew her into his room. Her teeth were chattering with fright. He switched on the light, bowed and announced with ceremony: 'Dr Fabian has the pleasure of welcoming Dr Battenberg to his apartment.' Then he threw himself on the bed and bit the pillow to choke his laughter.

'No!' she said, behind him. 'That can't be true. Then she was convinced in spite of herself, and broke into a Tyrolese clog-dance.

He stood up and watched her. 'You mustn't smack yourself so loud on the bottom,' he said, with dignity.

'That's the right way to do it,' she answered, and went on dancing as authentically and loudly as she could. Presently, she walked gravely to the table, sat down on a chair, made a movement as though to straighten her non-existent frock, and said: 'The menu, please.'

He produced plates, knives, forks, bread and sausage and biscuits, and played the attentive head-waiter while she ate. Afterwards she rummaged about on his bookshelves, tucked some books under her right arm, gave him her left, and ordered majestically: 'Take me back at once to my apartment.'

Before switching off the light, they arranged that she should rouse him next morning. It was agreed that she was to tweak his ear till he awoke. Next evening they would meet again in the flat. Whoever was there first would make a pencilled cross beside his door-handle. They decided that so far as possible they would keep matters a secret from the widow Hohlfeld.

Then Cornelia put out the light, and snuggled down beside him. 'Come!' she said. He stroked her limbs. She took his head in her hands, pressed her lips to his ear and whispered: 'Come! What was it Selow said? Vive la différence!'

XI

A SURPRISE AT THE FACTORY
HE MEETS AN ECCENTRIC ON THE KREUZBERG
LIFE IS A BAD HABIT

Next morning Fabian was at work a quarter of an hour before he was due to arrive. He whistled to himself as he glanced over his notes for the prize-competition, for which the board was now waiting.

The company was to distribute to the retailers a hundred thousand special packets of cigarettes at a very low price. These packets would be numbered and each would contain an assortment of six different brands without any indication of which brands they were. The purchaser had to guess how many cigarettes of each of the six well-known brands manufactured by the company were contained in the packet. If he bought one of the cheap packets, and wished to enter for the competition and win one of the prizes, he had to buy one packet of each of the six regular brands which had long been on the market, that is, he had to buy six packets in addition to the cheap packet. If a hundred thousand persons competed, they would buy automatically six hundred thousand normal packets of cigarettes, or seven hundred thousand packets in all. Moreover, there was the general rise in sales which usually follows a cleverly managed publicity stunt. Fabian began to make a rough calculation.

Just then Fischer came in. 'Hallo,' he said, and looked inquisitively over Fabian's shoulder.

'The draft of the prize-competition,' said Fabian.

Fischer put on the grey alpaca coat he wore in the office. 'Can I show you my couplets when you've finished?' he asked.

'Rather. I'm in a lyric mood this morning.'

There was a knock at the door, and Schneidereit, the decrepit, elderly factotum, sometimes alluded to as the discoverer of flat feet, shuffled into the room. Sulkily he placed a large yellow envelope on Fabian's desk and went out again.

The letter contained Fabian's papers, a note to the cashier, and a short letter with the following contents:

'Dear Sir, We find ourselves compelled to terminate your engagement as from today. The salary due to you at the end of the month will be paid to you immediately on application to the cashier. We have taken the liberty of enclosing herewith an unsolicited testimonial, and we seize this opportunity to state that you appear to possess exceptional qualifications for publicity work. Our present step is an unfortunate result of the reduced expenditure on advertising on which the board has decided. We thank you for the work you have done on behalf of this company and offer you all good wishes for the future.' Signature. Finish.

For some minutes Fabian sat without stirring. Then he got up, put on his coat and hat, thrust the letter into his pocket, and said to Fischer: 'So long. And good luck.'

'Where are you off to?'

'They've just sacked me.'

Fischer sprang to his feet. His face had gone green. 'You don't say so! Good Lord, my luck's in again!'

'You get less money,' said Fabian. 'They let you stay.'

Fischer went up to his ex-colleague and, giving him his moist hand, expressed his regrets. 'Well, it doesn't matter much to you, luckily. You're a smart chap, and you haven't got a wife tied round your neck.'

Suddenly Director Breitkopf was standing in the room. Seeing that Fischer was not alone, he hesitated and finally bade them both good morning.

'Good morning, sir,' returned Fischer, and bowed twice. Fabian pretended not to see Breitkopf. 'You'll find my plan for the prize-competition on my desk,' he said to Fischer. 'I bequeath it to you.' With that he left the scene of his labours and collected two hundred and seventy marks from the cashier. He remained standing for some minutes in the doorway before he went out into the street. Lorries were clattering past. A messenger-boy jumped from his bicycle and hurried into the building opposite. The house next door was latticed with scaffolding. Bricklayers were standing on planks, cleaning the grey, crumbling plaster. A file of bright-coloured furniture-vans turned ponderously into a side-street. The messenger-boy came out, hastily mounted his bicycle and rode away. Fabian stood in the doorway, thrust his hand into his pocket to make sure the money was there, and thought: what will become of me? Then, since he was not permitted to work, he went for a stroll.

He walked through the streets at random. About midday, he drank a cup of coffee at Aschinger's – he was not hungry – and started out afresh, although he would rather have crept miserably away and hidden himself in some deep forest. But there were no deep forests there. He tramped and tramped, working out his trouble through the soles of his feet. In the Belle Alliance-Strasse he recognized the house where he had lived for two terms as a student at the university. It stood there like an old acquaintance, whom one has not met for a long while and who waits with some embarrassment to see whether one will speak to him or not. Fabian climbed the stairs to find out if the old privy councillor's widow were still living there. But there was a fresh plate on the door. He turned back. The old lady's hair had been snow-white, and she had been very handsome. He recalled her foolish, regular, aged face. In the inflation winter he had had no money for heating. He had squatted up there buried in his overcoat, working at a paper on Schiller's system of morals and aesthetics. Occasionally the old lady invited him to a Sunday lunch and explained the domestic affairs of her wide circle of acquaintances. All his life he had been a poor, unfortunate devil and had excellent prospects of remaining one. Poverty had become a bad habit with him, like round shoulders or nail-biting with other people.

The previous night, before he fell asleep, he had thought to himself that, after all, perhaps he ought to sow a small packet of ambition somewhere in this town, since ambition bore fruit so quickly here; perhaps, after all, he ought to take himself a little more seriously, and furnish a snug three-roomed flat in the tottering house of the world, as though everything were as it should be; perhaps it was a sin to love life and never have a serious affair with it. Cornelia, the woman lawyer, had lain by his side and pressed his hand in her sleep. She told him in the morning that she had started up wide awake, in the middle of the night. For he had sat up in bed and declared energetically: 'I'll have the small advertisements illuminated.' Then he had lain down again.

He climbed slowly up to the plateau of the Kreuzberg and seated himself on a bench. It was commended to the care of the public. A little shield bore the words: 'Citizens, conserve your amenities.' The corporation had signed this ambiguous sentence, and the corporation ought to know. Fabian contemplated the trunk of a huge tree. The bark was furrowed by a thousand vertical wrinkles. Even trees had their cares. Two small schoolboys walked past the bench. The one held his hands clasped behind his back. 'Are we to put up with it?' he asked indignantly. The other took time to reply. At length he said: 'You can't do anything against those beasts.' Then they passed out of earshot.

An extraordinary figure was approaching from the other side of the gravelled square: an old gentlemen with a white Vandyke beard and a badly rolled umbrella. Instead of an overcoat, he wore a faded greenish cape, and his head was crowned with a greyish top-hat that might, years ago, have been black. The wearer of the cape made straight for the bench, murmured some formula of greeting and sat down beside Fabian. After a protracted fit of coughing, he drew circles in the sand with his umbrella. He made one of the circles into a cog-wheel, drew a straight line from its centre to the centre of another circle, made the sketch more and more complicated with curves and straight lines, wrote formulas above it and beside it, calculated, crossed out, calculated again, drew two lines beneath a number, and asked: 'Do you know anything about machines?'

'I'm sorry,' said Fabian. 'If anyone lets me wind up his gramophone he can be sure it will never go again. When I try to use a lighter it never lights. To this day I regard electric current as a liquid, as indeed the name seems to indicate. I shall never understand how it is possible for slaughtered oxen to go in at one end of a metal edifice, which works by electricity, and corned beef to come out at the other. By the way, your cape reminds me of my boarding school. Every Sunday we used to wear capes like that, and green caps, when we marched off to service at the Martin Luther Church. We all fell asleep during the sermon, except one boy whose job it was to wake us when the organist began to play the hymn-voluntary, or when the house-master went into the pulpit.' Fabian looked at his neighbour's cape and realized how this garment evoked the past. He saw the pale, plump headmaster. Every morning, at the beginning of service, before he sat down and opened his hymn-book, he bent his knees and laid his hands on his trouser-legs, as though to reassure himself that those carnal earthly envelopes were still there. Fabian saw himself of an evening, slinking through the school gates, running along the dusky streets, past the barracks, across the parade-ground, dashing up the stairs of a tenement building and pressing the door-bell. He heard his mother's tremulous voice inside the door: 'Who's there?' And his own breathless cry: 'It's me, mother! I just wanted to know whether you're better today.'

The old gentleman passed the tip of his badly-rolled umbrella across the sand until his calculations were erased. 'If you understand nothing of machines,' he said, 'perhaps you will understand me. I am a so-called inventor, an honorary member of five academies of science. I am responsible for many recent technical developments. With my help the textile industry now produces five times as much cloth per day as it used to do. Many people have made money out of my machines, including even myself.' The old gentleman coughed and tugged nervously at his moustache. 'I invented pacific machines and never noticed that they were guns. Capital increased daily, the works became more and more productive, but the number of employed workers grew smaller and smaller. My machines were guns; they put whole armies of workmen out of action. They shattered the claims of hundreds of thousands to a bare existence. When I was in Manchester, I saw the police riding down locked-out workmen, hitting them over the heads with their sabres. A little girl was trampled down by a horse. And it was all my fault.' The old gentleman pushed back the top-hat from his brow, and coughed. 'When I came back my family had me certified. They didn't like my beginning to give away money; they didn't like my saying I wouldn't have any more to do with machines. And so I left them. They have all they need. They live in my house by Lake Starnberg. I've been lost for six months. Last week I saw in the paper that my daughter had given birth to a child. So now I'm a grandfather, and wander about Berlin like a vagabond.'

'Old age is no defence against wisdom,' said Fabian. 'Unfortunately not all inventors are so sentimental.'

'I thought of going to Russia and putting myself at the disposal of the Soviets. But you can't get there without a passport. And if the authorities found out who I was, they would be all the more determined to keep me here. In my breast-pocket I have the sketches and calculations for a loom that would supersede all previous textile machinery. There are millions in this patched pocket of mine. But I would rather starve.' The old gentleman struck himself proudly on the chest, and coughed again. 'I shall spend the night at 93 Yorckstrasse. I shall go in just before the outer door is closed. If the porter asks me where I'm going, I shall say I'm visiting the Grünbergs. They live on the fourth floor. The husband drives a mail-van. I shall go upstairs, past the Grünbergs' flat, as far as the loft. There I shall sit down on the stairs. Perhaps the loft-door will be open. Perhaps there will even be an old mattress in a corner. Early tomorrow morning I shall come down again.'

'But how do you come to know the Grünbergs?'

'From the directory,' replied the inventor. 'I must, of course, know the name of one of the families in the house in case the porter asks me what I'm doing there. Next morning they often find out. But that century-old appeal to do honour to grey hairs and respect old age has worked, even with house-porters. Moreover I change my address daily. Last winter I used to teach physics in a private school. Unfortunately the lessons developed into a series of warnings against the miracles of technical science. That pleased neither the pupils nor the masters, so I preferred to spend three months warming myself in post offices. Now I have no more need of post offices. The weather is warm. I sit for hours at railway stations, watching the people who come and go and stay behind. It is all very interesting. I sit there and I am glad to be alive.'

Fabian wrote down his address and handed it to the old man. 'Take good care of that. And if a porter ever orders you off the stairs prematurely, come to me. You can sleep on my sofa.'

The old gentleman read the address. 'What will your land-lady say?' he asked.

Fabian shrugged his shoulders.

'You need not be afraid of my cough,' said the old man. 'When I spend the night on the dark stairs of houses, I never cough at all. I keep myself under control so as not to startle the people in the house. A queer way of living, isn't it? I began poor, then I became rich, and now I'm just a poor beggar again. It doesn't matter. You take it as it comes. Whether the sun shines on me here on the Kreuzberg or on my terrace at Leoni matters as little to me as to the sun itself.' The old gentleman coughed and stretched his legs. Fabian got up. 'I must go,' he said.

'What are you by profession?' asked the inventor.

'Unemployed,' returned Fabian, and walked off towards an avenue that led back into the streets of Berlin.

When he reached the flat in the evening, his legs were unsteady with the long hours of tramping. He wanted to go straight to Cornelia and tell her what had happened. The very thought of the coming scene stirred him deeply. Or perhaps he was merely hungry.

Frau Hohlfeld, the landlady, frustrated his intention. She was standing in the corridor, and whispered with unnecessary secrecy – but such was her habit – that Labude was there. Labude was sitting in Fabian's room. He evidently had a bad head. He had come to apologize because he had left the club on the previous night without taking leave of his friend. Actually his reason for coming was quite a different one. He wanted to know what Fabian thought of his affair with Selow.

Labude was a moral man, and it had always been his ambition to write a clean record of his career without notes and without errors. As a child he had never scribbled on blotting-paper. His sense of morality resulted from his love of order. The disillusionment he had suffered in Hamburg had upset the organization of his private life and thus disturbed his morals. His spiritual timetable was imperilled. His character had lost its handrail. Now he, who was useless and unhappy without an aim in life, came to Fabian, the expert in aimlessness. He hoped to learn from him how to experience unrest without becoming restless.

'You are looking bad,' said Fabian.

'I never closed my eyes all night,' confessed his friend. 'This Selow woman is both melancholy and vulgar in the same breath. She can sit on a sofa for hours, mumbling indecencies as though she were repeating a litany. It's more than I can listen to. She drinks alcohol in such quantities that it makes you tight to look at her. Then she remembers she's alone in the flat with a man, and makes me wish I'd taken out an insurance policy. And yet I'm sure her feelings are not those of a normal woman. At the same time, I don't think she's a lesbian. Curious though it sounds, I think she's a homosexual.'

Fabian let his friend go on talking. Nothing seemed to surprise him and therefore Labude grew calm. 'Tomorrow I'm going to Frankfurt for two days,' he told him, before he left.

'Rassow is coming too. We want to form an active group there. Meanwhile the girl can stay in my number-two flat. She's had a hell of a time in the last few months. She can have a good sleep. Good-bye, Jacob.' Then he went.

Fabian entered Cornelia's room. What would she say when she learned he had lost his job? But Ruth Reiter, the sculptress, was sitting there. She looked wretched, was not at all surprised to see him, and gave him a summary of what she had already told Fräulein Battenberg: Little Kulp had been taken to the infirmary. She had suffered internal injuries, and Wilhelmy, the wooden-legged candidate for death, had been lying since the previous night in her studio, gasping for breath and absorbed in the prospect of dying.

Cornelia had unpacked a few cups, plates, knives and forks from her trunk; she had bought something to eat and had laid the table invitingly. There was even a white cloth and a bunch of flowers. Ruth Reiter said she could not stay. But, before she forgot it – did anyone know where young Labude lived? It was obvious that she had come expressly to ask this question. She had hoped that her old school-friend would give her Fabian's address, and that Fabian would give her Labude's, for the servants at the villa in Grunewald had been unable to give her the information she wanted.

'I know where he lives,' said Fabian. 'But he was in my room down the corridor until a few minutes ago. He wouldn't allow me to give you his address.'

'He was here?' cried the sculptress. 'Good-bye!' She fled from the room.

'She misses Selow,' said Cornelia.

'She misses the rough treatment,' said Fabian.

'I don't.' She kissed him and drew him over to the table, where he was to admire her preparations for supper. 'Does that look nice?' she asked.

'Magnificent. Very fine. And, I say, do be nice and always ask me when you want me to admire something. I suppose you haven't a new frock on? Have I seen those ear-rings before? Was your hair parted like that yesterday – in the middle? If I like anything I never notice it. You have to rub my nose in it.'

'You're nothing but faults,' she cried. 'I should hate them all separately, but I love them all together.'

She told him at supper that she was to take up her new post on the following morning. She had been introduced that afternoon to a number of her new colleagues, theatrical experts, producers and directors, and she described the strange, rambling building, crammed to the attics with important people, who dashed from one conference to another and made life a misery for the evolution of the talking film. Fabian postponed his announcement till later.

When they had finished supper, she put on one side a plate containing two sandwiches, and said with a smile: 'Emergency rations.'

'You're blushing,' he said.

She nodded. 'So you do sometimes notice when there's something to admire!'

He proposed a short walk. She put on her things. Meanwhile he was wondering how he could tell her that he had lost his job. But the walk was never taken. As they reached the street, they heard someone cough behind them, and a strange man wished them 'Good evening.' It was the inventor with the cape. 'The description you gave me of your sofa,' he said, 'has taken all the fun out of stairs and lofts, at least for today. I made a detour round the Yorckstrasse and came here. I'm not at all happy about troubling you, for after all you're unemployed yourself.'

'You unemployed?' asked Cornelia. 'Is that true?'

The old gentleman made elaborate apologies; he had assumed the young lady was already informed.

'This morning I was dismissed.' Fabian let go Cornelia's arm. 'When I left, they handed me two hundred and seventy marks. After paying my month's rent in advance, we shall have a hundred and ninety marks left. Yesterday, I should have laughed.'

When they had packed the old gentleman on the sofa and placed the standard lamp at his side, for he wished to go on calculating at his mysterious machine, they bade him 'Good night' and went to Cornelia's room. Fabian returned to bring his guest a few sandwiches.

'I promise you I won't cough,' said the old man, in a whisper.

'Coughing is not prohibited. Your next-door neighbour pursues quite other forms of amusement without disturbing the repose of our landlady, a certain Frau Hohlfeld, who has not always had to let. What worries me is how we're going to arrange things in the morning. The landlady thinks her furniture most attractive, and she would be seriously annoyed if a stranger camped out all night on the sofa. Sleep well. I'll wake you in the morning. I shall think of something in the meanwhile.'

'Good night, my young friend,' remarked the old man, and produced his valuable papers from his pocket. 'Give my kind regards to your fiancée.'

Fabian could not understand why Cornelia seemed so happy. An hour later she was eating her emergency ration. 'Isn't life wonderful?' she said. 'What do you think about fidelity?'

'Empty your mouth before you use such long words!' He sat beside her, his arms round his knees, and looked down at the girl's outstretched figure. 'I think I'm only waiting to be given a chance and I should be faithful, and yet I thought till yesterday that I was too demoralized.'

'But that's a proposal,' she said softly.

'If you cry now I'll tan the seat of your pants!' he threatened.

She rolled out of bed, slipped on her little pink knickers and came and stood in front of him. She smiled through her tears. 'I'm crying,' she murmured. 'Now it's for you to keep your promise.' Then she bent down. He drew her on to the bed. 'My dear, my dear!' she said. 'Don't worry.'

XII

AN INVENTOR IN THE WARDROBE
NOT TO WORK IS A DISGRACE
HIS MOTHER MAKES A GUEST APPEARANCE

The inventor was up next morning when Fabian went to wake him. Washed and dressed, he was sitting at the table doing calculations.

'Did you have a good night?'

The old man was in excellent spirits, and shook hands with him. 'That sofa was born to be slept on,' he said, and stroked its brown back as though it were that of a horse. 'Must I go now?'

'Let me make you a proposal,' said Fabian. 'While I'm in my bath the landlady brings in the breakfast, and she mustn't meet you here or there'll be a row. As soon as she's gone you'll be my welcome guest again. Then you can stay here quietly for an hour or two. I shall have to leave you however, because I must look for work.'

'That's all right,' said the old man. 'If you don't mind, I'll take a look at your books. But where am I to go while you bathe?'

'I thought, in the wardrobe,' said Fabian. 'Wardrobes as a habitation have hitherto been the monopoly of comedies of adultery. Let us break with tradition, my honoured guest! Do you agree to my proposal?'

The inventor opened the wardrobe, looked in sceptically, and asked: 'Are you generally long in the bath?'

Fabian reassured him, pushed his winter overcoat and his only spare suit to one side, and invited his guest to enter. The old gentleman drew his cape round him, put on his hat, stuck the umbrella under his arm and crawled into the wardrobe, which creaked at every joint. 'And what if she finds me here?'

'Then I shall move out on the first.'

The inventor leaned on his umbrella and nodded. 'Now off to your tub,' he said.

Fabian locked the wardrobe, removed the key as a precaution, and called into the corridor: 'Frau Hohlfeld, breakfast!' When he reached the bathroom, Cornelia was seated in the bath covered with soap-suds. She laughed. 'You must rub my back for me,' she said. 'I've got such awfully short arms.'

'Cleanliness becomes a pleasure,' remarked Fabian, and soaped her back. Later she did the same for him. Finally they sat opposite each other in the water and played at making waves. 'It's awful,' he said,'the prince of inventors has been standing all this time in my wardrobe waiting to be released. I must hurry.' They climbed out of the bath and towelled each other till their skin was burning. Then they separated.

'I shall see you this evening,' she whispered.

He kissed her. He took leave of her eyes, her mouth and her neck, of every part of her body separately. Then he ran back to his room. Breakfast had arrived. He unlocked the wardrobe. The old gentleman climbed stiffly out, and coughed protractedly to make up for his previous abstinence.

'Now for the second part of the comedy,' said Fabian. He went out into the corridor, opened the outer door, slammed it to again, and cried: 'Uncle! How splendid of you to come and see me. Come in!' He ushered this imaginary person into the room, and nodded to the astonished inventor. 'There, now you've arrived officially. Sit down. Here's another cup.'

'So now I'm your uncle, am I?'

'Family connections always have a soothing effect on landladies,' Fabian explained.

'Well, the coffee is good. May I take a roll?' The old man began to forget the wardrobe. 'If I had not been certified, I would make you my sole heir, my dear nephew,' he said, and ate with great solemnity.

'I'm honoured by your hypothetical proposal,' returned Fabian. At the wish of his new uncle they clinked coffee-cups, and cried, 'Good health!'

'I love life,' confessed the old man, and became almost shy. 'I love life, and I love it all the more now I'm poor again. Sometimes I feel so happy I could eat the sunshine, or the breezes that stir in the parks. Do you know how that comes about? I often think of death, and who does that nowadays? No one thinks of death. We all allow it to take us by surprise, like a railway accident or some other unforeseen disaster. People have grown so blind. I think of it daily, for any day it may beckon to me. And because I think of it, I love life. That's a splendid invention, and I know all about inventions.'

'And what of your fellow men?'

'The world has scabies,' growled the old man.

'Love life and yet despise your fellow men – that seldom turns out well,' said Fabian, and stood up. He left his guest still drinking coffee, asked Frau Hohlfeld not to disturb his uncle, and went to the local employment exchange.

When he had passed through the hands of three officials, that is, after the lapse of two hours, he learned that he had come to the wrong place and must apply at a branch in the West End, which catered especially for office-workers. He took a bus to Wittenbergplatz and went to the place named. The information had been false. He found himself surrounded by a troop of unemployed nurses, kindergarten-teachers and stenographers, and, as the sole male applicant, aroused a great deal of attention.

He withdrew, went back into the street and found a shop, a few houses further down, that looked as though it were a branch of the Co-operative Society, but was in fact the particular employment exchange to which he had to apply. Behind what had been the counter an official was seated, and a long queue of unemployed clerks was standing in front of it. One by one they produced their cards and had them stamped.

Fabian was surprised to see how well these unemployed were dressed. Some of them could even be called smart, and if he had met them in the Kurfürstendamm he would undoubtedly have taken them for men of voluntary leisure. Presumably they combined their morning visit to the labour-exchange with a saunter through the fashionable shopping centres. It still cost nothing to look into shop-windows, and who could say whether one was unable, or merely unwilling, to buy. They wore their Sunday suits, and quite right too, for no one had more Sundays than they.

They bore themselves well as they stood in a long file, gravely waiting to pocket their cards. They went out as though they were leaving a dental clinic. Sometimes the official grumbled, and put a card on one side. Then an assistant took it into the next room, where an inspector sat enthroned, calling irregular applicants to account. From time to time a kind of porter appeared at this door and called out someone's name.

Fabian read the printed notices that hung on the walls. It was forbidden to wear arm-bands. It was forbidden to take return tram tickets from their original owners and make further use of them. It was forbidden to start political discussions or to take part in them. It was announced that a most nourishing meal could be obtained at a certain place for thirty pfennigs. It was announced that persons with such and such an initial had henceforth to come on such and such a day. It was announced that the places and times had been changed for those belonging to certain trades. It was announced. It was forbidden. It was forbidden. It was announced.

Gradually the room emptied. Fabian placed his papers in front of the official. The man said that he was not authorized to deal with advertising copywriters and recommended Fabian to apply at the exchange which catered for scientists and artists. He gave him the address.

Fabian took a bus to Alexanderplatz. It was nearly midday. At this new address he found himself in very mixed company. To judge by the notices displayed, they might be doctors, lawyers, engineers, agricultural experts or music teachers.

'I'm on the parish now,' said a little man. 'I get twenty-four-marks-fifty a week. That is, with my family, two-marks-seventy-two per head per week, or thirty-eight pfennigs per head per day. I've calculated it exactly in my abundant leisure. If things go on like this, I shall soon go in for burglary.'

'That's not so easy,' sighed his neighbour, a short-sighted youth. 'You've got to learn even to steal. I've done twelve months. Well, there are nicer places.'

'It's all the same to me, at any rate beforehand,' declared the little man, excitedly. 'My wife can't even give the youngsters a bit of bread to take to school. I can't put up with that any longer.'

'There's no sense in stealing,' said a tall, broad-shouldered man, who was leaning against the window. 'As soon as a middle-class man has nothing to eat, he wants to go straight over to the lumpen proletariat. Why don't you become class-conscious, you ugly little scrub? Haven't you found out yet where you belong? Help to prepare the way for a political revolution.'

'My children will all starve to death before that comes.'

'If you get locked up for stealing, these marvellous children of yours will starve still quicker,' said the man by the window.

91

The short-sighted youth laughed, and moved his shoulders apologetically.

'My shoes are all worn to bits,' said the little man. 'They're finished in a week with walking here every day, and I can't afford to take a bus.'

'Can't you get shoes from the parish?' asked the short-sighted one.

'I've got such sensitive feet,' said the little man.

'Go and hang yourself!' suggested the man by the window.

'He's got such a sensitive neck,' said Fabian.

The young man had placed a few coins on the table and was counting his wealth. 'Half my money goes every week in letters of application. There's stamps. Then there's stamps for reply. Every week I have to make twenty copies of my testimonials and get them authenticated. Nobody ever sends them back. You don't even get an answer. I suppose the chaps in the offices use my stamps to start collections.'

'But the government does all it can,' said the man by the window. 'Among other things they've started free courses in drawing for the unemployed. That's a real act of benevolence, gentlemen. First you learn to draw apples and beefsteaks and then you satisfy your hunger with what you've drawn. Art-training in place of grub.'

The little man seemed to have lost all sense of humour. He said despondently: 'That's no good to me. I'm a draughts-man.'

An official passed through the waiting-room, and Fabian, now grown cautious, inquired whether he had any prospect of being registered there. The official asked if he had a form from his local employment exchange. 'Haven't you signed on yet? You must do that first.'

'Now I must go back to where I started from five hours ago,' said Fabian. But the official was no longer there.

'They treat you politely,' said the youth, 'but you can't say the information they give is always accurate.'

Fabian took a bus to the employment exchange of the district where he lived. He had already spent one mark in fares, and was too angry to look out of the window.

When he arrived the office was closed. 'Let me have a look at your papers,' said the porter. 'Perhaps I can help.' Fabian gave his papers to this friend in need. 'Aha,' declared the doorkeeper, after studying them conscientiously, 'you're not unemployed at all.'

Fabian sat down on one of the bronze milestones that decorated the entrance.

'You've been given leave, so to speak, on full salary till the end of the month. They've paid you the money, haven't they?'

Fabian nodded.

'Then come back here in a fortnight's time,' suggested the other. 'Meanwhile you can try your hand at a few letters of application. Read the announcements of situations vacant in the newspapers. There's not much point in it, but it's not for me to say so.'

'Pleasant journey,' said Fabian. He took his papers and went into the Tiergarten, where he intended to eat a few sandwiches. As it turned out, he crumbled them up and threw them to the swans, which were taking their young ones for a swim in the new lake.

When, towards evening, he returned to his room, he found his mother waiting for him. She was sitting on the sofa. She put down the book she was reading, and said: 'Aren't you surprised, Jacob?'

They embraced. 'I had to come and see what you were doing,' she went on. 'Father's keeping watch to see that no one comes into the shop. I've been worried about you. You've given up answering my letters. You haven't written for ten days. I couldn't be easy in my mind, Jacob.

He sat down at his mother' side, stroked her hands and told her all was well with him.

She looked at him doubtfully. 'Am I in the way?' He shook his head. She got up from the sofa. 'I've put your clean things in the wardrobe. Doesn't your landlady ever do any dusting? I suppose she's still too much of a lady? What do you think I've brought you?' She opened her basket and placed various packages on the table. 'Black sausage,' she said. 'One pound. You know, from the Breitestrasse. Cold cutlet. I'm sorry I can't get into the kitchen, or I would warm it up. Gammon of bacon. Half a salami sausage. Aunt Martha sends her love. I went down to the garden to see her yesterday. A few tablets of soap from the shop. I wish business wasn't so bad. I believe people have given up washing themselves. And here's a tie. Do you like it?'

'You're such a dear,' said Fabian, 'but you mustn't spend so much money on me.'

'Don't talk so silly,' said his mother, putting the provisions on a plate. 'She's making us a drop of tea, your fine landlady. I asked her to. I must go back tomorrow night. I came by an express. It didn't take long. There was a little boy in our carriage. We did laugh. How's your heart? You're smoking too much! There's empty cigarette packets all over the place.'

Fabian watched her. She was so overcome that she harangued him like a policeman.

'I couldn't help thinking yesterday,' he said, 'of the time when I was at boarding-school and you were ill. I used to run home in the evenings, across the parade ground, to see how you were getting on. I remember once you had to push a chair in front of you and hold on to the back, or you couldn't even have opened the door to me.'

'You've had a lot of trouble with your mother,' she said. 'We ought to see more of each other. How are things in business?'

'I've drafted a scheme for a prize-competition. They'll make a quarter of a million marks on it.'

'And they pay you two hundred and seventy marks a month, the wretches!' His mother was indignant. There was a knock at the door. Frau Hohlfeld entered with the tea and placed the tray on the table. 'Your uncle's come back again,' she said.

'Your uncle?' asked his mother, in astonishment.

'I must say, it made me wonder,' declared the landlady.

'I hope you've not done yourself any harm in the process, madam,' said Fabian, and Frau Hohlfeld withdrew, insulted. Fabian fetched the inventor into the room. 'Mother,' he said, 'this is an old friend of mine. He spent last night on the sofa and, to cut short all formalities, I have appointed him my uncle.' He turned to the inventor. 'This is my mother, dear uncle. The best woman of the twentieth century. Sit down. I'm afraid I can't accommodate you on the sofa tonight. But I should like to invite you again for tomorrow, if that's convenient to you.'

The old gentleman sat down, coughed, hung his top-hat on the handle of his umbrella, and pressed an envelope into Fabian's hand. 'Put that in your pocket, as quick as you can,' he said. 'That is my machine. They're after me. My family are trying to put me back in the asylum. They are probably hoping to get these specifications from me and turn them into gold.'

Fabian put the envelope in his pocket. 'They're trying to shut you up in an asylum?'

'I don't mind,' remarked the old man. 'You can have a quiet time there. The park's magnificent. The medical superintendent is not a bad fellow, a bit mad himself, and an excellent chess-player. I've been there twice before. If I get tired of it, I shall clear out again. I beg your pardon, madam,' he said to Fabian's mother, 'I'm afraid I'm making a nuisance of myself. Don't be alarmed when they come to fetch me. You'll hear the bell in a moment. I'm quite ready. My papers are in good hands. And, by the way, I'm not mad; on the contrary, I'm too rational for my esteemed family. My dear friend, if you should change your address, write me a few lines to the Sanatorium at Bergendorf.'

The door-bell rang.

'There they are,' said the old man.

Frau Hohlfeld ushered two men into the room.

'I must apologize for disturbing you,' said the one, bowing. 'I have papers here – you are welcome to read them – which give me authority to remove Professor Kollrepp from your company. My car is waiting outside.'

'Why all this ceremony, my dear doctor? You've got thinner. I noticed you were on my track yesterday. Evening, Winkler. Well, we had better go down to the car. How's my dear family?'

The doctor shrugged his shoulders.

The old man walked over to the wardrobe, opened it, looked in and closed the door again. Then he went up to Fabian and took his hand. 'Thank you very much.' He went to the door. 'You have a good son,' he said to Fabian's mother. 'And that's more than most people can say.' The doctor and the warder followed him. Fabian and his mother looked through the window. A car was standing outside the house. The three men came out. The chauffeur helped the old inventor into a dustcoat. The cape was stowed away in the car.

'A queer man,' said Fabian's mother, 'but I'm sure he wasn't mad.' The car drove off. 'Why did he look into your wardrobe?'

'I shut him up there this morning, so that my landlady shouldn't know he was here,' said the son.

His mother poured out tea. 'But all the same it's rash of you to have complete strangers sleeping here. Something might happen so easily. I hope he hasn't made the things in your wardrobe dirty.'

Fabian wrote the address of the asylum on the envelope and locked it away. Then he sat down to the table.

After supper he said: 'Come on. Get ready. We're going to the pictures.' While the old lady was putting on her things he went in to see Cornelia, and told her of his mother's arrival. She was tired and already in bed. 'I shall sleep till you come back from the cinema,' she said. 'Shall you look in and see me?' He promised to do so.

The talkie Fabian and his mother saw was an inane stage-play, confined within two dimensions. This was the only sign of economy; the prodigality displayed in other directions exceeded all bounds. You had the feeling that the chamber pots under the beds were made of gold, although of course decency prevented such objects from being shown. His mother laughed a good deal, and that pleased Fabian so much that he laughed with her.

They walked home. His mother was in a good humour. 'If I'd been as well in the old days as I am now, my son, you'd have had a better time of it,' she said, after a while.

'It wasn't bad as it was,' he said. 'And anyhow it's over now.'

At home they quarrelled a little as to who should sleep in the bed and who on the sofa. Finally Fabian won. His mother made up the sofa for the night. He had to look in next door, he said. 'A young woman lives there, and she's a friend of mine.' He bade his mother good-night, in case she should be asleep when he returned, gave her a kiss and softly opened the door.

A minute later he came back. 'She's asleep,' he whispered, and mounted his sofa.

'That would have been impossible in my young days,' remarked Frau Fabian.

'Just what her mother said, too,' said her son, and turned his face to the wall. On the point of falling asleep, he suddenly got up, groped his way across the dark room, leaned over the bed and said what he had used to say years ago: 'Sleep well, mum.'

'And you,' she murmured, and opened her eyes. He could not see her. He groped his way through the darkness back to his sofa.

XIII

Next morning his mother called him. 'Get up, Jacob! You'll be late at the office.' He got up as quickly as he could, stood at the table to drink his coffee, and took leave of her.

'I'll tidy things up a bit meanwhile,' she said. 'Just look at the dust everywhere. And the loop's come off the back of your overcoat. You can go without a coat today. It's quite warm outside.'

Fabian leaned against the door-post, and watched his mother as she set to work. This industry of hers was composed of two factors – nervousness and love of order – and it reminded him of home. It filled the room; it suddenly recalled his childhood.

'Now just sit down for five minutes, and rest your hands in your lap,' he told her. 'Wouldn't it be nicer, if I hadn't to go out. We could go in the Tiergarten. Or to the Aquarium. Or we could stay here, and you could tell me what a funny boy I was when I was little. Do you remember when I scratched the bedstead all over with a pin, and then took your hand and led you in to show you the wonderful drawing I had made? Or when I gave you black and white cotton and a dozen needles and press-buttons for your birthday?'

'And a packet of pins and white and black machine-silk. It might have been yesterday,' she said, and smoothed the creases out of his coat. 'That suit wants pressing.'

'And I want a wife and seven jolly little kids,' he supplemented, with wise forethought.

'You run off to the office!' She put her hands on her hips. 'It does you good to work. I shall call for you at the office this afternoon. I'll wait outside. Then you can take me to the station.'

'It's a pity you can't stay longer than one day.' Again he came back.

His mother did not look at him. She found something to do on the sofa. 'I couldn't stand it there any longer,' she murmured. 'But now it will be all right again. What you need is more sleep. And you mustn't take life so seriously, my boy. It doesn't make things any easier.'

'Well, I must go now,' he said, 'or I shall be late.'

She looked after him from the window, and nodded. He waved and laughed and hurried on till he was out of sight. Then his pace slackened, and presently he stopped. A fine game of hide-and-seek he was playing with the old lady! Hurrying off when he had nowhere to go. Leaving her alone, up there in that horrible, unfamiliar room, when he knew that she would gladly give a whole year of her life for one extra hour of his company. She was to call for him at the office that afternoon. He would have to stage another little comedy for her benefit. She must not know that he had lost his job. The suit he was wearing was the only one he had bought for himself in thirty-two years. All her life she had scratched and toiled for him. Was that to go on for ever?

It came on to rain, so he took a stroll through the Kaufhaus des Westens. Big stores are extremely well adapted, though such is not their intention, to provide entertainment for such as have neither money nor umbrellas. He listened to a saleswoman playing skilfully on the piano. The smell of fish, which he had never been able to stand from early childhood, perhaps because of some pre-natal memory, drove him out of the provisions. A young man in furniture was determined to sell him a large wardrobe. It was a bargain, an opportunity never to be repeated. Fabian escaped from this monstrous suggestion, and fled to the bookstall. On one of the tables of second-hand books, he came across a volume of extracts from Schopenhauer. He turned the pages and gradually became immersed. The proposal of this crotchety uncle of humanity to ennoble Europe by a method of salvation derived from India was in truth a hare-brained scheme, but in that it resembled all the positive proposals that had hitherto been made, whether by philosophers of the nineteenth century or by economists of the twentieth. But apart from that, the old boy was without a rival. Fabian came to a typological disquisition and read:

'This is the distinction which Plato draws between

εὔκολος and δύσκολος – the man of *easy*, and the man of *difficult* disposition – in proof of which he refers to the varying degrees of susceptibility which different people show to pleasurable and painful impressions; so that one man will laugh at what makes another despair. As a rule, the stronger the susceptibility to unpleasant impressions, the weaker is the susceptibility to pleasant ones, and vice versa. If it is equally possible for an event to turn out well or ill, the δύσκολος will be annoyed or grieved if the issue is unfavourable, and will not rejoice, should it be happy. On the other hand, the εὔκολος will neither worry nor fret over an unfavourable issue, but rejoice if it turns out well. If the one is successful in nine out of ten undertakings, he will not be pleased, but rather annoyed that one has miscarried; whilst the other, if only a single one succeeds, will manage to find consolation in the fact and remain cheerful. But here is another instance of the truth, that hardly any evil is entirely without its compensation; for the misfortunes and sufferings which the δύσκολοι that is, people of gloomy and anxious character, have to overcome, are, on the whole, more imaginary and therefore less real than those which befall the gay and careless; for a man who paints everything black, who constantly fears the worst and takes measures accordingly, will not be disappointed so often in this world, as one who always looks upon the bright side of things.'

'What can I get for you?' asked an elderly saleswoman.
'Have you any cotton socks?' asked Fabian.
The elderly saleswoman looked at him sourly. 'On the ground floor,' she said. Fabian put the book back on the table and descended to the floor below. Was Schopenhauer right when he, he of all people, placed those two types of men on an equal footing? Was it not he who had stated in his Psychology that the feeling of happiness was nothing more than a minimum of mental unhappiness? Had he not in this sentence generalized his view of δύσκολοι against his better knowledge? . . .
There was a commotion in the department for porcelain and pottery. Fabian went to see what was amiss. A crowd of assistants, customers and loungers, were gathered round a little girl of about ten. She was crying; she was poorly dressed, and carried a school-bag. Trembling from head to foot, the child

looked round in terror at the circle of angry, agitated, adult faces.

The manager of the department came up. 'What's all this?'

'This impudent little creature was stealing an ash-tray. I caught her at it,' declared an elderly spinster. 'Look!' She held up the small bright-coloured object for the inspection of her superior.

'Off to the manager!' ordered the man in the tail coat.

'I don't know what children are coming to!' said an over-dressed woman.

'Off to the manager!' cried one of the saleswomen, and grasped the little girl by the shoulder. The child cried bitterly.

Fabian pushed his way through the circle. 'Let go of that child at once!'

'Excuse me,' said the manager of the department.

'What business is it of yours?' asked someone else.

Fabian rapped the saleswoman across the knuckles, making her loose her hold, and drew the little girl to his side. 'What made you take it?' he asked. 'And an ash-tray of all things? Have you started smoking cigars?'

'I hadn't any money,' said the child. Then she rose on tiptoe. 'It's my daddy's birthday today.'

'No money, so she simply steals. This is getting worse and worse,' said the overdressed woman.

'Give us the bill,' said Fabian to the saleswoman. 'We'll keep the ash-tray.'

'She ought to be punished,' maintained the departmental manager. Fabian went up to the man. 'I'll pay. If that's not good enough for you, I'll smash up your whole damned china-shop!'

The man in the tail coat shrugged his shoulders, the sales-woman made out the bill and took the ash-tray to the packing-counter. Fabian went to the cash-desk, put down the money and was given the parcel. Then he accompanied the child to the door. 'Here's your ash-tray,' he said. 'But take care it doesn't get broken. Once there was a little boy who bought a big casserole to give to his mother on Christmas Eve. When the moment arrived he took his casserole in his hands and sailed towards the half-open door. He could see the Christmas tree inside, all brightly lighted. Here mother, he said, and he was just going to say: here's the casserole. But there was a crash. The casserole had struck the door and was smashed to pieces. Here mother, he said, here's the handle. For the handle was all that was left of it.'

The little girl looked up at him, grasped the parcel firmly in both hands, and said: 'My ash-tray hasn't got a handle.' She curtsied and ran off. Presently, she turned round again, cried 'Thank you!' and disappeared.

Fabian went out into the street. It had stopped raining. He took up his position on the kerb and inspected the motor-cars. A car stopped. An old lady, smothered in parcels, hove herself ponderously from the seat and tried to get out. Fabian opened the door, helped her down from the step, raised his hat politely and stepped to one side.

'Here!' said a voice. It was the old lady. She pressed something into his hand, nodded and went into the store. Fabian opened his hand. It contained a ten-pfennig piece. He had unwittingly earned ten pfennigs. Did he look like a beggar already?

He pocketed the coin, stepped boldly back to the kerb, and opened the door of a second car.

'Here!' said the occupant, and gave him another ten pfennigs. This is developing into a profession, thought Fabian. Before fifteen minutes had passed, he had earned sixty-five pfennigs. Supposing Labude were to come by, he reflected, and see the authority on literary history opening car-doors. But he was not daunted by the thought. The only persons he would not have liked to meet were his mother and Cornelia.

'A little gift acceptable?' asked a woman, and handed him a silver coin. It was Frau Irene Moll. 'I've been watching you for some time, my son,' she said, and smiled maliciously. 'Another of our chance meetings. I didn't know you were having such a rotten time. You were in too much of a hurry when you declined my husband's offer, and you might at least have kept the keys. I was waiting to welcome you to my couch. This reluctance of yours makes me all the keener. Here, help me carry these parcels. You've had the tip.'

Fabian allowed himself to be loaded with packages, and followed her in silence.

'Now, what can I do for you?' she inquired, pensively. 'You've had the sack, eh? I'm not the one to bear a grudge. Unfortunately we can't reckon on Moll any longer. He's taken ship to France or somewhere. And now the Criminal Investigation Department is lodging with us. Moll misappropriated his clients' money for his own purposes. He's been doing it for years. I would never have believed it of him. We underestimated him.'

'How do you live now, then?' asked Fabian.

'I've opened a pension. You can get big flats very cheap now. The furniture was given me by an old friend, that is to say the friend is old though the friendship is young. All that belongs to him is a few peep-holes in the doors.'

'And who lives in this remarkable pension?'

'Young men. Board and lodging free. And thirty per cent of the proceeds into the bargain.'

'What proceeds?'

'My young men's unchristian association is frequented with real enthusiasm by ladies of the highest society. They are neither slim nor lovely, and you would scarcely believe that they had ever been young. But they are rich. And, however much I demand, they pay up. They wouldn't miss coming, even if they had first to rob or murder their husbands. My boarders make money, the furniture-dealer looks on, and the ladies satisfy their passions. Three of my young men have already been bought out. They have a good income, flats of their own, and, on the quiet, of course, a *petite amie*. One of them, a Hungarian, was acquired by the wife of a wealthy industrialist. He lives like a prince. If he plays his cards rightly, he'll have made his fortune within twelve months. Then he can get rid of the old scarecrow.'

'I see, a male brothel,' said Fabian.

'In these days it has much more *raison d'être* than a women's house,' declared Irene Moll. 'Besides I've dreamt, since I was a young girl, of owning such an establishment. I'm quite satisfied. I've got money, I engage new boarders almost daily, and every applicant for a position has to come to me for a sort of entrance examination. I don't take anybody. Real talent is hard to come by. It's easier to find persons with natural gifts. I shall have to start continuation classes.'

She stopped. 'Here we are.' The pension was situated in a large and elegant block of flats. 'I should like to make you an offer. You haven't the qualifications for a boarder, my dear. You're too finicky, and besides you're too old for the job. My clients prefer boys of twenty. And then you suffer from false pride. But I could make room for you as my secretary. I find the books need keeping in order. You could work in my private rooms, and you could live there too. What do you think of it?'

'Here are the parcels,' said Fabian. 'I'm afraid if I listen to you any longer I shall be sick.'

At that moment two young men came out of the building. They were smartly dressed. On catching sight of Frau Moll, they hesitated and took off their hats.

'Gaston, is this your day off?' she asked.

'Mackie said I could come and see the car No. 7 has promised him. I shall be back in twenty minutes.'

'Gaston, go to your room immediately. Is this the way to behave? Mackie will go alone. Upstairs with you! No. 12 has made an appointment for three o'clock. You'd better sleep till then, do you hear?'

The young man went back into the house; his companion bowed again, and went his way.

Frau Moll turned to Fabian. 'So you want to refuse me again?' She took the parcels from him. 'I'll give you a week to consider it. You know the address. Think it over. If you're fond of starvation, of course, that's your affair. But you would be doing me a personal favour. Truly you would. The more you resist, the more the idea attracts me. There's no hurry. I have plenty of amusement on hand for the time being.' She went into the house.

'This borders on the inevitable,' murmured Fabian, as he turned away.

He lunched on sausage and potato-salad in a little beerhouse. As he ate, he read the newspapers provided by the proprietor and made notes of situations vacant. Then he bought paper and envelopes in a musty stationer's shop and composed four letters of application. After posting them he found it was time to meet his mother, and set off, tired out, for the cigarette-factory.

'Hello, you here again?' said the porter.

'I arranged to meet my mother here,' answered Fabian.

The porter winked. 'You can rely on me,' he said.

It was embarrassing to Fabian that the man seemed to see through his little comedy. He walked quickly into the block of offices, sat down in a window-niche, and looked every five minutes at his watch. Whenever he heard footsteps he shrank back against the window-frame. It was ten minutes off closing time. The staff were in a hurry. They did not notice him.

He was on the point of leaving his hiding-place, when once more he heard footsteps and voices approaching.

'At tomorrow's board meeting I shall report on the plans you prepared for the prize-competition, my dear Fischer,' said one of the voices. 'Your scheme is well worth considering. We shall know how to value your services.'

'That's very kind of you, director,' replied the other voice. 'But as a matter of fact I inherited the scheme from Dr Fabian.'

'What you've inherited is your property as much as any other, Herr Fischer.' The director's voice had grown unfriendly. 'Don't you like my proposal? Have you any objection to a rise in salary? Well then. Besides, the scheme needs a number of improvements. I'm just going to dictate a summary into the machine, using your material as a basis. Believe me, it's going to make a stir, this prize-competition of ours. You can go now. You're a lucky man.'

'Schiller says, "The master's work is never done",' remarked Fischer. Fabian stepped out from his niche. Fischer retreated a step in alarm. Director Breitkopf ran his finger round his collar. 'I'm less surprised than you,' said Fabian, and went towards the stairs.

'Here he is,' said the porter, who was chatting with Fabian's mother. She had put down her suitcase, and placed her travelling-bag, her hand-bag and her umbrella on top of it. She nodded to Fabian. 'Been hard at work?' she asked. The porter smiled good-humouredly, and sauntered into his office.

Fabian shook his mother by the hand. 'We've half an hour to spare,' he said, and picked up the luggage.

When they had taken possession of a corner-seat (in the middle of the train, for Frau Fabian thought it best to reduce the ill effects of any possible railway-accident well in advance) they walked up and down in front of the compartment.

'Not too far away.' She caught her son by the sleeve. 'You can easily have your case stolen. Just turn your back and it's gone before you can look round.' Finally Fabian became even more mistrustful than his mother, and peered steadfastly through the window at the luggage-rack.

'Now I can be off again,' she said. 'I've sewn the loop on to your coat, and your room looks fit to live in again. Frau Hohlfeld seemed to be offended, but it's no use worrying about that.'

Fabian ran to one of the refreshment-wagons and brought back a ham-sandwich, a packet of biscuits and two oranges. 'What a spendthrift!' she said. He laughed, climbed into the compartment, managed to slip a twenty-mark note unseen into her handbag, and returned to the platform.

'When do you think you're going to come back home again?' she asked. 'I'll give you all your favourite dinners, a different one every day, and we'll go down to Aunt Martha in the garden. There's not much doing in the shop.'

'I'll come as soon as I can,' he assured her.

Then she was looking out of the carriage window. 'Mind you take care of yourself, Jacob,' she said. 'And if things up here go wrong, just pack up your things and come home.'

He nodded. They looked at each other and smiled as people smile on railway stations; it is much the same as at the photographer's, except that there is no one present with a camera. 'Look after yourself,' he whispered. 'It was nice to have you.'

There were flowers on the table, and a letter. He opened it. A twenty-mark note dropped out, and a scrap of paper. 'A little present. Love. Mother,' was written on it. There was something else at the bottom of the sheet: 'Eat the cutlet first. The sausage will keep for some days in grease-proof paper.'

He put the twenty-mark note in his pocket. There was his mother in the train; very soon she would find the twenty-mark note he had slipped into her handbag. Mathematically considered, the result equalled nothing. For both were now as poor as they had been before. But good deeds are beyond book-keeping. The moral and the arithmetical equations work out differently.

The same evening Cornelia asked him for a hundred marks. She had met Makart in the corridor at the film-offices. He had come to see his rivals to negotiate some film distribution rights. He had spoken to her; had told her she was the very type he had been looking for for a long time. For the next film his company was making, of course. Would she come to see him at his office the following afternoon? The producer and the director would be there. Perhaps they might give her a trial.

'At lunch-time tomorrow I must get a new hat and jumper. I know you haven't much money left, Fabian. But I can't let this chance slip by. Just think, supposing I became a film actress. Can you imagine it?'

'Yes,' he said, and gave her his last hundred-mark note. 'I hope the money will bring you luck.'

'Me?' she asked.

'Us,' he amended, to please her.

XIV

That night Fabian had a dream. He probably dreamed more often than he thought he did. But this time Cornelia woke him up, so he remembered his dream. A few days ago there had been no one to wake him from his dreams. No one, until he slept beside Cornelia, to shake him anxiously in the dead of night. Truly, in his time, he had slept with many women and girls, but this was different.

In his dream, he was hurrying down an endless street. The tops of the houses were out of sight. The street was quite empty, and the houses had neither windows nor doors. And the sky was remote and strange, like the sky above a deep well. Fabian was hungry, thirsty and dead tired. He knew the street was endless, but he went on walking; he wanted to get to the end of it.

'It's no good,' said a voice. He looked round. The old inventor was standing behind him, with his faded cape, his badly rolled umbrella, his greyish top-hat.

'How do you do, dear Professor?' cried Fabian. 'I thought you were in the asylum.'

'This is the asylum,' said the old man, and struck the wall with the crook of his umbrella. It gave out a tinny sound, and a door opened where no door had been.

'My latest invention,' said the old man. 'Permit me to lead the way, dear nephew. I'm quite at home here.' Director Breitkopf was squatting in the porter's office, with his hands on his belly. 'I'm going to have a child,' he groaned. 'My secretary's been careless again.' Then he struck three times on his bald pate, which gave forth a sound like a gong.

The professor stuck his badly-rolled umbrella deep into the director's throat and proceeded to open it. Breitkopf's face expanded like an air-balloon, and burst.

'I'm very much obliged,' said Fabian.

'Don't mention it,' returned the inventor. 'Have you seen my machine?' He took Fabian by the hand and led him down a corridor, illumined by a bluish neon-light, and so into the open air.

In front of them towered a machine as vast as Cologne Cathedral. Before it were standing workmen, stripped to the waist. They were armed with shovels, and were shovelling hundreds of thousands of babies into a huge furnace where a red fire was burning.

'Come to the other end,' said the inventor. They travelled across the grey courtyard on moving bands. 'Look,' he said, and pointed into the air.

Fabian looked up. Huge, red-hot Bessemer converters were sinking downwards, turning over automatically and emptying their contents on to a horizontal mirror. The contents were alive. Men and women were spilled on to the glittering glass; they rose to their feet and stared spell-bound at their tangible and yet unreachable reflections. Some bent down and waved their hands to their other selves as though in greeting. One drew a pistol from his pocket and fired. He had taken careful aim at the heart of his own image, but he shot himself in the big toe and his face was contorted with pain. Another turned completely round. Evidently he was trying to turn his back on his reflection. The attempt failed.

'A hundred thousand a day,' explained the inventor. 'And yet I've cut down the hours and introduced a five-day week.'

'All mad?' asked Fabian.

'That is a matter of terminology,' answered the professor. 'One moment – the coupling is not working properly.' He went up to the machine, thrust his umbrella through a hole, and prodded the works. Suddenly the umbrella disappeared; it was followed by the cape, which dragged the old man after it. He was gone. His machine had swallowed him up.

Fabian travelled back across the grey courtyard on the moving band. 'There's been an accident!' he shouted to the half-naked workmen. Then a baby rolled out of the furnace. It wore horn-rimmed spectacles and held a badly rolled umbrella in its little hand. A workman picked up the baby on his shovel and flung it back into the glowing furnace. Fabian travelled back across the yard, and stood beneath the swaying Bessemer converters, waiting for his old friend, again transformed, to come back to him.

He waited in vain. Instead of the inventor, it was himself, a second Fabian, but with the cape, umbrella, and top-hat, that dropped from one of the huge converters, and ranged himself with the other men and women, staring, like them, at his reflection in the mirror. This reflection, the third Fabian, hung head downwards from the soles of his feet, and stared up from the mirror at the face of the second Fabian. The latter jerked his thumb over his shoulder towards the machine, and said: 'Mechanical soul-migration. Kollrepp patent.' Then he went over to the real Fabian, who was still standing in the yard, walked straight into him and was no longer visible.

'Fits like a glove,' Fabian admitted. He took the umbrella from the machine-man, the invisible occupant of his body, pulled his cape straight, and was once more the sole examplar of himself.

He looked across at the shining mirror. Suddenly the people standing on it sank as though into a transparent bog. They opened their mouths, apparently screaming with fright, but no sound came from them. They sank beneath the surface of the mirror. Their reflections fled like fish in a pool, head-foremost, grew smaller and smaller, and vanished completely. Now it was the people themselves who were standing beneath the mirror, and they looked as though they were imprisoned in amber. Fabian went up close. What he saw was no longer a reflection: these submerged creatures were merely separated from him by a sheet of glass, beneath which they went on living. Fabian knelt and looked down.

Fat women with deep creases across their naked bodies were sitting at tables, drinking tea. They wore openwork stockings, and little straw hats on the backs of their heads. They glittered with bangles and ear-rings. One old woman had put a golden ring through her nose. At other tables fat men were sitting in top-hats, half-naked, hairy as apes, some in mauve underpants, and all with big cigars between their thick lips. The men and women were staring greedily at a curtain. The curtain was drawn aside, and youths with heavily made-up faces, wearing tight-fitting bathing-suits, strutted with the affectation of mannequins along a raised catwalk. They were followed by young girls, also in bathing-suits, who smiled coyly and laid themselves out to show every curve they possessed. Fabian recognized some of them: Fräulein Kulp, the sculptress, Selow; even Paula from Haupt's Dance Hall was among them.

The old women and men screwed their opera-glasses into their eyes, sprang up, fell over chairs and tables, rushed towards the catwalk; they struck at those who got in their way and neighed like mares and stallions. The fat, bejewelled women snatched at the youths, threw themselves screaming to the floor, knelt in imploring attitudes, spread out their fat legs, plucked their diamonds from arms and fingers and ears and held them entreatingly towards the whorishly smiling young men. The old men spread out their gorilla-arms and grabbed, generally at the girls, but sometimes at the youths, embracing whomever they caught, their faces purple with excitement. The floor was strewn with underpants, varicose veins, sock-suspenders, bright rags of bathing-suits, fat limbs with deep creases, distorted faces, grinning scarlet lips, slim brown arms, convulsively twitching feet. It was as though a living Persian carpet were spread on the earth.

'Your Cornelia is among them,' said Frau Irene Moll. She was sitting at his side, eating miniature young men out of a large carton. First she ripped off their clothes, and it looked as though she were tearing the paper wrappings from caramels. Fabian looked round for Cornelia. All the rest were writhing in a wild heap on the floor. She alone was on the catwalk. She was resisting a fat brute of a man, who tried with one hand to force open her mouth, and with the other to press into it the lighted end of his cigar.

'It's no good her struggling,' said Frau Moll, turning over the contents of her carton. 'That's Makart, the film magnate. Money's no object with him. His wife poisoned herself.' Cornelia tottered, and fell into the turmoil beside Makart.

'Why don't you jump in after her?' said Frau Moll. 'But you are afraid the sheet of glass might break. You are always afraid of breaking the glass between you and other people. You take the world for a shop-window.'

Cornelia had vanished from sight. But now Fabian saw Wilhelmy, the candidate for death. He was naked, and his left leg was artificial. He was standing on a four-poster bed, sailing like a surf-rider across the struggling mass. Kulp seized hold of the bed. He waved his crutch and beat her on the head and hands till she lost hold and sank back streaming with blood.

Wilhelmy tied a line to his crutch, attached a bank-note to one end of the line, and threw out his bait. The men and women below leapt up like fish, snapped at the note, fell back exhausted and leapt again. There! A woman had caught the note in her mouth. It was Selow. She screamed shrilly. The hook had pierced her tongue. Wilhelmy pulled in his line; with distorted face Selow was drawn nearer and nearer the bed. But the sculptress arose behind her, seized her with both arms and dragged her back. Her tongue stretched far out of her mouth. Wilhelmy and the sculptress both tried to pull the girl towards them. Her tongue grew longer and longer, like a red strip of rubber, and so taut that it threatened to tear. Wilhelmy gasped for breath, and laughed.

'Wonderful!' cried Irene Moll. 'Just like a tug-of-war. We live in an age of sport.' She crumpled up the empty carton. 'Now I'll eat you,' she said. She wrenched off his cape. Her fingers worked up and down like scissors, slitting Fabian's suit. He struck her on the head with the crook of his umbrella. She staggered and released him. 'But I love you,' she whispered, and began to weep. The tears squeezed out of the corners of her eyes like tiny soap-bubbles; they grew bigger and rose into the air, shining and iridescent.

Fabian got up and left her.

He found himself in a great room that had no walls. Innumerable steps rose from one end of the hall to the other. Every step was crowded with people. They were looking attentively upward, their hands in each other's pockets. All robbing their neighbours. Each was groping cautiously in the pockets of the man in front, and, as he did so, was being robbed in turn by the man behind him. All were quite quiet, but all were hard at work. They thieved industriously and allowed others to thieve from them. On the lowest step was the little girl of ten; she extracted a brightly painted ash-tray from the coat-pocket of the man in front of her. Suddenly Labude was standing on the topmost step. He raised his hands, looked down the whole flight, and cried: 'Friends! Fellow Citizens! Decency must triumph!'

'Of course!' yelled the others in chorus, and went on picking each other's pockets.

'Those who side with me put up their hands!' cried Labude.

They all put up one hand, but went on stealing with the other. The little girl on the lowest step was the only one who put up both hands.

'I thank you,' said Labude, and his voice shook with emotion. 'The age of human dignity is dawning. We must never forget this moment!'

'You're a fool!' cried Cornelia. She reached Labude's side, dragging a tall, handsome man behind her.

'My best friends are my worst enemies,' said Labude sadly. 'I don't care. Reason will triumph, whether I fail or not.'

Shots rang out. Fabian looked up. All round him were roofs and windows, and everywhere sinister figures with revolvers and machine-guns.

The people on the steps threw themselves down at full length, but they went on stealing from each other. There was a fresh crackle of shots. Some were hit, and died with their hands in other people's pockets. The stair was littered with corpses.

'They are no great loss,' said Fabian to his friend. 'Let us go!' But Labude still stood there in a hail of bullets. 'Nor am I, now,' he whispered. Looking up at the windows and roofs, he shook his fist at them.

From the gables and dormer-windows a storm of shots came down. Wounded men were hanging from the windows. Two athletic figures were struggling on one of the gable-ends. They strangled and bit each other till the one reeled and both came crashing down. He heard the impact of their hollow skulls. Aeroplanes were swooping under the roof of the hall and throwing lighted torches into the houses. The roofs took fire. Green smoke poured out of the windows.

'Why are they doing all this?' The little girl he had seen at the store took Fabian's hand.

'They want to build new houses,' he replied. Then he took the child on his arm, and went down the steps, climbing over dead bodies. Half-way down he encountered a little man. He was jotting down figures on a writing-block and his lips moved as he reckoned them up. 'What are you doing here?' asked Fabian.

'I sell the scraps,' was the answer. 'Thirty pfennigs per corpse. Five pfennigs extra if the character's not much worn. Are you authorized to do business?'

'Go to the devil,' cried Fabian.

'Later,' said the little man, and went on with his reckoning.

At the foot of the steps, Fabian put the little girl down. 'Now go home,' he said. The child ran off, skipping and singing.

He went up the steps again. 'I'm not making a penny,' muttered the little man, as he passed him. Fabian quickened his pace. Above him, the houses were falling in. Tongues of fire rose from the heaps of brickwork. Flaming beams sagged and dropped, as though into cotton-wool. He still heard occasional shots. Men in gas-masks were crawling through the debris. When two of them met, they raised their rifles, took aim and fired. Fabian looked round. Where was Labude? 'Labude!' he shouted. 'Labude!'

'Fabian!' cried a voice. 'Fabian!'

'Fabian!' cried Cornelia, and shook him. He awoke. 'Why were you calling Labude?' She stroked his forehead.

'I was dreaming,' he said. 'Labude is in Frankfurt.'

'Shall I switch on the light?' she asked.

'No. Go to sleep quickly, Cornelia. You must look pretty tomorrow. Good-night.'

'Good-night,' she said.

And then both lay awake for a long time. Each knew the other was awake, but neither spoke.

XV

A MODEL YOUNG MAN
ON THE MEANING OF RAILWAY STATIONS
CORNELIA WRITES A LETTER

Next morning, when Cornelia set out for her work, he sat by the open window. She had a portfolio under her arm and stepped out briskly. She had a job, she was earning money. He sat by the window and allowed the sun to tickle his skin. The sun shone warm, as though the world were in the best possible order. Nothing disturbed its equanimity.

Cornelia was already some distance off. He must not call her back. If he did so, if he leaned out of the window and called: Come back! I don't want you to work, I don't want you to go to Makart. What then? She would answer: What do you mean? Either give me money or stop hindering me. He was helpless. He put out his tongue at the sun.

'What are you doing here?' asked Frau Hohlfeld, who had entered unnoticed.

Fabian said coldly: 'I'm catching flies. They're large and crisp this year.'

'Aren't you going to work?'

'I've retired. From the first of next month I shall appear in the Treasury deficit as an unexpected item of additional expenditure.' He closed the window and went and sat on the sofa.

'Unemployed?' she asked.

He nodded, and took some money from his pocket. 'Here are the eighty marks I owe you for next month.' She took the money hastily. 'There was no hurry about it, Herr Fabian,' she said.

'Oh yes, there was.' He arranged his remaining notes and coins upon the table and counted them. 'If I put my capital in the bank,' he said, 'they would pay me interest of three marks a year. It's hardly worth it.'

The landlady grew talkative. 'It said in the paper yesterday that an engineer had put forward a scheme to lower the level of the Mediterranean by seven hundred feet. That would bring large tracts of land above the surface, like before the ice-period, and they could be colonized and millions of people settled there. And if they built a series of small dams a through railway service could be run from Berlin to Capetown.' Frau Hohlfeld was still deeply impressed by the proposals of the engineer and spoke with great enthusiasm.

Fabian banged the arm of the sofa till the dust rose in clouds. 'All right,' he cried. 'Who's for the Mediterranean? Let's lower its level! Are you coming, Frau Hohlfeld?'

'I should love to. I haven't been there since my honeymoon. Lovely country. Genoa, Nice, Marseilles, Paris – though Paris is not on the Mediterranean, of course.' She gave the conversation a twist: 'I expect Fräulein Battenberg was very sad about it, wasn't she?'

'What a pity she's gone! We could have asked her.'

'A fascinating girl, and so distinguished! She reminds me of the Queen of Romania when she was young.'

'You've guessed it.' Fabian rose and conducted his landlady to the door. 'They say she's her daughter. But please, don't tell anyone!'

That afternoon he was sitting in the offices of a great newspaper concern, waiting for Herr Zacharias to find time for him. Herr Zacharias was an acquaintance of his, who had once told him, after they had been discussing the true nature of advertisement: 'If I can ever do anything for you, just look in.' As Fabian thoughtlessly turned the pages of one of the periodicals that graced the waiting-room, he recalled their conversation. Zacharias had agreed enthusiastically with a statement of H.G. Wells, to the effect that the growth of the Christian church was due in some measure to skilful propaganda: he had also supported Wells's contention that the time has come when advertisement should not be used merely to increase the consumption of soap and chewing-gum, but should be widely applied in the service of ideals. Fabian had answered that the capacity of the human race for education was a doubtful quantity, and that the propagandist's gifts for popular education and the educationist's talent for propaganda were both very questionable. Rational thinking could be imparted only to a limited number of people and they were rational already. Zacharias and Fabian had disputed with some heat, till they found their discussion had become excessively academic. The two possible results – the triumph or defeat of such ideal propaganda – presupposed the spending of a great deal of money, and no one would provide money for ideals.

Messengers busily threaded their way through the labyrinth of corridors. Cardboard cylinders dropped with a clatter from metal tubes. The telephone rang without ceasing. Visitors came and went. Employees ran from one room to another. A director hastened down the steps with a staff of obsequious officials.

'Herr Zacharias will see you.'

A messenger conducted him to the door. Zacharias's handshake was full of temperament. It was this young man's most conspicuous quality that he did everything he had to do with extraordinary intensity. His enthusiasm never cooled. Whether he was arguing or brushing his teeth, whether he was spending money or laying plans before his superiors, he was always in top gear. Everyone who came near him was infected by this lack of a sense of humour. A talk about tying ties would suddenly become the most exciting topic of the day. And when his superiors discussed business with Zacharias, they realized the immense importance of their vocation, their own firm, and their particular job. Nothing could stop the man's progress. It is improbable that the work he did himself was of any importance. He served as a catalytic agent for the organisation and as a stimulant for the persons round him. He was becoming indispensable, and at twenty-eight had a salary of two thousand five hundred marks a month. Fabian told him what there was to tell.

'There's nothing vacant,' said Zacharias, 'and I should like so much to oblige you. Besides I am sure we should get on splendidly together. Now what shall we do?' He pressed his hands to his temples like a soothsayer on the point of receiving inspiration. 'What do you think of this? Supposing I gave you a job here as my personal assistant, and paid you out of my own pocket? I could do with a man like you. They expect me to make a dozen suggestions every day. I'm not an automatic machine. Can I help it if other people have fewer ideas than I? If it goes on like this I shall chafe my brain into blisters. I've just bought a nice little car, a Steyr, six cylinder, with a special body. We could drive every day into the country for an hour or two, and lay eggs. I like driving. It steadies the nerves. I could manage to scrape up three hundred marks. And as soon as there's a vacancy here, you could have it. What do you say?'

Before Fabian could reply, Zacharias went on again: 'No, that won't do. They would say I'm keeping a ghost writer. All the fellows here are out for my blood. They're all waiting outside my door with an axe ready to land me one on the nob. Now what can we do? Can't you think of anything?'

Fabian said: 'I could go and stand in Potsdamerplatz with a large placard in front of me. Something of this sort: Young Man Unemployed. Give him a chance. He can do anything. Or I could paint it on a huge balloon.'

'If you meant that seriously, it would be worth while!' cried Zacharias. 'But it's no good, because you don't believe in it. The only things you take seriously are the really serious things, and I doubt whether you take those seriously. It's a great pity. With your brains, I should have been a managing director before now.'

Zacharias used a very subtle technique in dealing with people who were superior to him: he frankly accepted their superiority, he even insisted on it.

'How does it help me that I've more brains than you?' asked Fabian, dejectedly.

Zacharias had not expected this rhetorical question. If he was frank himself, that was enough. Here was this fellow casually dropping in, asking for advice, and then throwing his weight about!

'It's a pity you took that in bad part,' said Fabian. 'I didn't mean to offend you. I'm not vain about my abilities. They've just managed to bring me to starvation-point. It will be another fortnight before I sink to the level of getting conceited about them.'

Zacharias got up and accompanied his visitor with marked geniality as far as the stairs. 'Call me up tomorrow about twelve o'clock. No, I've got a conference on then, just after two. Perhaps I shall think of something in the meanwhile. So long.'

Fabian would have liked to telephone Labude, but he was in Frankfurt. Fabian had taken care not to tell him anything of his troubles. Labude had troubles of his own. He wanted to hear his friendly voice, that was all. A chat about the weather between friends can work wonders. His mother had gone back. The queer old inventor, with his cape, was on the way to the lunatic asylum. Cornelia was buying herself a new hat to please one or two film people. Fabian was alone. Why could he not escape from himself till further notice? He wandered aimlessly about the city, but presently he found himself standing outside the place where Cornelia was employed. Annoyed with himself, he walked on, and caught himself glancing sideways into every milliner's shop. Was she still in her office? Or was she trying on hats and jumpers?

At Anhalter Station he bought a newspaper. The man in the kiosk had a friendly air. 'Do you want an assistant?' asked Fabian.

'I shall have to take up knitting,' said the man. 'My turnover's just half what it was a year ago, and things weren't too flourishing then. People don't read newspapers now, except at the barber's and when they're sitting in cafés. I ought to have been a baker. The barbers haven't started giving away loaves yet.'

'Someone suggested a short time ago that bread should be supplied to every house by the state, like the water supply,' said Fabian. 'You wait, the day will come when even the bakers will not be safe from starvation.'

'Would you like a roll?' asked the man in the kiosk.

'I can manage for another week,' said Fabian. He thanked him and entered the station. He looked at the time-tables. Should he spend what he had left on a railway-ticket, and go back to his mother? But perhaps Zacharias would think of something before the morning. When he came out of the station, he found himself confronted once more by those lines of streets, those masses of brickwork, all that hopeless, pitiless labyrinth, and he turned giddy. He leaned against the wall, not far from a group of porters, and closed his eyes. But now the noise tormented him. It was as though the trams and omnibuses were driving right through his body. He turned back, ascended the steps to the waiting-room, and laid his head on a bare wooden bench. Half an hour later he felt better. He left the station, took a tram home, threw himself on the sofa and fell asleep immediately.

It was evening when he awoke. The hall-door had just closed with a slam. Was Cornelia coming in? No. Someone ran quickly down the stairs. He went over to the other room and stopped short on the threshold.

The wardrobe stood open. It was empty. Her trunks were gone. Fabian switched on the light, though it was scarcely dusk. On the table, weighed down by a vase of flowers which were waiting to be thrown away, was a letter. He nodded, took the letter, and went back to his room.

'Dear Fabian,' wrote Cornelia. 'Is it not better for me to go too soon than too late? I've just been standing beside you as you lay on the sofa. You were asleep and you are still sleeping as I write these words. I should like to stay, but suppose I did! A few weeks and you would be most unhappy. You would not be troubled so much by poverty itself as by the thought that poverty can be of such importance. So long as you were alone nothing could hurt you, no matter what happened. Things will all come right again. Are you very miserable?

'They want to give me a part in the next film. I shall sign the contract tomorrow. Makart has taken two rooms for me. It can't be helped. He talked about it as though he were ordering a hundredweight of coal. He's fifty and looks like a retired, overdressed wrestler. I feel as though I had sold myself to the medical schools. I've half a mind to come back to your room and wake you. No, I'll let you sleep. I shan't let it get me down. I shall pretend to myself I am being examined by a doctor. I must let him have his way, it can't be helped. The only way to get out of the mud is to get yourself thoroughly muddy. And we do want to get out of it!

'I said, We. Do you understand? I'm leaving you so as to be able to stay with you. Will you still be fond of me? Will you still want to look at me and still be able to take me in your arms, in spite of Makart? I shall be waiting for you tomorrow afternoon from four o'clock onwards at the Café Schottenhaml. What will become of me if you don't come? Cornelia.'

Fabian sat quite still. The room darkened. There was a pain at his heart. He clung fast to the knobs of the chair-arms, as though he were resisting some power that tried to drag him away. He regained control of himself. The letter was lying on the carpet at his feet, shining dimly in the darkness.

'But Cornelia,' he said, 'I was going to change my ways.'

XVI

The same evening he took the underground and went north-ward. He stood by the carriage-window, staring into the black tunnel where now and then little lamps flashed past. He looked out on the populous platforms of subterranean stations. And when the train rose out of the tunnel, he stared at grey lines of houses, down dusky side-streets and into lighted rooms, where strangers sat at their tables, waiting for the fulfilment of their destinies. He stared at the gleaming network of rails athwart which they sped, at the main-line stations where red lines of sleeping-cars thought wearily of the long road before them, at the silent Spree, at the theatre façades made bright with garish neon-signs, and at the purple sky itself, starless above the city.

Fabian saw all this as though it were his eyes and ears alone that were moving through Berlin, while he himself was far, far away. His senses were acute, but his heart was numbed. He had sat there a long while in his furnished room. Somewhere in this inscrutable city was Cornelia. In bed with a man of fifty, her eyes closed in submission. Where? He longed to tear down the walls of every house till at last he found them. Where was she? Why had she condemned him to remain inactive? Why had she done so at one of the rare moments when the urge to action was upon him? She did not know him. She had chosen to act wrongly herself rather than demand that he should act rightly. She thought he would suffer a thousand blows rather than once uplift his arm. She did not know that he was crying out to serve, to accept responsibility. But where were those whom he could have served? Where was Cornelia. Lying with a fat old man, making herself a whore so that her dear Fabian should have time and inclination for idling. She gave him back magnanimously that very freedom from which she had freed him. Chance had thrown a person in his way for whom he could act at last, and that person had thrust him back into unwanted, accursed freedom. They had helped each other, and now there was no help for either. As soon as his work had acquired a meaning for him, because he had found Cornelia, he had lost it. And because he had lost it, he had lost Cornelia too.

Thirsting, he had carried a cup in his hand, and been unwilling to bear it because it was empty. And at last, when he scarce dared hope any longer, fate had relented and filled the cup. He had bent his head and tried to drink. Then, because he had not wished to bear the cup, fate had snatched it from him, and the water had been spilt upon his hands and run down upon the earth.

Hurrah! Now he was free. He laughed so loudly, so angrily, that his fellow-passengers edged away, a little intimidated. He got out. It mattered not where he got out, he was free! Cornelia, God knew where, was paying the price for success or despair or both. In the Chausseestrasse, he came to a row of police-barracks, and saw, through the open gateways, green lorries, headlights flashing. Policemen clambered into the lorries, and stood in close, silent ranks, resolute. Several of the lorries rattled off northwards. Fabian followed them. The street was full of people. Shouts were hurled at the lorries, shouts like stones. The police stared straight ahead.

At Weddingplatz, they closed the Reinickendorfer Strasse, up which a crowd of workmen was approaching. Behind the cordon, mounted police were waiting for the word to attack. Uniformed workers, waiting, leather straps beneath their chins, for civilian workers. Who drove them against each other? The crowd of workmen was drawing near, their songs swelled louder and louder, then the police advanced, step by step, a yard between each man. The singing gave place to an angry roar. He could not see, but he felt what was happening by the noise and its sudden crescendo: Out there in front, the police and the workmen were on the point of meeting. A minute passed and shrill outcries confirmed his fear. They had met, the police were using their truncheons. Now the horses swung into motion and trotted into vacancy. Their hoofs clattered on the roadway. A shot rang out. A splintering of glass. The horses were galloping. The crowd at Weddingplatz strove to press after them. A second cordon closed the end of Reinickendorfer Strasse and moved slowly forward, clearing the square. Stones were flying.

A sergeant was stabbed. The police drew their rubber truncheons and advanced at the double. Three lorries arrived with reinforcements. The men sprang from the slowly-moving vehicles. The workmen broke and ran, only to halt round the edges of the square and in the streets that led into it. Fabian pushed his way through the living wall and walked off. The noise receded. Three streets further on, and it seemed as though quiet and order reigned everywhere.

Several women were standing in a doorway. 'Hey, you!' cried one. 'Is it true they're fighting in Weddingplatz?'

'They are taking each other's measure,' he answered, and went on.

'Damn me! I'll bet our Franz is mixed up in it,' cried the woman. 'Just wait till he gets home!'

There was an unexpected break in the line of house-fronts, a gap between the solid old tenement buildings; it was the entrance to a fair-ground, Uncle Pelle's Amusement Park.

The noise of barrel-organs submerged the chattering of girls, who lounged, arm-in-arm, in a long chain, outside the entrance. Bold-looking lads, with their caps over one ear, prowled about, making pointed remarks. The girls were flattered; they giggled and gave unmistakable response.

Fabian passed through the gateway. The ground resembled a laundry-yard. Acetylene flames leapt unsteadily, throwing the paths and booths into semi-darkness. The earth was heavy and covered with coarse stubble. The roundabouts were draped in waterproof-sheets for lack of custom. Men in rough jackets, old women with kerchiefs, children who should have been in bed long ago, trotted along the paths between the booths.

A lucky wheel spun noisily. The crowd stood close packed, their eyes glued to the rotating disc. It moved slower, crawled past the last few numbers, and stopped.

'Twenty-five!' shouted the proprietor.

'Here, here!' An old woman, with spectacles low on her nose, held up her ticket. They gave her the prize. What had she won? A pound of lump sugar.

The wheel whirred again.

'Seventeen!'

'Hello, that's me!' A young man waved his ticket. He received a quarter of a pound of coffee. 'Something for mother,' he said with satisfaction, and moved off.

'Now comes the special prize! The winner can choose whatever he wants!' The wheel wavered, ticked, stopped, no, moved to the next number.

'Nine!'

'Here!' A factory girl clapped her hands. She read through the rules. 'The special prize consists of five pounds of best quality wheat-flour, or a pound of butter, or three quarters of a pound of coffee, or a pound and three quarters of lean bacon.' She asked for the pound of butter. 'Not bad for ten pfennigs,' she laughed. 'Something worth carrying home.'

'Get ready for the next turn,' shouted the proprietor. 'Anybody not got a ticket? Who wants a ticket? Here you are, granny! This is the beggar's Monte Carlo. Tickets ten pfennigs. Not a mark, not half a mark, only ten pfennigs!'

Across the way was a similar attraction. But the prizes consisted of meat and sausage, and the tickets cost twice as much.

'The first prize, ladies and gentlemen, the first prize, this time, consists of half a Hamburg goose!' screamed the butcher's wife. 'Twenty pfennigs! Try your luck, friends!' Armed with a huge knife, her assistant was cutting thin slices from a Schlack-wurst, and distributing them as samples to the buyers of tickets. The onlookers felt their mouths water. They dug in their purses for twenty pfennigs and handed them over.

'What do you say to roast goose?' asked a man without collar and tie, turning to a woman.

'Waste of money,' she said. 'We never have any luck, Willie.'

'Oh, chuck it,' he said, 'you never know.' He bought a ticket, put the slice of sausage he received with it into the woman's mouth, and looked expectantly at the wheel.

'The draw will now take place!' screamed the butcher's wife. The lucky wheel hummed. Fabian passed on. Above a big tent was the announcement: 'Hippodrome. Dancing. Admission twenty pfennigs.' He went in. The booth consisted of two rings. The one was raised above the other on piles. Up there people were dancing. There was a brass band in the middle, playing as though the bandsmen had just had a violent quarrel. The girls stood leaning against the rails. The young men came and seized them. There was no standing on ceremony. The lower circle was a sanded ring, where three discarded old nags trotted round to the strains of the band. They were prevented from falling asleep by a ring-master in a top-hat, who brandished his whip and constantly urged them on. On a little one-eyed white horse was a woman, seated astride. Her skirt had worked up high above her knee. She was a bad rider and laughed every time she threatened to lose her balance.

Fabian sat down on one side of the ring and drank a glass of beer. Each time the horsewoman passed him she pulled down her skirt. Her exertions were in vain, for her skirt soon worked up again. When she passed Fabian's table for the fourth time, she smiled slightly and let her skirt stay where it was. On the next occasion, the horse stopped in front of his table and stared with its blind eye into his beer-glass. 'There's no sugar there,' said the woman, and looked into Fabian's face. The ring-master cracked his whip and the little white horse shuffled off again.

Scarcely had the woman dismounted, when she took a seat with exaggerated lack of intention at the next table, diagonally in front of Fabian, where he could not overlook her bodily charms. His eyes remained fixed on her figure, and suddenly the pain within him awoke from its narcotic. Where was Cornelia? Was the embrace in which she lay repulsive to her? Was she taking her pleasure in a strange bed while he sat here? He jumped to his feet, knocking over the chair. The woman at the next table looked into his face again. Her eyes opened wide, she pursed her lips, slightly opened her mouth, and passed the tip of her moist tongue along her upper lip.

'Coming with me?' he asked reluctantly. She came with him. They said little, but went into the 'theatre'. It was a wretched booth. 'Personal Appearance of the famous Rheingold Singers. Smoking permitted. Children must stand at evening performances.' The place was half full. The audience kept their hats on, smoked cigarettes and allowed themselves to be moved to tears in the darkness by the unspeakably inane and insincere romanticism, for which they had paid the sum of thirty pfennigs. They had more feeling for the trumpery fiction on the stage than for their own genuine misery.

Fabian put his arm round the strange woman. She snuggled up to him, breathing hard, so that he should hear her. The play was very sad. A smart young student – played by Director Blasemann in person, though he was grey-haired and past fifty – came home drunk to his lodgings every morning. It was all that damned champagne! He sang student's songs, ordered pickled herring, was sternly rebuked by the porter's wife, and gave his last thaler to an old and gouty opera-singer on condition that she moved off elsewhere.

But fate stalked forward as fast as it could. The old opera-singer was the mother of this grey-haired student! Who else could she have been? It was twelve long years since he had seen her, but he received an allowance from her every month and thought she was still, as formerly, engaged at the Royal Opera House. Of course he did not recognize her. But mother's eyes see deeper! She knew at once: it was he. But the climax of the play was postponed. A love affair intruded. The student loved and was loved in return, the latter function being performed by Fräulein Martin, the pretty seamstress who lived opposite, and sang like a lark while she worked the treadle of her sewing-machine. Ellen Martin, the singing skylark, weighed a good fifteen stone. She danced out of the wings, while the stage bent beneath her, and sang a duet with Director Blasemann, the student. Their most successful number began as follows:

> 'Little sweetheart, don't be lonely,
> You shall be my one and only!'

The young couple, numbering together about a hundred summers, shoved each other ponderously to and fro before a backcloth that was meant to represent a courtyard. Then he proposed marriage to her, but she was sad because he habitually drove away elderly opera-singers. Then they proceeded to the next verse.

The audience applauded. The woman Fabian had put his arm round turned slightly towards him and surrendered her breast. 'Isn't it lovely?' she said. He took her to mean the play. A solemn stillness fell once more upon the auditorium. The old, bent, gouty opera-singer, who paid for her son to study medicine and belong to an exclusive students' corps, tottered out of the wings, managed to reach the courtyard, and put up one finger. The pianist responded, and a sentimental song of mother-love was about to be rendered.

'Let's go,' said Fabian, and released the strange woman's brassiere.

'What already?' she asked in surprise, but she followed him.

'This is where I live,' she said, when they reached a great

block of flats in the Müllerstrasse. She unlocked the door. 'I'll come up,' he said.

She objected, but her tone was unconvincing. He pushed her inside the outer door. 'What will my landlady say? Oh, you are in a hurry. Well, be quiet then!' The name on the door was Hetzer.

'Why are there two beds in your room?' he asked.

'Ssh! They might hear us,' she whispered. 'My landlady's got nowhere else to put it.'

He undressed. 'Why all this fuss?' he asked.

She seemed to think some coquetry indispensable, and was as coy as an elderly virgin. At last they were lying side by side. She had put out the light before she finished undressing. 'Just a moment,' she whispered. 'Don't be cross.' She switched a flashlight on, spread a cloth over his face and examined him by the light of the torch, like an old panel doctor. 'I'm sorry I have to do this,' she declared, 'but you can't be too careful nowadays.' After this no further obstacles stood in their path.

'I'm an assistant in a glove shop,' she told him, a little later. 'Will you stay all night?' she asked, when another half-hour had passed. He nodded. She disappeared into the kitchen: he could hear her washing. She brought in some warm soapy water, washed him carefully with a housewife's zeal, and climbed back into bed. 'Doesn't it annoy your landlord if you heat water in the kitchen?' he asked. 'Leave the light on.'

She told him scraps of news, asked where he lived, and called him 'sweetheart'. He scrutinized the furniture. In addition to the beds, there was a plush sofa with violent curves, a washstand with a marble top, a terrible coloured print, which depicted a plump young woman in her nightdress, playing with a rosy baby on a polar bear's skin, and a wardrobe with a mirror in the door, which functioned imperfectly. Where is Cornelia? he thought, and once more fell upon his naked but half-scared companion.

'You're enough to frighten a woman,' she whispered afterwards. 'Do you want to kill me? But it's wonderful.' She knelt at his side, looked with wide-open eyes into his indifferent face, and kissed him.

When, wearied to death, she had fallen asleep, he still lay awake, alone in a strange room. He looked attentively into the darkness, and thought: Cornelia, what have we done?

XVII

'I told you a lie,' said the woman, next morning. 'I don't go to business at all. And this flat belongs to me. And we're all alone. Come into the kitchen.'

She poured out coffee, buttered the rolls, tapped him affectionately on the cheek, put on her apron, and they sat down together at the kitchen table. 'Taste nice?' she asked brightly, though he had not yet eaten anything. 'You look pale, sweetheart. And no wonder! Have a good meal. It'll make you big and strong again.' She laid her head on his shoulder and pursed her lips like a flapper.

'You were afraid I should run off with the sofa, or get a knife and slit you open?' said Fabian. 'But how come these two beds in your room?'

'I'm married,' she confessed. 'My husband travels in knitwear. He's in the Rhineland now. Then he's going on to Württemberg. He'll be away at least another ten days. Will you stay here all the time?'

He drank his coffee and said nothing.

'I need somebody,' she declared vehemently, as though she had been contradicted.

'He's never here, and when he is here it's not worth it. Stay with me these ten days. Make yourself at home. I'm a good cook, and I've got enough money. What would you like for dinner today?' She began to clear up, looking anxiously across at him.

'Do you like calves' liver with fried potatoes? Why don't you answer?'

'Have you a telephone?' he asked.

'No,' she said. 'Do you want to go? Do stay! It was so lovely. I've never known it so lovely.' She dried her hands and stroked back his hair.

'I'll stay,' he agreed. 'But I must telephone.'

She said he could telephone from the butcher's, and would he bring back half a pound of fresh calves' liver, but with no veins in it. Then she gave him money and cautiously opened the door of the flat. She found the stairs deserted, and let him go.

'Half a pound of fresh calves' liver, but with no veins in it,' he said, when he reached the butcher's. While they served him, he rang up Zacharias. The telephone was greasy.

'No,' said Zacharias, 'I haven't thought of anything. But I'm not giving up hope, old man: that would be too absurd. Listen, look in here again tomorrow. Things may move quickly. At all events we can have a chat. How will that suit you? So long.'

Fabian was handed the calves' liver. The paper was bloody. He paid, and carried the packet of meat cautiously into the house. A neighbour was polishing the door-handle, so he proceeded as far as the fourth floor. A few minutes later he came down. The woman he had spent the night with opened the door without waiting for his ring, and drew him quickly into the flat. 'Thank the Lord,' she said softly. 'I thought that gossiping old devil would catch us out. Go and sit in the living-room, sweetheart. Would you like to read the paper? I'll finish clearing up.'

He placed the change he had received on the table, sat down in the living-room and read the newspaper. He could hear the woman singing. After a while, she brought him cigarettes and kirsch, and looked over his shoulder. 'Dinner at one,' she said. 'I hope you're making yourself quite comfortable.'

Then she vanished again and went on singing in the next room. He read the official report of the disturbances in the Reinickendorfer Strasse. The sergeant that had been stabbed had died in hospital. Three of the demonstrators had been seriously injured. Several others had been arrested. The leading article spoke of irresponsible elements that constantly tried to incite the unemployed to violence, and of the grave problem with which the police were confronted. Despite unceasing efforts in certain quarters, it would be fatal to reduce the budget for that branch of the police entrusted with the protection of life and property. Events such as those of yesterday provided incontrovertible proof of the need for preventive thought and action.

Fabian looked round the little room. The furniture was

ornamented wherever there was space for ornamentation. On the sideboard were three letter-files. The table was resplendent with a brightly-coloured glass dish with a waved edge, containing picture-postcards. Fabian took the card that was uppermost. It showed a picture of Cologne Cathedral, and he thought of the poster for the cigarette company.

'Dear Mucki,' he read. 'I hope things are going well and you've got enough money. I've landed some pretty good orders. I'm off to Düsseldorf tomorrow. Love and kisses, Kurt.' He put the card back on the dish, and drank a glass of kirsch.

At dinner he cleared his plate to avoid displeasing Mucki. She was as delighted as if a dog had emptied its platter. Afterwards there was coffee.

'Won't you tell me anything about yourself, sweetheart?' she asked.

'No,' he said, and went into the living-room. She ran after him. He was standing by the window.

'Come on the sofa,' she said. 'Somebody might see you. And don't be bad-tempered.'

He sat down on the sofa. She brought him the coffee, sat down at his side, and unbuttoned her blouse. 'Now for the dessert,' she said. 'But please don't bite me again.'

About three o'clock he went out.

'Are you quite sure you'll come back?' She stood before him, straightening her skirt, pulling up her stockings, and looking at him pleadingly. 'Swear that you'll come back!'

'I expect I shall,' he said, 'but I can't promise.'

'I shall wait for you for supper,' she told him. Then she opened the door.

'Quick!' she whispered. 'While the coast's clear.'

He ran down the stairs. The coast is clear, he thought, and had a sense of disgust for the house he was leaving. He took a tram to the Grosser Stern, crossed the Tiergarten to the Brandenburg Gate, and lost himself again in the park. The rhododendrons were in bloom. He found himself in the Siegesallee. The Hohenzollern dynasty and the sculptor Begas seemed indestructible.

Outside the Café Schottenhaml he turned back. What was there left to discuss? It was too late for talking. He walked on, came to the Potsdamer Strasse and stood undecided at Potsdamerplatz. He hurried up the Bellevuestrasse and found himself once more outside the café. This time he went in. Cornelia was sitting there as though she had been waiting for years. She waved feebly.

He sat down. She took his hand. 'I didn't think you were coming,' she said, shyly. He looked past her in silence. 'It wasn't right of me, was it?' she whispered, and looked down. The tears were falling into her coffee. She pushed the cup aside and wiped her eyes.

He looked away. Between the two baroque staircases that led to the upper floor, the walls were crowded with flocks of gaudy parrots and humming-birds. They were made of glass, and roosted on glass twigs and lianas, waiting for the evening and its lamps when that fragile, primitive forest would burst into light.

Cornelia whispered: 'Why don't you look at me?' She pressed her handkerchief to her lips, and her weeping sounded like the far-away whimpering of a child in despair.

The café was empty. What guests there were were sitting outside under the large red sunshades. There was no one near but a waiter. Fabian looked into her face. Her eyelids flickered nervously. 'Do say something,' she said, in a harsh voice.

His mouth was dry. His throat was constricted. He swallowed with difficulty.

'Say something,' she repeated, very softly, and folded her hands on the cloth, between the nickelled coffee-trays.

He still remained silent.

'What will become of me?' she whispered, as though she was speaking to herself and he was no longer there. 'What's to become of me?'

'A woman who has got what she wants and is still unhappy,' he said, speaking much more loudly than he had intended. 'Are you surprised? Isn't this what you came to Berlin for? This city is a mart. If you want something you must give what you have.'

He waited for a while, but she did not speak. She took a compact from her bag, but let it lie unopened. He had gained control of himself again. His feelings soon wearied and ceased to trouble him, evading the urge to set things right. He looked back at what had been, as though it were a disordered room, and began, coldly and meanly, to clear it up. 'You came here with an aim in view which you have managed to attain more rapidly than you dared to hope. You have found a powerful man to finance you. He is not only financing you, but giving you a chance to make good in your profession. I don't doubt your success. When you succeed, he will get back the money he has, so to speak, invested in you; you will also earn money yourself, and one day you will be quits with him.' Fabian felt surprised and shocked at his own words. Perfectly clear, he thought, except that I should have dictated the punctuation.

Cornelia looked at him as though she were seeing him for the first time. Then she released the catch of the compact, examined her face in the little circular mirror and with the powdery white puff dusted her tear-stained, childishly astonished face. She nodded to him to proceed.

'What will happen then,' he said, 'what will happen when you've no further need of Makart, is more than I can tell you. In any case, it's beside the point. You will work, and when a woman is at work there is not much left of her. You will become more and more successful, more and more ambitious, but the higher you climb the greater the danger of falling. Probably you will have to give yourself to other men. There are always male obstacles in a woman's path which she can only scale by lying down with them. You will get used to it. You created the precedent yesterday.'

He found me in tears, and he goes on beating me, she thought with surprise.

'But I'm not here to discuss the future,' he said, and made a conclusive gesture as though disposing of the idea. 'We have still to speak of the past. You did not consult me yesterday before you went. Why should you be interested now in what I think? You knew you were a burden to me. You knew I wanted to get rid of you. You knew I was keen to have a mistress who slept in other men's beds to earn the money I haven't got. If you were right, I was a scoundrel. If I was not a scoundrel, then everything you did was wrong.'

'It was wrong,' she said, and got up. 'Good-bye, Fabian.'

He followed her, very dissatisfied with himself. He made her suffer because he had a right to do so, but was that any reason? He overtook her in the Tiergartenstrasse and they walked on in silence, sorry for themselves and each other. Suppose she asks me, shall she come back, he thought. What am I to say? I still have about fifty-six marks.

'It was horrible last night,' she said suddenly. 'He was so hateful! What will come of it, if you're not fond of me any more?

There would be no need for us to worry now, and yet things are worse than before. What shall I do, if I know you don't want to have any more to do with me?'

He took her by the arm. 'First of all, pull yourself together. The advice is old but still sound. You have cut your own head off; take care that at least you've not done it for nothing. And forgive me for having hurt you so just now.'

'Yes, yes.' She was still wretched and yet happy again. 'And can I come to you tomorrow afternoon?'

'All right,' he said.

At that she threw her arms round him in the street, kissed him, whispered 'Thank you,' and ran away sobbing.

He stood still. A passer-by shouted 'Lucky man!' Fabian wiped his mouth with his hand. He felt sick. What had touched Cornelia's lips since he last saw her? Did it matter that she had brushed her teeth? Could hygiene remove this feeling of nausea?

He crossed the street and entered the park. Morality was the best cleanser. It was not enough to gargle with hydrogen peroxide.

And then, for the first time, he remembered where he had been the previous night.

He did not wish to return to the Müllerstrasse. But the mere thought of his lodgings, of the widow Hohlfeld's curiosity, of Cornelia's empty room, of the long, lonely night that awaited him, while for the second time Cornelia was deceiving him, drove him northwards through the streets to the Müllerstrasse, to the house of that woman whom he did not wish to see again. Her face beamed. She was proud that he had returned to her, and glad to have him back again.

'That's fine,' she greeted him. 'Come, you must be hungry.' She had laid supper in the living-room. 'We generally take our meals in the kitchen,' she said. 'But what's the good of having a three-roomed flat?' There was sausage and ham and Camembert cheese. Suddenly she put down her knife and fork. She said: 'Hey presto!' and produced a bottle of Moselle. She poured it out and clinked her glass against his. 'To our baby!' she cried. 'He's got to be like you, and if it doesn't turn out to be a boy, you'll have to do pack-drill.' She emptied her glass and refilled it. Her eyes began to shine. 'Lucky I met you,' she said, and drank again. 'Wine makes me so excited.' She fell on his neck.

132

There was a jingle of keys outside. Footsteps approached along the passage. The door opened. A man came in; he was of middle height and heavily built. The woman jumped up. His face darkened. 'I wish you both a good appetite,' he said, and went towards the woman.

She moved backwards, and, before he could reach her, tore open the bedroom door, sprang through, and slammed and bolted it behind her.

The man cried: 'You wait! I'll tan your hide for you!' He turned towards Fabian, who had risen in embarrassment. He said: 'Please sit down. I'm the husband.' They sat facing each other for a while in silence. Then the man took up the Moselle bottle, carefully examined the label, and filled himself a glass. He drank and said presently: 'The trains are very crowded at this time of year.'

Fabian nodded agreement.

'But this is good wine. Did you like it?' asked the man.

'I'm not very fond of white wine,' explained Fabian, and got up.

The other followed him. 'You're not going?' he asked.

'I don't want to intrude any longer,' returned Fabian.

Suddenly the traveller sprang at his throat and tried to throttle him. Fabian struck him in the teeth with his fist. The man released his hold, sat down and took his face in his hands.

'I'm sorry,' said Fabian, miserably. The man just groaned, spat blood into his handkerchief, and was fully occupied with himself.

Fabian left the flat. Where was he to go now? He went home.

XVIII

Although Fabian unlocked the door very quietly, Frau Hohlfeld was waiting for him in the corridor. She was wearing a morning frock, for it was evening, and she was extremely agitated. 'I left my door open so that I should hear you,' she said. 'The police have been here. They came to fetch you.'

'Police?' he asked, in surprise. 'When was that?'

'Three hours ago, and about an hour ago they came back again. You are to go immediately. Of course, I told them that you were not at home last night, and I said Fräulein Battenberg left her room yesterday without a word and has simply vanished.' The widow was about to take a step nearer but instead of that she stepped back. 'It's terrible,' she whispered, in an agitated voice. 'What have you done?'

'My dear Frau Hohlfeld,' he answered. 'Your imagination is running away with you. It would just suit you, wouldn't it? A little drama of passion with fatal results. Frau Hohlfeld in deep mourning in the witness-box, photographs of two of her lodgers in all the newspapers, the murderer, Fabian, in the dock. Don't let your imagination run away with you!'

'Well,' she said, 'it's none of my business.' His obstinacy pained her deeply. Two years this man had been living with her, and she had cared for him like her own son. And now he did not even think it necessary to open his heart to her.

'Where am I to go?' he asked.

She gave him a slip of paper.

He read the address.

'There, you see!' she cried triumphantly. 'Why did you turn so pale?'

He wrenched open the door and dashed downstairs. At Nürnbergerplatz he stopped a taxi, and gave the address. 'Drive as fast as you can!' he cried. The car was old and ramshackle,

134

and jolted over the smooth street. Fabian pulled down the window. 'Faster!' he shouted. He tried to smoke, but his hand shook and the draught blew out the match. He leaned back and closed his eyes. From time to time he opened them to see how far they had got. Tiergarten, Tiergarten, Tiergarten. Brandenburg Gate. Unter den Linden. They had to stop at every street corner. The red light glowed out on every traffic signal just as they reached it. He felt as though they were travelling through semi-liquid glue. It was better once they had passed Friedrichstrasse. At last the University, the State Opera House, the Cathedral and the Castle lay behind them. The car turned to the right and stopped. Fabian paid the fare and ran, like a hunted animal, into a tenement-house.

A stranger opened the door. Fabian gave his name. 'At last!' said the stranger. 'I am Detective Inspector Donath. We can't get on without you.'

Five young women were sitting in the first room he entered, and a policeman was standing near them. Fabian recognized Selow and the sculptress. 'At last!' cried Selow. The room was a wreck, glasses and bottles lying about the floor.

In the next room, a young man rose from the writing-table. 'My assistant,' explained the inspector. Fabian looked round and started violently. Labude was lying on the sofa, with closed eyes, his face white as chalk. There was a wound in his temple. His hair was matted with blood.

'Stephan,' said Fabian softly, and sat down beside the body. He placed his hand on the icy hand of his friend, and shook his head.

'But Stephan,' he said, 'you can't do this.'

The two detectives went and stood by the window.

'Dr Labude has left a letter for you,' said the inspector. 'Will you please read it and let us know if there is anything in it that concerns us. We agree with you that this is probably a case of suicide, and the five young women, whom for the moment we have detained, claim that they were in the next room when the shot was fired. All the same, the case doesn't seem to be quite cleared up. Perhaps you noticed that the next room was pretty well wrecked. What's the meaning of that?'

The assistant handed Fabian an envelope. 'Will you be so good as to read the letter? The girls maintain that the room was wrecked in the course of a private quarrel. They say Dr Labude had nothing to do with it, and was not even there. He had left them and come in here, saying he wanted to write a letter.'

'There are indications that these young ladies' relations with each other are of a rather unusual sort,' explained the inspector. 'I assume they had some kind of jealous quarrel. They informed the police immediately of what had happened, and waited here for us instead of running away, which makes it improbable that they were directly implicated. Will you read the letter?'

Fabian opened the envelope and took out a folded sheet of paper. As he did so, a bundle of banknotes fell to the floor. The assistant picked them up and put them on the sofa.

'We'll wait in the next room,' said the inspector thoughtfully, and they left Fabian alone. He got up and switched on the light. Then he sat down again, and gazed at his dead friend, whose face, yellow, and rigid in its fatigue, lay just beneath the lamp. His mouth was a little open, his lower jaw had dropped. Fabian unfolded the sheet of paper and read:

'Dear Jacob, I went to the University at midday today to ask about my research thesis, but the Professor was away again. Weckherlin, his assistant, was there, however, and he told me that my thesis had been turned down. The Professor had described it as totally inadequate, and said that if he passed it on to the faculty, it would only be imposing on them. He also said that there was nothing to be gained by advertising my failure. This work has taken me five years. I've been working for five years on something which they wish to bury in secret out of consideration for my feelings.

'I thought of telephoning you, but I was too ashamed. I have no talent for receiving sympathy – even at that I'm no good. I realized it a short time ago, after the talk we had about Leda. You would have shown me that my misfortune was microscopically small. I should have appeared to agree with you, and we should each have been deceiving the other.

'The rejection of my work means my ruin, materially and psychologically, but especially the latter. Leda repulsed me, and now the University does the same. On all sides I am repudiated as inadequate. That is more than my ambition can stand. That breaks me, Jacob, mind and body. It is no good citing statistics of how many great men have been unsuccessful in their studies and unhappy in their love affairs.

'Politically, my trip to Frankfurt was a sickening failure. It ended in a free fight. When I got back yesterday, Selow was lying in bed and Ruth Reiter was here and several other women were lending a hand. And now, as I write, they are throwing tumblers and vases at each other in the next room. When I survey my present situation, I can only say that everything about it is distasteful to me. I have been expelled from the circles where I belong, and those that would accept me I do not wish to enter. Do not be angry with me, dear friend; I am leaving it all. Europe does not need me. It will survive or go under without my assistance. We live in a time when economic horse-trading can alter nothing; it can only hasten or delay the final breakdown. We stand at one of those rare turning-points of history, where a new way must be found of looking at life: all else is useless. I have no longer the courage to allow myself to be made fun of by political experts who let the continent die under their hands, while they potter about with their petty remedies. I know I am right, but that is no longer enough. I have become ridiculous, a candidate for manhood who has failed in both subjects, love and work. Let me get rid of myself! The revolver I took from the Communist the other day, by the Märkisches Museum, shall reap fresh laurels. I took it so that no harm should be done. I ought to have been a teacher, for children are the only persons ripe for ideals.

'Well, good-bye, Jacob. I had almost written, in all seriousness, I shall often think of you. But that is all over now. Do not blame me for disappointing us so. You are the only person I ever knew and yet loved. Remember me to my father and mother, and especially to *your* mother. If you should happen to meet Leda, do not tell her that I was so hard hit by her unfaithfulness. Let her think I was only hurt for the moment. There is no need for everyone to know everything.

'I would ask you to look after my affairs, but there is nothing to look after. My parents are to close my No. 2 flat; they can do what they like with the furniture. I found two thousand marks in my desk just now. Take it. It is not much, but it will be enough for a holiday somewhere.

'Good-bye, my friend. Live better than I did. Make a job of it.

Your Stephan.'

Fabian gently stroked the dead man's forehead. His lower jaw had dropped still further. His mouth was gaping wide. 'Life is a chance, death is a certainty,' Fabian whispered, and smiled to his friend, as though he still wished to comfort him.

The inspector quietly opened the door.

'Excuse my troubling you again.' Fabian gave him the letter. He read it, and said: 'Now I can send these girls home.' He handed the letter back, and went into the next room. 'All right,' he said. 'I won't keep you any longer.'

'Just a moment,' cried a feminine voice. 'I have a weakness for corpses.' The five women crowded through the door, and stood in silence round the sofa.

'He ought to have his chin bound up,' said one of the girls, presently. Fabian did not know her. The sculptress ran into the other room and came back with a table-napkin. She bound up Labude's jaw, closing his mouth, and tied the ends of the napkin in a knot above his hair.

'A dead man with a toothache,' remarked Selow, and laughed unpleasantly.

Ruth Reiter said: 'It's a shame. There's Wilhelmy lying in my studio, getting better every day, the swine, in spite of the fact that the doctors have given him up. And this healthy young chap goes and does himself in.'

The assistant herded the women out of the room. The inspector sat down at the writing-table to draft his report. His assistant came back again. 'Wouldn't it be better to get a car and have him taken to his parents' place?' he asked. He stooped down. The banknotes had fallen from the sofa and were lying on the floor again. He picked them up and stuck them in Fabian's pocket.

'Have his people been informed?' asked Fabian.

'Unfortunately we couldn't get hold of them,' replied the assistant. 'Herr Labude is away from home; the servants don't know where. His mother is in Lugano. They've wired to her.'

'All right,' said Fabian. 'Let us take him home!'

The assistant telephoned to the nearest fire-station. Then they waited in silence, all three, till the ambulance came. The

138

attendants packed Labude on to a bier and carried him down-stairs. A group of curious neighbours was waiting outside the house. The bier was lifted into the ambulance, and Fabian sat down beside his friend's prostrate body. The detectives took their leave. He shook hands with them. An attendant folded up the steps and shut the door. Fabian and Labude were driving through Berlin together for the last time.

The window was down, and within its frame appeared the Cathedral. Then the scene changed. Fabian saw Schinkel's Guardhouse, the University, the National Library. How long ago was it since they drove this way together in a taxicab?

It was the night they took the revolvers from two rowdies out there by the Märkisches Museum. Now Labude was lying on his bier, and they were driving through the Brandenburg Gate without his being aware of it. Two tight straps held him in his place. His head dropped slowly to one side. He seems to be meditating, thought Fabian. He lifted Labude's head back on to the pillow, and let his hand rest beside it. A dead man with toothache, Selow had said.

When the ambulance stopped outside the Grunewald villa, the servants were standing at the door. The housekeeper was crying, the butler walked with dignified steps in front of the attendants, the maids followed behind, keeping step with the gravity of the hour. They carried Labude to his room and laid him on the sofa. The butler threw open the windows. 'A woman's coming in the morning to lay him out,' said the housekeeper; and now the maids too were crying. Fabian gave the attendants money. They saluted and went away.

'Herr Labude has not come back yet,' remarked the butler. 'I have no idea where he is. But he'll see it in the newspapers.'

'Is it in the newspapers?' asked Fabian.

'Yes,' returned the butler. 'Frau Labude has been informed. She will reach Berlin at midday tomorrow, if she is strong enough to stand the journey. The express has just reached Bellinzona.'

'You had better go to bed,' said Fabian. 'I shall stay here all night.' He drew up a chair to the sofa. The others left him. He was alone.

So Labude's mother was now in Bellinzona? Fabian sat down at his friend's side. What a punishment for a bad mother! he thought.

XIX

Despite the napkin, which seemed to hold Labude's face together, his appearance was changing. The cheek-bones began to protrude, as though the flesh were becoming fluid and seeping away inside. The eyes had sunk deep into their shadowed sockets. The nostrils fell in and looked pinched.

Fabian leaned forward. Why are you changing? he thought. Is it to take the sting from our leave-taking? I wish you could speak; there is so much I would ask you, old friend. Are you at rest now? Are you still content to be dead, now you have died? Or have you repented of it? Do you wish to make undone what is done for all eternity? I used to think that, when I stood by the body of one I had loved, I should fail to comprehend that he was dead. I used to think: How shall I realize that he is no longer here, when he still lies visible before me with his collar and tie, wearing the same old suit? How shall I realize that because he once forgot to breathe he has become a lump of flesh, and in three days' time will be cast thoughtlessly into the fire? And, when that time comes, shall I not cry aloud for help to save him from the flames? . . . But now, Stephan, I cannot understand my fear that I could ever doubt the reality and extent of death. You are dead, old friend. There you lie, visibly fading, like a badly-fixed photograph of yourself. They will throw this photograph into a furnace, called a crematorium. You will be burned, and no one will cry for help – not even I.

Fabian went over to the writing-desk and took a cigarette from a yellow wooden box that had stood there for years. On the wall was an engraving: it was a portrait of Lessing. 'You are to blame for this,' said Fabian to the man with the wig, and pointed to Labude. But Gotthold Ephraim Lessing ignored this reproach, which reached him a hundred and fifty years after his death. He looked straight ahead with a grave expression, full of character. His broad, peasant face did not move a muscle. 'All right,' said Fabian, and turning his back on the picture, resumed his seat beside his friend.

'Listen,' he said to Labude. 'That was a man.' And he pointed backwards with his thumb. 'He bit and fought and struck round him with his pen, as though his goose-quill were a cavalry sabre. He was built for fighting; you were not! He did not live for his own sake; he had no private interests; he asked nothing for himself. And when at last he remembered his own self, when he turned to fate and demanded a wife and child, then his world fell in upon him and buried him. And that was right and proper. If a man would live for others, he must be a stranger to himself. He must be like a physician, whose waiting-room is filled with people, day and night, and among them there must be one whose turn never comes, who waits without complaint: that is himself. Could you have lived like that?'

Fabian stroked his friend's knee, and shook his head. 'I wish you happiness, for you are dead. You were a good man, a decent fellow and my friend, but what you wished above all things to be, that you were not. Your character existed in your own imagination, and, when that failed you, there was nothing left but the pistol and what lies here on the sofa. Listen! Soon an embittered struggle will begin, first for mere bread and butter, then for the plush sofas; the one side will strive to retain them, the other side to secure them. Titanic blows will be struck and finally they will hack the sofas to pieces, so that no one shall possess them. There will be mountebanks on all sides among the leaders, men who invent proud phrases and grow drunk with the sound of their own voices. There may be two or three real men among them. If they tell the truth twice running they will be hanged. But you would not even have been hanged, you would have been killed with laughter. You were not a reformer and you were not a revolutionary. But don't let that trouble you.'

Labude lay as though he were listening. But he only seemed to be doing so. Fabian's harangue died away; he was growing tired. Why weren't you satisfied to find beauty where beauty is? he thought. Then this stroke of bad luck with Herr Lessing would never have hurt you so. Then you might have been sitting in Paris now, instead of lying here. Then your eyes would have been open, and you would have been looking happily down from the Sacré-Coeur upon the glittering boulevards, with their swirl of hot air above them. Or we two would have been sauntering through Berlin. The trees have put on their new green coats; the blue sky is veneered with gold; the girls have trimmed themselves to whet the appetite, and if one of them sleeps with a film magnate, there are others as good to be found. My old inventor was in love with life. I never told you how he stood in my wardrobe. He kept his hat on, and held his umbrella in his hand as though he were afraid it would rain.

Fabian could not have been long asleep, when he started up. He heard voices in the street and went over to the window. A car stopped outside the gate, the butler came out of the house and opened the car door. Herr Labude got out; he had a newspaper in his hand and held it out towards the butler. The butler nodded, and pointed up to the window where Fabian was standing. A woman tried to get out of the car, but Herr Labude thrust her back on to the seat. The car began to move off, and as it went the woman pressed her face against the window. Herr Labude entered the house. The butler followed, with arms anxiously outstretched lest it should be necessary to support his master.

Fabian went into the corridor; he did not wish to be present when the father found his son lying there. Herr Labude came up the stairs. He held firmly to the rail; the old butler walked behind him, still with arms outstretched protectively, but Labude's father did not falter. He went, without a glance at Fabian, into the lighted room. The butler closed the door and bent his head, listening in case he should be needed. But no sound came from the room. Fabian and the butler stood outside, each in his own place; they did not look at each other, they listened intently. Their sympathy was alert, waiting for some sound, some cry of grief. But they heard nothing. The scene behind the door remained an enigma.

The bell rang. The butler disappeared into the room, and came back into the corridor. 'Herr Labude wishes to speak to you.' Fabian went in. Old Labude was sitting at the desk, his head resting in his hand. After a while he sat up, rose to greet his son's friend, and smiled a forced smile. 'I have no contacts with tragedy,' he said. 'All the cases I have pleaded in the courts, the whole routine of the law, has given a false brightness to the bit of sympathy my egoism has left me, and in that brightness all else is reflected but genuine compassion.' He turned away and looked at his son, and it seemed as if he were trying to ask pardon of the dead. 'It's no good reproaching myself,' he went on. 'I was not the kind of father to live for his son. I am a pleasure-seeking old man, who is in love with life. And life has not lost its meaning because this has happened.' He pointed with outstretched arm to the body. 'He knew what he was doing, and if he thought it best, we others have no need to shed tears.'

'The sober way in which you speak,' said Fabian, 'almost makes me feel that you are reproaching yourself. There is no call for that. The tangible cause of Stephan's suicide was something beyond our influence.'

'Do you know anything of it? Did he leave letters?' asked Herr Labude.

Fabian said nothing of the letter. 'The information was contained in a brief note,' he said. 'The Professor has rejected Stephan's research-thesis.'

'I've never read it. I've never had time. Was it so bad?' asked the other.

'It is one of the best and most original pieces of literary criticism I know,' replied Fabian. 'Here it is.' He took a copy of the manuscript from the bookshelf and placed it on the desk.

Herr Labude turned over the pages, then he rang, asked for the telephone-directory, and ran his finger down the columns of names. 'It's very late,' he said, as he went to the telephone, 'but that can't be helped.' He got his number. 'Can I speak to the Professor?' he asked. 'Then I wish to speak to your mistress. Yes, even if she has gone to bed. This is Herr Labude speaking.' He waited. 'I beg your pardon for disturbing you,' he said. 'I hear your husband is away. In Weimar? Oh, at the meeting of the Shakespeare Society. When will he be back? I shall take the liberty of calling on him tomorrow at the University. You don't happen to know whether he has read my son's thesis?' He listened for some time, then he said 'Good-bye,' hung up the receiver, and turned to Fabian.

'Do you understand that?' he said. 'The Professor said at dinner the other day that the thesis on Lessing was extremely interesting, and he was eagerly waiting to get to the end of it and read the author's conclusions. They do not seem to have heard of Stephan's death.'

Fabian sprang agitatedly to his feet. 'He praised it? People don't praise a work and then reject it.'

'At all events, it is more usual for people to accept a work they have privately condemned,' returned Herr Labude. 'Will you leave me now? I shall stay with my boy and read his manuscript. He's been working at it for five years, has he not?' Fabian nodded and shook his hand. 'There's the cause of death,' said old Labude, pointing to the portrait of Lessing. He took the picture from the wall, stared at it for a moment, and smashed it, without visible agitation, against the corner of the writing-desk. Then he rang the bell. The butler came. 'Sweep this rubbish away and bring some sticking-plaster,' he ordered. His right hand was bleeding.

Fabian gave one more look at his dead friend. Then he went out and left the two alone.

He was too tired to sleep, and he was too tired to muster the sense of bereavement which the day required of him. The knitwear-traveller in the Müllerstrasse was holding his cheek. Wasn't his name Hetzer? His wife was lying in bed unsatisfied; Cornelia was again with Makart. Fabian saw these things like living pictures, in two dimensions, far away on the horizon of his mind. And even Labude, lying dead on the sofa somewhere in a villa in Grunewald, was at the moment only an idea. His sorrow had burnt down like a match and gone out. He recalled a similar state of mind in his childhood. When, as a little boy, he had cried for a long time over some trouble that seemed vast and irreparable, the reservoir that supplied the pain had grown empty. His feeling died away, as sometimes the life died out of his fingers after a heart-attack. The sorrow that filled him was insensible, the pain was cold.

Fabian walked down the Königsallee and came to the Rathenau Oak. There were two wreaths hanging on the trunk. At this turn in the road a wise man had been murdered. 'Rathenau had to die,' a National Socialist writer had once said to him. 'He had to die, his hubris was to blame for it. He was a Jew and wanted to be German Foreign Minister. Imagine a

144

nigger from the French Colonies as a candidate for the Quai d'Orsay – that would be just as impossible.'

Politics and love, ambition and friendship, life and death, nothing moved him. Alone with himself, he strode down the nocturnal street. Rockets were soaring into the sky above Luna Park, and falling in bright fiery sheaves towards the earth. Half-way down, the brightness expired, vanishing without trace, and fresh rockets soared hissing into the air. There was a notice at the entrance to the Park: 'Attempt by Fernando, World's Champion Marathon Dancer, to beat his own record. He will dance for 200 hours. Wine not compulsory.'

Fabian went into a beer-house, near the Halensee railway-cutting. The conversation of those sitting around him appeared utterly meaningless. A small illuminated Zeppelin, bearing in letters of light the words, 'Trumpf Chocolate,' passed above their heads towards the city. A train with brightly lighted windows rolled by beneath the bridge. Buses and tramcars followed each other in a long line down the street. At the next table a man was telling stories. His neck bulged over his collar, and several women, who were listening to him, screamed as though mice had run up their skirts.

What's the good of it all? he thought. He hurriedly paid the bill, and went home.

A number of letters were lying on the table; his applications for employment had all been rejected. There were no vacancies. We much regret . . . Yours faithfully. Fabian washed his hands and face. Later, he found himself sitting motionless on the sofa, holding the towel in front of his wet face and staring under its lower edge at the carpet. He dried himself, threw aside the towel, lay down and fell asleep. The light was on all night.

XX

CORNELIA IN A PRIVATE CAR
THE PROFESSOR KNOWS NOTHING
FRAU LABUDE FAINTS

When he awoke next morning and found the light still burning,
the events of the previous day had vanished from his mind. He
felt wretched and depressed, but he did not know why. He shut
his eyes, and then, very gradually, his misery took shape. All
that had happened came back to him, as though someone
outside had thrown it through his window-pane. He had
forgotten it out of sheer exhaustion. Now the memories in his
conscious mind sank deeper, growing and changing as they
sank; it was as if they were gaining in specific weight; then they
dropped like stones upon his heart. He turned to the wall and
covered his ears.

Frau Hohlfeld made no fuss when she brought in the breakfast, although the light was still on and Fabian was lying on the
sofa instead of in bed. She put the tray on the table and switched
off the light, observing in all she did the ritual prescribed for the
sickroom. 'I offer you my deepest sympathy,' she said. 'I've just
read it in the paper. A terrible blow for you! And his poor father
and mother!' The tone and pitch of her voice were well meant.
Her sympathy was sincere. It was more than he could stand.

He overcame his repugnance and murmured 'Thank you.'
He remained lying on the sofa until she left the room, then he
got up and dressed quickly. He had to speak to the Professor. A
suspicion had been gnawing at his mind since the previous
evening; it seemed groundless, yet it had grown more and more
unbearable. He must go to the University. As he left the house,
a big private car drove up.

'Fabian,' cried a voice. It was Cornelia. She waved to him
from the car, and got out as he went towards it.

'My poor Fabian,' she said, and stroked his hand. 'I couldn't
endure it till this afternoon, and he lent me his car. Am I
disturbing you?' Then she lowered her voice. 'The chauffeur is

keeping watch.' And asked more loudly: 'Where do you want to go?'

'To the University. He killed himself because his thesis was rejected. I must speak to the Professor.'

'I'll drive you there. May I?' she asked. 'Drive us to the University,' she said to the chauffeur. They got into the car and drove off towards the town. 'How did you get on last night?' asked Fabian.

'Don't speak of it,' she begged. 'All the time I had a feeling that some harm was threatening you. Makart was telling me about the part I am to play, but I scarcely listened, I was too much troubled by my forebodings. It was like the sense of oppression before a thunderstorm.'

'What sort of part is it?' He did not take up the question of Cornelia's forebodings. He hated the practice of lifting the veil of the future as though it were the coverlet of a bed, and still more the retrospective pride with which people say: I told you so. How vulgar to worm oneself thus into the confidences of fate! His dislike was not concerned with the truth or otherwise of such forebodings. He regarded it as presumptuous for a person to attempt this misplaced intimacy with what was still hidden. In spite of his usual passivity, this had nothing to do with an uncomplaining acceptance of the inevitable.

'A very extraordinary part,' she said. 'Just think, in this film I have to be the wife of a man who, to satisfy his perverse imagination, demands that I shall constantly change. He is a pathological case, and forces me to act sometimes as an inexperienced girl, sometimes as a sophisticated woman, now as a common drab and now as a smart, brainless, pleasure-seeker. Gradually it comes out, though he and the audience know it before I do, that I am really quite a different woman from what I had believed. He and I are both astonished, for I go on changing, finally against his will, and become at last what I have really been all the time. It comes out that essentially I am vulgar and domineering, and he meets a tragic end in the conflict which he had originally conjured up.'

'Is that Makart's idea? Look out, Cornelia, he's a dangerous man. At present he wants you only to act this series of transformations, but he is secretly speculating on the chances of your actually becoming such a woman.'

'There would be no tragedy in that, Fabian. Such men need

to be crushed. This film will be an education that will last me for life.'

He searched his pockets, found the bundle of notes, counted out a thousand marks and gave them to Cornelia. 'Here, Labude left me some money. Take half of it. It makes me feel more comfortable.'

'If only we had had this money three days ago,' she said.

Fabian observed the chauffeur, who kept watch on them by constantly peering into the little concave driving-mirror. 'Your governess will end by driving us into a tree . . . The show's in front!' he shouted, and for a time the chauffeur gave up observing them.

'I shall come without him this afternoon,' she said.

'I don't know whether I shall be in,' he answered.

She leaned shyly towards him for a moment. 'I shall come in any case, perhaps you'll need me.'

When they reached the University, he got out. She drove on with her warder.

The Professor's factotum opened the door to him. The Professor had not yet arrived, but was expected back from Weimar at any moment. Was his assistant there? Yes.

Herr Labude and his wife were sitting in the waiting room. She looked very old. When Fabian spoke to her she began to cry. 'We never troubled about him,' she said.

'It is no good reproaching yourself,' returned Fabian.

'He was of age, wasn't he?' asked Herr Labude. His wife began to sob, and he frowned. 'I read Stephan's thesis last night,' he said. 'I don't know the subject, and I cannot judge whether his premises are sound, but there can be no doubt that the conclusions he draws are shrewd and intelligent.'

'The premises from which he argues are quite sound,' said Fabian. 'It is an outstanding piece of work. I wish the Professor would come.'

Frau Labude was crying quietly to herself. 'He's dead now,' she said. 'He had a reason for taking his life; why do you want to rob him of it? Come, let us go!' She rose to her feet and took hold of the two men. 'Leave him in peace!'

But her husband said: 'Sit down, Luise.'

And then the Professor came. He had a certain old-fashioned elegance, and his eyes stood a little too far out of his head. The

148

factotum followed him up the stairs, carrying his suitcase. 'This is terrible,' said the Professor. With head bent sideways, he went up to Labude's parents. Frau Labude sobbed aloud as he took her hand, and even her husband was moved. 'I think we've met before,' said the old professor of literature, turning to Fabian. 'You were his friend.' He unlocked the door of his private room and invited them to enter. 'Excuse me,' he said, and washed his hands as though for a medical consultation, while they sat silent round the table. The factotum held the towel ready.

As he wiped his hands, the Professor said: 'I am not at home to anyone.' The factotum went out, the Professor took a seat. 'I bought a newspaper this morning in Naumberg,' he said, 'and the first thing I saw was the report of your son's tragic death. Is it too indiscreet if I ask the obvious question: What in heaven's name could have driven him to do such a thing?'

Herr Labude clenched his fist as it lay on the table. 'Can't you guess?' he asked.

The Professor shook his head. 'I haven't the faintest idea.'

Labude's mother threw up her hands and clasped them above her head. Her mute glance implored the men to desist.

But the barrister leaned forward in his chair. 'My son shot himself because you rejected his thesis.'

The Professor drew a silk handkerchief from his breast-pocket and passed it across his brow. 'What!' he asked, in a toneless voice. He stood up and stared at them with his prominent eyes, as though he feared they had taken leave of their senses. 'But that is impossible,' he whispered.

'No, it is quite possible!' cried Herr Labude. 'Put on your coat and come with us. Come and see the boy! He is lying on the sofa, as dead as a man can be!'

Frau Labude's eyes were fixed and staring. 'You are killing him a second time,' she said.

'This is terrible,' murmured the Professor. He seized Herr Labude by the arm. 'I rejected his thesis? Who told you that? Who told you that?' he cried. 'I passed on his work to the faculty with a note saying it was the most mature piece of literary criticism I had seen for years. I wrote in my report that, as the author of this work, Dr Stephan Labude must be taken with the utmost seriousness by expert critics. I wrote that, with this brilliant study, Dr Labude had rendered invaluable services to modern research. I wrote that I had never before received a work of such importance from a student, and that I was taking immediate steps to have it included in the list of university publications. Who said I rejected it?'

Labude's parents sat without stirring.

Fabian got up. He was trembling all over. 'One moment,' he said hoarsely. 'I will fetch him.' Then he ran out, down the stairs, into the catalogue room. Dr Weckherlin was bending over a card-index, sorting the cards, which bore the titles of books recently acquired by the library. He looked up angrily, screwing up his short-sighted eyes. 'What do you want?' he asked.

'The Professor wants you immediately,' said Fabian. The other made no move to get up, but simply nodded and went on sorting the cards. Then Fabian grasped him by the collar, dragged him from his chair, and hustled him out through the door.

'What on earth are you doing?' he cried. But instead of answering, Fabian struck him in the face with his fist. Weckherlin raised one arm to protect himself and, without further opposition, stumbled up the stairs. Outside the Professor's room he drew back, hesitating, but Fabian wrenched open the door. The Professor and Labude's parents started up from their seats. The assistant was bleeding from the nose.

'I must put a few questions to this gentleman in your presence,' said Fabian. 'Dr Weckherlin, did you tell my friend Labude yesterday that his thesis had been rejected? Did you tell him the Professor had said it would only be imposing on the faculty to pass it on to them? And did you tell him the Professor wished to reject it privately and thus avoid advertising his failure?'

Frau Labude moaned and slid swooning from her chair. The men took no heed of her. Weckherlin had retreated as far as the door. The others bent forward, waiting for his answer.

'Weckherlin,' said the Professor in a whisper, leaning heavily on the back of a chair.

The assistant's broad, pale face grew twisted, as though he were trying to smile. He opened his mouth and closed it again repeatedly.

'Well?' asked the Professor, in a threatening voice.

Weckherlin put his hand on the latch of the door, and said: 'It was only a joke!'

Then Fabian cried out. It was an inarticulate sound like the cry of an animal. Next moment he sprang forward and struck at Weckherlin with both fists, repeatedly, careless of where the blows fell. Insensate, like an automatic hammer, he struck and struck again. 'You scoundrel!' he screamed, and struck the other in the face with both fists. Weckherlin was still smiling, as though in apology. He had forgotten that his hand was on the latch, forgotten that he wished to flee from the room. Under the rain of blows his knees gave for a moment. He pulled himself up by the latch and thus the door clicked open. Not till then did he recall his desire to escape. He squeezed through the door into the corridor. Fabian followed. Step by step, they neared the stairs that led to the ground floor, the one striking, the other bleeding.

A crowd of students had gathered at the foot of the stairs, attracted by the noise that reached them from the rooms above. They stood silent, waiting, as though they felt the justice of what was happening there. 'You swine!' cried Fabian, and struck the assistant under the chin. Weckherlin tipped over backwards, his head hit one of the steps with a dull thud, and he rolled clattering down the wooden staircase. Fabian ran down after him and tried to throw himself upon him. But several of the students sprang forward and held him fast. 'Leave go!' he screamed, and tore like a maniac at the arms that held him. 'Let go of me! I'll kill him!' Someone put his hands over Fabian's mouth. The Professor's factotum was kneeling beside Weckherlin, who attempted to sit up, but fell back with a groan. They dragged him into the catalogue room.

The Professor and Labude's father were standing at the head of the stairs. Through the open door could be heard a series of long-drawn, plaintive cries. Stephan's mother had recovered from her swoon.

'So it was all a joke!' said Herr Labude, and laughed a despairing laugh.

The Professor said firmly, as though at last he had found a way out, 'Dr Weckherlin is discharged.' The students released Fabian. His head dropped forward. Perhaps he intended it as a bow of farewell. Then he went out.

XXI

FROM LAW-STUDENT TO FILM-STAR
AN OLD ACQUAINTANCE
HIS MOTHER SELLS SOFT SOAP

It had been only a joke!

Herr Weckherlin had played a silly practical joke, and Labude had died of it. It was not really suicide. A subordinate official in the Department of Middle High German had killed Fabian's friend. He had dropped poisoned words into his ear, like arsenic into a drinking-glass. He had aimed at Labude, for a joke, and pulled the trigger. And the unloaded gun had fired a deadly bullet.

As he hurried down the Friedrichstrasse, Fabian could still see Weckherlin's face in front of him, with its cowardly smile, and he asked himself in retrospective surprise: Why did I thrash that fellow? As though I had to destroy him! Why did my rage against him exceed my sorrow for Labude's futile death? Surely a man who is the unintentional cause of such a tragedy deserves pity rather than hate? Will he ever be able to sleep peacefully at night?

Gradually Fabian understood the instinct that had impelled him. Weckherlin had not done it unintentionally. He had wanted to injure Labude, not to kill him, but to injure him. The dullard had revenged himself on his talented rival. The lie he had told had been a bomb. He had thrown it at Labude, and run off to a safe distance to watch the explosion with malicious joy.

Weckherlin had been discharged, he had also been thrashed. But would it not have been better if he had retained his job and been spared his thrashing? Would it not have been better, now that Labude was dead, if Weckherlin's lie had survived? Yesterday his friend's death had filled Fabian with sorrow, today it filled him with a turbulent restlessness. The truth had been revealed, and who was the better for it? Labude's parents now knew that their son had been the victim of an infamous lie – were they the better? Before they knew the truth there had been no untruth. Now justice had triumphed and his death had become a tragic absurdity. Fabian thought of Labude's funeral and shuddered: he saw himself in the procession, he recognized Labude's parents behind the coffin, the Professor was there, Labude's mother was sobbing. She tore the black crepe veil from her black hat, and fell forward, whimpering.

'Look out!' cried someone angrily. Fabian felt himself jostled, and stood stock still. Ought he to have hushed up Weckherlin's action instead of revealing it? Ought he to have locked his knowledge of the situation within his heart, and kept it secret from Labude's parents? Why had Labude been so conscientious, why had he been so orderly, even in those last letters of his? Why had he always given a name to his motives? Fabian walked on. He turned into the Leipziger Strasse. It was midday. Clerks and shop-assistants were surging down the pavements, storming the buses. The lunch-hour was short.

If only this Weckherlin had never interfered, if only Labude had heard the Professor's true estimate of his work -- then he would not be dead – even more, his success would have spurred him on, soothed his disillusionment with Leda and provided a vent for his political ambitions. Why had he worked for five years on that thesis? Because he wanted to prove to himself what he could do. He had reckoned on this success, weighed it psychologically, included it as a factor in his development, and his reckoning had been right. And yet he had rather believed Weckherlin's lie than his own conviction.

No, Fabian did not wish to be present when they conveyed his friend into the beyond. He must get away from here. He stared at a passing car. Was that Cornelia? Sitting there beside the fat man? His heart missed a beat. It was not she. He must go, wild horses would not hold him back.

He went to the station. He did not call at the widow Hohlfeld's. He left everything in his room, just as it was. He did not call again on Zacharias, that vain, deceitful young man. He went to the station.

The express left in an hour's time. Fabian bought a ticket, bought some newspapers, sat down in the waiting-room and glanced over the headlines.

At some economic congress a demand had been made for far-reaching international agreements. Was this merely window-dressing? Or were these people gradually beginning to understand what everyone else knew? Did they recognize that reason was the most rational solution? Had Labude been right after all? Perhaps there was really no need to wait for the moral uplifting of fallen humanity? Perhaps the aim of the moralists, of whom Fabian was one, was actually attainable by economics. Were the demands of morality unrealizable simply because they were meaningless? Was the question of a world-order merely a question of business organization?

Labude was dead. He had been an enthusiast in such matters. They had fitted into his plans. Fabian sat in the waiting-room, thought his friend's thoughts and remained apathetic. Did he want conditions to improve? He wanted men and women to improve. What did he care for the betterment of conditions, unless it were reached through the betterment of people? He wished every man and woman ten chickens per day in the stewing-pot; he wished them all a water-closet with a loud-speaker; he wished them seven motor-cars, one for each day of the week. But what was achieved thereby, unless something more were achieved? Did they want to persuade him that people were made good by living under good conditions? If that were so, the masters of oilfields and coal-mines should be perfect angels!

Had he not once said to Labude: When you've got your Utopia the people there will still be punching each other on the nose? . . . Was that Elysium, where each barbarian had an average income of twenty thousand marks, a worthy aim for human endeavour?

As he sat there, defending his moral principles against opportunism, those doubts, which for some time had been eating like worms into his mind, began to stir again. Were those decent, humane, normal people, whose existence he desired, desirable in themselves? Did not this heaven on earth, whether attainable or unattainable, take on an infernal aspect in the mere process of conceiving it? Could one endure an age thus gilded with nobility? Would it not be more likely to drive one crazy? Perhaps that economic scheme of uncompetitive self-interest was an ideal, not only easier to realize, but also easier to bear. Perhaps his Utopia had only a relative significance and, as a reality, was as undesirable as it was unattainable. Was it not as though he said to humanity, as a man might say to his mistress:

'I should like to give you the moon!'? A praiseworthy utterance, but what disaster if the lover should proceed to fulfil it! What would the unfortunate mistress do with the moon, when he handed it to her? Labude had stood on solid ground; he had tried to march forward and stumbled. He, Fabian, was floating in the air, because he lacked weight and substance; yet he was still alive. Why did he go on living, when he did not know what he was living for? Why was his friend dead, when he had known why he lived? Life and death still came to the wrong people.

In the theatre-notes of the newspaper lying on his knee, he caught sight of Cornelia again. 'Law Student as Film Star,' was printed in big letters under the photograph. Dr Cornelia Battenberg, he was further informed, had been discovered by Edwin Makart, the well-known film magnate; she would be starring in a new film, which was to be taken in hand in a day or two, entitled: 'The Masks of Frau Z.'

'Good luck,' whispered Fabian, and nodded to the photograph. He met her again in another paper. She wore a magnificent summer fur, and was seated at the wheel of a car which he had seen before. By her side was a tall, fat man, probably the discoverer in person. The caption confirmed his suspicion. The face was brutal and cunning, like that of a self-made devil. Edwin Makart, the man with the divining rod – such was the editorial comment – with his latest discovery, Cornelia Battenberg. As a former student of law she represented the latest and most fashionable type, the intellectual German woman.

'Good luck,' repeated Fabian, and stared at the photograph. How long ago it all was! He stared at it as though he were staring into a grave. An invisible and ghostly pair of scissors had snipped through every tie that bound him to this city. His profession was gone, his friend was dead, Cornelia had fallen into another's hands; what was there left for him here?

He carefully cut out the photographs, tucked the cuttings away in his wallet, and discarded the newspapers. Nothing held him back; everything drew him to the place whence he had come: to his home, his birthplace, his mother. He was still sitting in the Anhalter Station, but he had left Berlin long ago. Would he ever come back? . . . A group of persons approached and sat down at his table. He got up, walked past the barrier and found a seat in the train. It was waiting for the signal to start.

Away! The minute hand of the station-clock jerked forward. Away!

Fabian sat by the window and looked out. The fields and meadows swirled past like objects on a turntable. The telegraph-posts dropped curtsies to him. Sometimes the little peasant children, standing barefoot in the dancing landscape, waved mechanically. In a meadow a horse was grazing. A foal was prancing along the fence, swinging its head. Then they passed through gloomy, pine-woods. The trunks were overgrown with grey lichen. The trees stood there as though they were stricken with leprosy and had been forbidden to leave the wood.

He felt that someone was trying to attract his attention. He turned and looked round the compartment. His fellow travellers, people of no particular interest, were sitting listlessly there, full of their own concerns. Yet someone's eyes were upon him. Then he discovered Frau Irene Moll outside in the corridor. She was smoking a cigarette and smiling at him. He made no response and she beckoned.

He went to her.

'It's a perfect scandal the way we two run after each other,' she said. 'Where are you going?'

'Home.'

'Be polite, and kindly ask me where I am going?'

'Where are you going?'

She leaned against him and whispered: 'I'm clearing out. One of my boys has split on me. I heard of it this morning from a police-officer whose wages I have doubled. Come with me to Budapest.'

'No,' he said.

'I've got a hundred thousand marks. We need not go to Budapest. Suppose we go to Prague and then back to Paris. We'll stay at Claridge's. Or we'll go to Fontainebleau and rent a little villa there.'

'No,' he said. 'I'm going home.'

'Come with me,' she begged. 'I've got some jewellery too. When we're broke we can blackmail the old hags who used to patronize my *pension*. I've got some interesting information. Peep-holes have their uses. Or would you rather go to Italy? What do you say to Bellagio?'

'No,' he said. 'I'm going to my mother.'

'You damned fool,' she whispered, angrily. 'Do you want me to kneel down and say I love you? What have you got against me? Am I too enlightened for you? Would you rather have some little white lamb? I'm sick of taking the first man that comes along. I like you. We're always running into each other. That can't be pure accident.' She took his hand and caressed his fingers. 'Do come!'

'No,' he said. 'I will not come. I wish you a pleasant journey.' And he turned to go back into his compartment.

She held him fast. 'What a pity! What a terrible pity! Some other time perhaps.' She opened her handbag. 'Do you want some money?' She tried to press a wad of bank-notes into his hand. He clenched his fist, shook his head, and went back to his seat.

For some time she remained standing outside the door of his compartment, watching him. He looked out of the window. They passed through a village.

It was nearly six in the evening when he arrived. He walked out of the station and saw the Church of the Three Kings. It seemed to look down at him disdainfully, as though it were asking: Why is there no one to meet you? Why have you no luggage?

He walked along the Dammweg and under the old railway-bridge. An endless goods train clanked past above him, making the stone arches groan. The house where Schanze, the schoolmaster, used to live had just been repainted. The grey frontage of the other houses was still unchanged, just as he had known it from childhood. In the corner house, which belonged to Frau Schröder, the midwife, a new shop had been opened; it was a butcher's. There were still flower-pots in the window.

Slowly he approached the house where he had been born. How familiar the street was! He knew all the houses, all the courtyards, all the cellars and lofts; he was at home here, everywhere. But the people who came and went were strangers to him. He stopped. Above a shop-window was the single word 'Soap'. There was a notice gummed to the window-pane: 'Reduction in Price of Toilet soap,' he read. 'Our Lavender Soap reduced from 22 pfennigs to 20. Torpedo Soap from 28 pfennigs to 25.' He went up to the shop door.

Behind the counter was his mother, and in front of it two

women. His mother bent down for a packet of washing-powder and put it on the counter. She cut a bar of washing soap in two. Then she took a sheet of paper and a wooden spoon, ladled soft soap from a cask, weighed it and wrapped it up. The smell of soap came out to him in the street.

He pressed down the door-handle. The bell tinkled. The old woman looked up and her hands fell suddenly to her sides.

He went up to her and said in a trembling voice: 'Mother, Labude has shot himself.' And suddenly the tears were running down his face. He opened the door that led into the back room, closed it again, sat down in the armchair by the window and looked out into the yard. Then he laid his head slowly on the windowsill and wept.

XXII

'What's wrong with him?' asked his father, next morning.

'He's out of a job,' said his mother. 'And his friend has committed suicide. You know, Labude, the man he met in Heidelberg.'

'I never knew he had a friend,' said his father. 'Nobody tells me anything.'

'You never listen,' said his mother. Then the shop bell rang. When Frau Fabian came back, her husband was reading his paper.

'And then he's had a disappointment with a girl,' she went on. 'But he won't tell me much about that. She studied to be a lawyer and now she's gone into the films.'

'Waste of money for her education,' said Fabian's father.

'A pretty girl,' said his mother. 'But she's living with a film-man, a big fat chap. It makes me sick.'

'Will he be here long?' asked his father.

She shrugged her shoulders and poured out the coffee. 'He's given me a thousand marks. Labude left it him. I shall put it by. The boy's had a bad time; it's no use denying it. And it's not because of Labude nor the film-actress. He's no belief in God – that's what's the matter with him. He has no resting place.'

'When I was his age I had been married nearly ten years,' said his father.

Fabian walked up the Heerstrasse, past the garrison church and the barracks. The round, gravel-strewn space in front of the church was quite empty. When had it happened? When was it that he had stood there, one among thousands of soldiers, in slacks, his helmet on his head, parading for a field-grey sermon, only seventeen, waiting to hear the message of the German God to his armies? He stopped at the gateway of what had been the artillery barracks, and leaned against the iron railings. Parades for fatigue-duties, gun-drill, night operations, pay; lectures on war loan; how much this bleak yard had witnessed! Here he had heard old soldiers, before they were marched off in full equipment for the third or fourth time, bet each other a loaf of bread that they would be back first. And a week later they had turned up again, in ragged uniforms, with a genuine Brussels dose of the clap. Fabian left the railings and walked on past the pompous old grenadier and infantry barracks. He reached the grounds of the school where for years he had been a pupil and boarder before he was introduced to anti-clockwise rifling, field binoculars and gun-carriage trails. Here was the street that dropped down to the town. How often he had raced down it of an evening, without leave, to get home to his mother for a few minutes! School, church, cadets' college, military hospital, every building on the outskirts of this town had been a barrack.

The big, grey building, with its tiled and pointed corner-towers, was still there, looking as though it were filled to the roof with the troubles of childhood. The windows of the headmaster's house were still hung with white curtains, in contrast to the rows of blank, undraped windows, which belonged to the class-rooms, common-rooms, locker-room and dormitories. As a child he had almost expected that side of the building where the headmaster's house was to sink into the ground, so weighty had seemed to him the presence of those curtained windows. He passed through the gateway and up the steps. Voices, shrill and gruff, came to him from the class-rooms. They filled the empty corridor. Choral-singing and the tones of a piano were wafted down from the first floor. Fabian disdained the broad, central staircase and climbed the narrow steps in the wing. Two little boys were coming towards him.

'Heinrich!' cried one. 'The Stork wants you at once; you are to fetch the exercise-books.'

'Let him wait a bit,' said Heinrich, and vanished with exaggerated slowness through a swaying glass door.

The Stork, thought Fabian. Nothing had changed. The same masters were still there, with the same nicknames. Only the pupils were not the same. Year after year they came, and were trained and educated. Early mornings, the house-master's bell. Then the hunt began: dormitory, wash-room, locker-room, dining-hall. The youngest laid the tables, fetched the tins of butter from the refrigerator and the enamelled coffee-pots from the lift. The hunt proceeded: common-room, dusting, class-room, lessons, dining-room. The youngest spread the tables for the midday meal. The hunt proceeded: recreation, gardening, football, common-room, preparation, class-room, dining-hall. The youngest spread the tables for supper. The hunt proceeded: common-room, preparation, wash-room, dormitory. The sixth-form boys were allowed to stay up two hours longer, and smoked cigarettes in the grounds. Nothing had changed, except the boys.

Fabian reached the third floor. He opened the door of the main hall. Morning prayers, evening prayers, the strains of the organ, the Kaiser's birthday, Sedan celebrations, Battle of Tannenberg, flags on the tower, Easter reports, boys leaving to join the army, courses of military training for seniors, and again the strains of the organ, and speeches full of sonorous piety. The air was permanently saturated with unity and justice and freedom. Were the boys still compelled to stand to attention when a teacher passed? Two hours' leave on Wednesdays and three on Sundays. And if your leave was cancelled, were you still grabbed by the janitor, given a pair of scissors, and set to work transforming daily newspapers into toilet paper?

But had he never been happy here? Had he never felt anything but that lie which stealthily filled the place, that evil, secret power that transformed whole generations of children into obedient officials and narrow-minded bourgeois? Yes, there had been happy times, but in spite of the system. He left the hall and climbed the dark, spiral staircase that led to the wash-rooms and dormitories. The iron bedsteads stood in a long row. The night-shirts hung folded above them with military precision. You must have order. At night the sixth-form boys had come up after their stroll out in the grounds and forced their way into the beds of frightened youngsters from the second and third. The little boys had held their tongues. You must have order. He went to the window. Down below, where the river threaded its way through the valley, the old town was shining with all its towers and terraces. How often he had crept to this window when the other boys were asleep and tried to find the house where his sick mother was lying! How often he had pressed his forehead against the panes and fought down his tears! It had done him no harm, neither the prison-house nor the suppression of his tears. No, it had done him no harm. They had never managed to crush his spirit. A few boys had shot themselves, but not very many. Many more died during the war. Others had died later. Today, half his class was gone. He went down the stairs, left the building and entered the grounds. Here they had trotted along behind a hand-cart, each armed with a giant broom, a shovel, or a pointed stick, sweeping up faded leaves and stabbing bits of paper. The grounds were large and sloped down to a little stream.

Fabian followed the old familiar paths; he sat on a bench, looked up at the tree-tops, and then walked on again, struggling in vain against the effort of the things about him to transmute him back into what he once had been. The walls, the rooms, the trees, the flower-beds that surrounded him were not realities, they were memories. He had left his childhood here, and now he found it again. It sank down upon him from the branches and walls and towers and took possession of his soul. He walked deeper and deeper into that dismal magic. He came to the skittle alley; the skittles were set ready for a game. Fabian looked round; he was alone. Then he took one of the bowls from the box, drew back his arm, ran forward and sent it rolling down the alley. It jumped a little in places. The alley was still uneven. Six skittles fell with a clatter.

'What do you think you are doing?' asked an angry voice. 'Strangers have no business here!' It was the headmaster. He had scarcely changed, except that his Assyrian beard had grown still whiter.

'I beg your pardon,' said Fabian. He raised his hat and began to walk away.

'One moment,' cried the headmaster. Fabian turned. 'Aren't you one of our old boys?' He held out his hand. 'Of course! Jacob Fabian! I'm glad to see you. Well, this is nice! Have you felt homesick for your old school?' They shook hands.

'A terrible time,' asserted the headmaster. 'A godless time. The righteous have much to bear.'

'Who are the righteous?' asked Fabian. 'Give me their address.'

'You are still the same,' said the headmaster. 'You were always one of my best pupils and one of the least respectful. And what have you achieved in life?'

'The government is on the point of granting me a small pension,' said Fabian.

'Unemployed!' cried the headmaster, severely. 'I expected more of you.'

Fabian laughed. 'The righteous have much to bear.'

'If only you had taken your teaching examinations,' said the headmaster, 'you would not be standing here without a profession.'

'I should be without a profession in any case,' returned Fabian, with some agitation '– even if I were practising one. I can tell you in confidence that the human race, with the exception of parsons and pedagogues, hardly knows whether it's on its head or its heels. The compass is broken. But you don't notice it here. You go up and down in your lift from the first form to the sixth, as you have always done; what need have you of a compass?'

The headmaster thrust his hands under the tails of his frock coat. 'I am horrified,' he said. 'Is there no work for you to do? Go away and form your character, young man! Why did we study history? Why did we read the classics? You must round off your personality.'

Fabian regarded the well-fed, complacent old man and smiled. Then he said: 'You with your rounded-off personality!' – and went.

In the street he met Eva Kendler. She had two children with her, and had grown quite plump. It surprised him that he recognized her.

'Jacob!' she cried, and blushed. 'You haven't changed a bit. Say "good morning" to uncle!' The children held out their hands and curtsied. Two little girls. They resembled their mother more closely than she did herself.

'It must be at least ten years since we met,' he said. 'How are you? When did you get married?'

'My husband is house-surgeon at the Carola hospital,' she explained. 'He can't make much progress there, and he can't afford a practice of his own. He may go to Japan with Professor Wandsbeck. If things go well, I shall follow later with the children.' He nodded and looked down at the two little girls.

'Those were wonderful times,' she said softly. 'Do you remember when my parents were away? I was seventeen then.

163

How time flies!' She sighed and straightened the little girls' sailor collars. 'Before you begin really to have a life of your own, you have all the responsibility of your children. We shan't even get to the seaside this year.'

'That's terrible,' he said.

'Yes,' she agreed. 'Well, we must be going. Good-bye, Jacob.'

'Good-bye.'

'Shake hands with uncle.'

The little girls curtsied and pressed close to their mother, and all three walked away. Fabian stood for a while where he was. The past had come round the corner, holding two children by the hand, grown strange, scarcely recognizable. 'You haven't changed a bit.' That is what the past had said to him.

'How did you get on?' asked his mother. They had had lunch and were standing in the shop, unpacking a case of bleaching powder.

'I went up by the barracks. I looked in at the school, too. Then I met Eva. She's got two little children. Her husband is a doctor.'

His mother counted the packets as she stowed them on the shelf. 'Eva? She used to be such a pretty girl. Now what happened that time? You stayed away from home for two days.'

'Her parents were away, and I had to give a course of instruction which lasted for several days. It was her first, and I performed my task most conscientiously and with a true moral earnestness.'

'I was very worried,' said his mother.

'But I sent you a telegram.'

'There's something horrid about telegrams,' she declared. 'I sat there holding it in my hands for half an hour before I could bring myself to open it.' He handed up the packets and his mother piled them on the shelves. 'Wouldn't it be better if you looked for a job here?' she asked. 'Do you really want to go back to Berlin? Don't you like it here now? You could have the living-room. Besides the girls here are nicer and not so flighty. Perhaps you'll find a wife for yourself.'

'I don't know yet what I shall do,' he said. 'Perhaps I shall stay here. I want to work. I want to be active. It's time I had

164

some object in front of me. And if I can't find one, I'll invent one. I can't go on like this.'

'People never worried about such things in my time,' she said. 'Then a man's aim was to make money and marry and have children.'

'Perhaps I shall get used to that,' he said. 'What's that phrase of yours?'

She stopped work. 'Man is a creature of habit,' she said emphatically.

XXIII

PILSNER BEER AND PATRIOTISM
TURKISH BIEDERMEIER
FABIAN IS TREATED GRATIS

Fabian went down that evening to the old part of the town. From the bridge he looked once more on those world-famous buildings that he had known since he was first able to think; what had been the Royal Castle, what had been the Royal Opera House, what had been the Chapel Royal; everything belonged to the past. The moon moved slowly from the spire of the castle-tower to the spire of the church, as though it were sliding along a wire. The terrace along the river bank was overgrown with ancient trees and venerable public buildings. The town, with its life and its culture, had retired from active affairs. The panorama resembled an expensive funeral procession. In the Altmarkt he ran into Wenzkat. 'There's a class reunion at the Ratskeller next Friday,' said Wenzkat. 'Will you still be here?'

'I hope so,' said Fabian 'I'll look in if I can manage it.' He hurriedly attempted to walk on, but Wenzkat asked him to have a drink. His wife had been away for a fortnight at some health resort. They went to Gassmeier's and drank Pilsner.

After the third glass, Wenzkat became political. 'It can't go on like this,' he growled. 'I've joined the Stahlhelm. I don't wear a badge. I have to think of my practice: it wouldn't do to show my colours in public. But that makes no difference. We are in for a last despairing struggle.'

'When you people begin,' said Fabian, 'we shall never get to the struggle. The despair will set in straight away.'

'You may be right,' cried Wenzkat, banging his fist on the table. 'Then we shall all go under, and to hell with it!'

'I don't know whether the whole nation will agree to that,' objected Fabian. 'Where do you get the audacity to condemn sixty million people to ruin, simply because you're fond of a scrap and possess the sense of honour of an insulted turkey-cock?'

'Look at the world's history,' said Wenzkat emphatically. 'It's always been the same.' He emptied his glass.

'Yes, that's what history amounts to from beginning to end!' cried Fabian. 'It makes one ashamed to read the stuff, and we should be still more ashamed to cram it into children. Why must we always do things as they were done in the past? If that had been carried out consistently we should still be sitting in trees.'

'You are no patriot,' said Wenzkat.

'And you are a blockhead,' said Fabian. 'And that is much worse.'

Then they drank another beer, and prudently changed the subject.

'I've got a good idea,' said Wenzkat. 'Let's go to a brothel.'

'Are there still such places left? I thought they were forbidden.'

'Of course they're forbidden,' said Wenzkat. 'And of course there are some left. The one thing does not exclude the other. You'll have a good time.'

'I've no intention of having a good time,' asserted Fabian.

'We'll have a bottle of champagne with the girls. The rest is optional. Be a sport. Come along. And keep an eye on me; I don't want to land myself in any trouble.'

The house was in a little narrow lane. As they were standing outside, Fabian remembered that this was the place where the officers of the garrison had held their orgies. That was twenty years ago. The house appeared quite unchanged. With luck, the same girls would be there. Wenzkat rang the bell. They heard footsteps approaching the door, then an unwinking eye stared through the peep-hole. The door opened. Wenzkat looked round him anxiously. There was no one in sight. They went in.

They passed an old woman, who murmured a greeting, and climbed the narrow wooden staircase. The manageress appeared. 'Evening, Gustav,' she said. 'So you've looked in again, have you?'

'A bottle of bubbly,' said Wenzkat. 'Is Lily still here?'

'No, but Lotte is. Her bottom is quite broad enough for you. Sit down!'

The room to which they were conducted was hexagonal and furnished in the Biedermeier–Turkish style. The lamp shed a crimson light. The walls were panelled and decorated with tarsia and naked women, and a low couch extended on each side. The two men sat down.

'Trade seems bad,' said Fabian.

'Nobody's got any money,' explained Wenzkat. 'Besides this business is out of date.'

Three young women entered the room and addressed themselves to the regular customer. Fabian sat in a corner, watching the scene. The housekeeper brought the champagne in ice and filled the glasses. 'Good health!' she cried, and they all drank.

'Lotte,' said Wenzkat. 'Get your things off.'

Lotte was a plump young person with merry eyes. 'Good,' she said, and the three girls went out together. A moment later they came back naked, and sat down between the two visitors.

Wenzkat jumped up and struck Lotte on the bottom with the flat of his hand. She squealed, kissed him and hustled him with earnest adjurations towards the door. They both disappeared.

Now Fabian was sitting at table with the manageress and two naked women, chatting and drinking champagne. 'Is it always as quiet as this?' he asked.

'We had crowds here when the choral festival was on,' said the blonde, fingering her nipples thoughtfully. 'I had eighteen men in one day. But at ordinary times it's enough to bore you to death.'

'It's like being in a nunnery,' said the little dark girl, and moved nearer Fabian.

'Another bottle?' inquired the manageress.

'I don't think so,' he said. 'I've only a few marks on me.'

'Oh, rot!' cried the blonde. 'Gustav's got plenty of money. Besides he can always have tick.' The manageress went out to fetch a second bottle.

'Are you coming with me?' asked the blonde.

'I told you the truth just now when I said I have no money.' He was glad there was no need to tell lies.

'It's the limit!' she cried. 'I didn't come to a knocking-shop just to let my pussy close up again. Come along! You can leave the money next time you pass this way.' Fabian refused.

Shortly afterwards Wenzkat came back and sat down beside the blonde. 'You needn't come and sit by me now,' she said, in a hurt voice.

Then Lotte appeared holding both hands over her buttocks.

168

'The swine!' she grumbled. 'Always knocking people about. Now it'll be another three days before I can sit down.'

'Here's another ten marks,' said Wenzkat. She bent down to slip the money into her shoe and, as she did so, he dealt her another slap. She gave him a furious glance and stepped forward to return the blow.

'Sit down,' he commanded. Then he snuggled up to the blonde and put his arm round her waist. 'Well, shall we?' he asked.

She looked at him searchingly. 'But I don't put up with any thrashing,' she said. 'I'm for doing things the proper way.'

He nodded. She rose and walked on ahead, swinging her hips.

'I was to keep an eye on you,' said Fabian.

'Oh Lord,' replied the other. 'A man must drown his sorrows somehow.' Then he followed the woman.

The manageress brought the second bottle and filled the glasses. Lotte complained about Wenzkat and showed the marks he had made. The little dark-haired girl whispered to Fabian: 'Come up to my room.' He looked at her. Her eyes were fixed upon him, wide and grave. 'I've got something to show you,' she said quietly, and they went out together.

This little naked person's room was furnished as tastelessly and as Turkishly as that from which they had come. The bedspread was smothered with printed flowers and thickly edged with lace. There were absurd pictures on the walls. The air was warmed by an electric radiator. The window was open. Three pots of flowering plants stood on the sill.

The woman closed the window, went up to Fabian, put her arms round him and stroked his face.

'What did you want to show me?' he asked. She showed him nothing. She simply looked at him.

He patted her kindly on the back. 'But I have no money,' he assured her. She shook her head, unbuttoned his waistcoat, lay down on the bed and regarded him expectantly, without stirring.

He shrugged his shoulders, took off his suit, and lay down beside her. She put her arms around him, breathing a sigh of relief. She gave herself to him very gently and her grave eyes hung on his face. He became embarrassed. It was as though he had persuaded a virgin into a rash act. She did not speak, but presently her lips parted and she moaned. Even that she did with great restraint.

Afterwards, she brought a bowl of water, poured chemicals into it from two flasks and held the towel ready for him.

Wenzkat was sitting between Lotte and the blonde. He nodded to Fabian. He was tired. They finished the bottle and took their leave. Fabian pressed two two-mark pieces into the hand of the little dark-haired girl. 'That's all I have with me,' he murmured. She looked at him earnestly.

Then they went all together to the head of the stairs. Wenzkat was getting noisy again; he was a little drunk. Suddenly Fabian felt a hand in his pocket. When he reached the street, he felt in the same pocket and found his two two-mark pieces there.

'Would you believe it?' he said. 'I gave that girl a few marks, and now she's put the money back in my pocket.'

Wenzkat yawned noisily and said: 'Love at first sight. And she probably needed it. By the way, Jacob, if you come to the reunion, don't say anything about this! And don't forget, Friday evening at the Ratskeller.' Then they parted.

Fabian took another walk. The streets were almost deserted. The trams were returning empty to the depots. He stopped on the bridge and looked down into the river. The arc-lamps threw quivering reflections, looking like a series of little moons that had fallen into the water. The river was high. There must have been rain in the mountains. On the hillsides, all round the town, were many twinkling lights.

While he was standing there, Labude was lying on his bier in a villa in Grunewald and Cornelia in a four-poster with Herr Makart. They were both very far away. Fabian was under a different sky. Here Germany had no fever. Here its temperature was below normal.

XXIV

HERR KNORR HAS CORNS
THE *Daily Post* NEEDS CAPABLE MEN
LEARN TO SWIM!

The following day he happened to be at the baker's, and from there he telephoned Wenzkat's office. Wenzkat was in a hurry. He was just going to the courts. Fabian asked if he happened to know anyone who had a directorship to give away.

'Why don't you call on Holzapfel?' asked Wenzkat. 'He's on the *Daily Post.*'

'What does he do there?'

'He's sporting editor, and he also writes the musical criticism. He may know of something. And remind him of Friday evening. So long.'

Fabian went home and told his mother he was going to the old part of the town to see Holzapfel, who was on the *Daily Post.* Perhaps Holzapfel could help him. His mother was in the shop, waiting for customers. 'That would be very nice, my dear,' she said. 'God bless you.'

A sudden swerve of the tram caused him to cannon into a tall, lanky man, who was standing next to him 'I think we've met before,' said the man, and held out his hand. He was a certain Herr Knorr, a former lieutenant of the reserve. To him had fallen the task of training a company of volunteers, among whom had been Fabian. He had flayed those lads of seventeen, as though he drew royalties from death and the devil.

'Put down your hand,' said Fabian, 'and quickly, or I shall spit on it.' Herr Knorr, a carrier by profession, followed this well-meant advice and laughed awkwardly. They were not alone on the platform of the tram. 'What have I done to you?' he asked, though he knew very well.

'If you were not so tall,' said Fabian, 'I would land you one. But as I cannot reach your confounded face, I must find some other way of expressing my feelings.' With that he trod so violently on Herr Knorr's corns that the latter pressed his lips together and turned very pale. The onlookers laughed. Fabian got off and walked the rest of the way.

Holzapfel, Fabian's former classmate, seemed extraordinarily grown-up; he was drinking bottled beer and scrawling hieroglyphics on a few galley-proofs. 'Sit down, Jacob,' he said. 'I've got to correct the tips for today's winners, and also a column of piano-recitals. Haven't seen you for a long while. Where have you been hiding yourself? Berlin, eh? I wish I could get up there now and then. Can't manage it. Always lots of work and lots of beer. Blisters on my brain, blisters on my backside, the youngsters always getting older and the girls always getting younger. Hope I don't get a dose of pneumonia.' As he mumbled thus to himself, he went quietly on with his corrections and his beer. 'Koppel's got a divorce. He found out his wife was deceiving him with two other men. He was always good at maths. Bretschneider's sold his chemist's shop and bought himself a bit of land. He grows redcurrants and new potatoes. We all spend our money on what we like best. There, the concerts can wait.' He rang for a messenger and sent the proofs of the racing-tips to the composing-room. Then Fabian told him he was looking for work; his last job had been in advertising. But it was all the same to him. The main thing was to find something here at home.

'You don't understand music. Nor boxing,' reflected Holzapfel. 'Perhaps we can use you on the literary side, as assistant dramatic critic or such like.' He got on the telephone and spoke to the director. 'Go and have a talk to the chap,' he urged. 'Tell him something nice. He's conceited but teachable.'

Fabian thanked him, reminded him of the class-reunion and sent up his name to Director Hanke. 'Dr Holzapfel is a school-friend of yours?' asked the director. 'You've studied literature? There's nothing free at the moment. But that makes no difference, if you are really efficient. I can always use a really efficient man. Work as a free-lance for a fortnight. I'll introduce you to the literary editor. If he turns your articles down, that's bad luck on you. Otherwise, you'll be very welcome as an outside contributor.' He was about to ring the bell.

'One moment, director,' said Fabian. 'Thank you for offering me this chance, but I would rather work on the publicity side. For instance, you might institute an advisory service for advertisers, which would supply ideas for attractive advertisements, or even work out complete advertisement campaigns. Then the circulation of the paper could be increased by skilful and systematic advertising. We could collaborate with the bigger buyers of space to arrange profitable prize-competitions, and organize boxing and similar popular entertainments for subscribers.'

The director listened attentively, then he said: 'Our biggest shareholders are not in favour of these Berlin stunts.'

'But they are in favour of increasing the circulation!'

'Not by such gimmicks,' declared the director. 'All the same, I'll speak to our advertising manager. After all, in the long run we shall have to apply these methods to some extent, so perhaps we ought to adopt them now, in modest doses. Come in again tomorrow at eleven. I'll see what I can do. Bring a few samples of your work with you. And testimonials, if you keep such goods in stock.'

Fabian got up and thanked him for the interest he had shown.

'If we engage you,' said the director, 'you must not expect anything fantastic in the way of salary. Two hundred marks is a lot of money in these days.'

'To the employees?' asked Fabian, curiously.

'No,' said the director, 'to the shareholders.'

Fabian sat in the Café Limberg, drank a tot of cognac and meditated on what he had done. It was a thoroughly crazy idea. If they were gracious enough to engage him, he would be helping to extend the influence of a reactionary newspaper. He could not persuade himself that publicity attracted him for its own sake, apart from the objects it served. He could not deceive himself so completely. Then could he chloroform his conscience, day by day, for the sake of a pair of hundred-mark notes every month? He was not a man of Münzer's kidney.

His mother would be pleased. She wanted him to become a useful member of society. A useful member of Society Ltd! He could not do it. He had not fallen so low as that. Earning money was not yet for him the whole meaning of life.

He determined to hide from his parents the fact that he could find a safe niche with the *Daily Post*. He did not want to find a safe niche with anyone. By heaven, he would not knuckle under! He determined to write to the director to that effect, and as soon as he had made up his mind he felt better. He could take the remaining thousand marks left him by Labude, and go to the Erzgebirge and stay there in some quiet little homestead. The money would last for six months or even longer. He could tramp about, within the limits imposed by his weak heart. He knew, from schoolboy excursions, the mountain-ridge, the summits, the toy towns. He knew the forests, the upland pastures, the lakes and the wretched, poverty-stricken villages. Other people went to the South Seas; the Erzgebirge were cheaper. Perhaps, up there, he would find himself again. Perhaps, up there, he would grow into the semblance of a man. Perhaps, on those lonely forest paths, he might find an object for which he could stake his life. Perhaps he could manage even with five hundred marks. Then he could leave the other five hundred for his mother.

Away then, to the bosom of nature! Up and away! By the time he came back, the world would have taken a step forward, or maybe two steps back. Whichever way it went, no situation could be worse than the present. However it changed, it would offer him wider prospects, either of work or of conflict. He could not go on standing there helpless like a child stuck in a bog. And yet the time had not come to help, to seize hold upon life, for where should he seize it, with whom should he ally himself? He wanted to pay a visit to solitude, and listen from the mountains for the starter's pistol, which should give the signal for him and those like him.

He left the café. But was not this plan of his a mere escape? Was there not always, everywhere, a stage for those who wished to act? For what had he been waiting all these years? Perhaps for the realization that he had been born and ordained a spectator, and not, as he still believed, an actor in the world's theatre.

He loitered before shop-windows, looked at clothes, hats, rings, and saw nothing. He came to himself again outside a corset shop. When all was said and done, living was a most entertaining activity. The baroque buildings of the Schloss Strasse were still there. Their builders and first tenants were long since dead. Lucky it wasn't the other way about!

Fabian began to cross the bridge.

Suddenly he saw a little boy balancing on the parapet.

He quickened his steps. He began to run.

The boy tottered and cried out shrilly; his knees gave way, he threw up his hands and fell from the parapet down into the river.

A few pedestrians who had heard the cry turned round. Fabian leaned over the wide stone balustrade. He saw the child's head, and his hands beating the water. He threw off his coat and jumped in to rescue him. Two tramcars stopped. The passengers swarmed out, and watched to see what would happen. Agitated figures ran up and down the bank.

The little boy swum ashore, howling.

Fabian sank. Unfortunately he could not swim.

Fabian and the Guardians of Morality*

This book is not meant for innocents of whatever age. The author repeatedly draws attention to the anatomical differences between the sexes. In several chapters he causes ladies and other women to run around without any clothes on. He repeatedly draws attention to what is known rather off-puttingly as intercourse. Nor does he scruple to refer to abnormal sexual practices. He omits nothing which might lead the guardians of morality to express the view that the author is a purveyor of filth.

To this the author replies: I am a moralist.

Personal experience and other observations have led him to the conclusion that events of an erotic nature should loom large in his novel. Not because he desired to provide a photographic image of life, for he neither wished to do this, nor has he done it. But he wanted very much to depict life in its proper proportions. His respect for this task may have taken precedence over his delicacy of feeling. He finds this justifiable. The guardians of morality, whether masculine, feminine or neuter, have once again leapt into action. Inspired by their psychoanalytical training, they are running amok through the countryside in droves, just like bailiffs, sticking fig-leaves over every keyhole and on every walking-stick. But it is not just secondary sexual characteristics that they find objectionable. It is not enough for them to accuse the author of pornography; they also condemn him as a pessimist, and in the eyes of moral guardians of every persuasion, that is the very worst that can be said of someone.

They want each citizen to put all his hopes into one great pot. And the less these hopes weigh, the more they try to make him offer up. And because nothing which occurs to them can be

---

* This statement was intended as an epilogue to the novel, but was rejected by the original German publisher. It was first published in the left-wing weekly, *Die Weltbühne* (edited by Carl von Ossietzky), vol. 27, no. 43, 1931.

made to yield nourishment when people cook away at it, and because what has occurred to them in the past has long since been consigned to the rubbish heap of history, our moral guardians ask themselves: what need have we then of writers, those clerks of the imagination, if not for this purpose? To all of this the author replies: I am a moralist.

He discerns but one ray of hope, and he names it. He sees that his contemporaries, like stubborn mules, are running backwards towards a yawning abyss in which there is enough room for all the nations of Europe. And so, like a number of others before and alongside him, he cries out: Watch out! Grip the handrail on your left with your left hand!

If people do not gather their wits (and each individual must gather his own, and not just leave it to others), and if they do not at long last take the decision to move forwards, away from the abyss and towards reason, where in all the world will we be able to discover any genuine grounds for hope? Hopes which a decent person can swear by, as he would swear by his mother. The author loves candour and reveres the truth. He has candidly depicted a certain state of affairs and truthfully expressed his opinion of it. Before the horrified guardians of morality destroy his book in a fit of rage, they should pay heed to what he has repeatedly asserted here.

He maintains that he is a moralist.

OTHER NEW YORK REVIEW CLASSICS

For a complete list of titles, visit www.nyrb.com or write to:
Catalog Requests, NYRB, 435 Hudson Street, New York, NY 10014

* Also available as an electronic book.